Minds Unmasked

ONE MILFORD PUBLISHING

ISBN: 978-1-6847-0042-4 (sc)
ISBN: 978-1-6847-0041-7 (e)

Lulu Publishing Services rev. date: 03/28/2019

Contents

Photograph by Preston Christy

*** *** ***

Lift Off

"**H**oney, come here! I think I got it!"

"You did?!? How did you do it?" He was astonished as he looked over the thousands of lines of code in awe.

"I don't really know, honestly. It was mostly trial and error. Here, I'm going to boot it up."

With one hit of the enter key, the limp robot sprung to life. Its inner blue lights shone through the clear accents, contrasting with the base matte grey plates. The bright LED eyes projected simulated emotions that the internal computer decided it should be portrayed to feel.

"Booting up.... Hello! I am LYS. I am an automated co-pilot created by Dr. Cynthia Albedo and Mr. Wallace Albedo. How may I be of assistance?"

"Oh my god! You did it!" The couple jumped for joy, as their long term project finally showed signs of life. "How did you get it to sound just like you?"

"Oh, that?" She brushed off her shoulder. "I sampled every possible syllable that LYS will ever need to say. I programed her to merge the syllables together almost perfectly, so she doesn't sound too robotic. You need to take some credit, too. If it weren't for the computer you built in her body, and the voice box you added two days ago, none of this would have been possible." She smiled back at him, beaming with pride.

✳✳✳

"Captain, your heart rate and blood pressure are increasing. I suggest taking a few deep breaths to calm your nerves. If it persists, I suggest--"

"I'm fine, LYS. It's just a launch. I've done plenty of these."

Please, for the love of God, stop talking soon, Wallace thought to himself. LYS' occasional chime-ins caused his patience to dwindle the closer they got to the launch.

"Are the calculated paths clear? What's the situation?"

"We will begin the launching process in T-10 minutes. Projected course is clear. No interfering debris. Everything looks good." His wife's voice rang through the cockpit with a hint of a metallic resonance. It was almost a perfect recreation of her vocals, but not quite.

The captain strapped himself into his seat. Facing straight up to the sky, he fastened his restraints. "I'm going to miss a whole lot in 30 years. It's kind of exciting to think of what society becomes." His hands caressed his heart locket as he shut his eyes, "So much to catch up on."

"I cannot keep you updated on what's going on as we go. The ship can only hold a steady signal to earth for so long, and with the velocity that this ship travels, it won't be physically possible once we've left the atmosphere."

He hesitated for a minute, not paying much attention to what LYS was saying.

"Honey, how long will I stay in contact with Earth once I leave orbit?" Their past conversation rung fresh in his mind.

"That's the thing, it's physically impossible to send information that fast without the use of tachyon particles, but we both know those are all theoretical. We can only talk for a few minutes after we break contact. You will be traveling so fast, the delay will grow as the signal decreases until it's basically non existent. I'll be with you through your launch, though." She looked at him and saw his face drop with disappointment. "I'm sorry."

"No worries, I'm just happy we can be together for my final moments after take off."

He snapped back to reality, "Yeah, we knew that when we designed you and the ship's long distance communication systems." All of his attention was focused on the metal chain clasped in his hand, opening his fingers, the locket that laid in his palm revealed a picture of Cynthia in her mid thirties. She was holding hands with a younger version of the space pilot. Despite the picture's small size, it showed very fine details on their faces.

Seeing his wife was all the captain needed in order to over run his brain with memories. Memories of their wedding day. Memories of her coming home with her second PHD. Memories of planning and working on this mission. She was so beautiful in absolutely every way possible. The way her eyes would light up with excitement while talking about thermonuclear fusion. The way her hair would flow like waves on a beach. The way she smiled when the Captain told her she looked stunning. They would spend so many late nights coding together in the light of the our electric fireplace. It was just the two of us, and we were happy, Wallace thought to himself.

"Preparing to launch in T-5 minutes." LYS booted up the flight controls. As the computer shifted everything to manual, the cockpit flickered to light. The flashing dials and switches LYS turned on drew Wallace's attention back to the cockpit, away from his beloved memories. Suddenly, the main screen turned on, revealing a somewhat old, but very muscular man in a uniform. His shoulders were completely covered in a rainbow of ribbons and medals Wallace could only assume denoted his valor. A part of Wallace wished that his wife was on the other end and that she miraculously got better, but instead, he had the Vice Admiral in her place.

"You ready for this, champ?" The voice boomed, causing Wallace to jump back from the surprisingly loud speakers. He shook his head ever so slightly, finding it ironic how much money had been spent on this mission, and how many test runs they'd had of this scenario and yet, they somehow couldn't get the volume of the speakers correct? The devil is in the details, Wallace thought to himself as he raised his eyes to meet those of the Vice Admiral. As her peered into the scene, he couldn't help but let his mind wander. Compared to Cynthia, the Admiral obviously knew much less of how to work the intercom system, Wallace silently judged, his wife constantly on his mind.

"As ready as I'll ever be, Vice."

"Relax, it will be just like the simulations. I'm sure you are aware of your mission, but I am contractually obligated to repeat it back to you." The Vice Admiral always had a way to make people laugh, while also sounding completely serious at the same time. "You will be traveling to planet C-97Y0. It is 14.2 light years away, so once your path is confirmed to be clear, you will give LYS the order to put you into a cryogenic sleep. Are you clear?"

"Yes Sir!"

"Good. When you wake up, you will undergo tests pertaining to the surface and whether or not we can terraform. You will be too far from Earth to send or receive signals, so you will be alone with LYS. It will guide you through the final stage of the mission, and initiate the cryosleep going to and from the planet. You will be launching soon." He shifted a little, "I'll see you in 30 years, pal."

The radio coms went silent. It was just Captain Wallace, LYS, and the sky with the occasional, small, cumulus cloud. A wave of happiness washed over the captain as he thought of the time he spent with Cynthia. In their infrequent moments of down time, the captain and his wife used to look up at those clouds and see little animals or objects.

"Look at that! Do you see it? It's a baby!" She used to get so excited over every discovery.

"Where? I don't see it?"

"It's right there." Her arm pointing up to the sky outlined the shape of a baby in the fetal position. "Do you see it?"

"I see the cloud you are referring to, but it doesn't line up right. Where are the arms?"

"You are always so literal." She said with a chuckle, "It's a baby."

For someone as advanced in science and math as she was, she had the imagination of a child, Wallace recalled with a smile. She was always able to see images and patterns in everything, and to this day, it still amazed him.

"Preparing to launch in T-1 minute."

The captain shook his head as he came back to his senses. This was his life story, he thought, nothing he could do in his future could come close to being as important as the mission. Thinking back to himself, he quickly recalled all the preparations that had gone into getting this mission off the ground over the past ten years. Everything he'd learned, everything he'd gained, everything he'd lost. Cynthia. All flashed through his mind in what seemed to be his last seconds of calm before the tumultuous launch began.

The radios booted up again with the voice of the Vice Admiral. Along with everyone in that control room, he was extremely nervous going into the launch. None of their stresses compared to that of Wallace's.

"Launch Commencing in 10..."

Sweat began to bead on his brow as he tried to comfort himself, repeating over and over again that it would be just like the simulations.

"9...8...7...6...5..."

This is my chance to make a difference in the world. He looked out the large front window and saw smoke as it engulfed the majority of the window.

"4..."

Breathe. Just breathe; he kept repeating to himself, over and over again, his heart racing as the seconds ticked away from him.

"3...2... 1..."

"Do it for Cynthia."

"And we have lift off."

All went silent. The shuttle started to rattle. Captain Albedo's knuckles changed from a pale pink to a bright white as he gripped the controls tighter and tighter, his breathing intensified. The roar of the rocket engines erupted through the ship, amplified from the inner metallic walls.

Stay calm Wallace. Stay calm, he tried to stop his heart from pounding through his chest

"Your blood pressure is increasing, Captain"

"Shut. Up. For. A second!" Every word was being strained as his chest weighed down on his lungs. Every second that passed pressed his chest against his ribcage more and more. His head started to ache as the blood was pushed to the back of his brain. Any kind of movement was impossible as he shot away from the Earth in the rocket.

Wallace's final thoughts as his ship flew through the sky were, "I can't breathe."

***

"Stay conscious, Captain. We are approaching the thermosphere. Only a little bit more until we have exited the majority of Earth's gravitational field."

"Please... Just... Be... Quiet... For a moment." Air was leaving his mouth just as fast as it was coming in.

As the intense weight on his chest dissipated, a wave of nausea hit the captain. Floating in his seat, the only thing holding him from moving around the cockpit was his restraints.

The radio sparked back to life after a second of static. "Stage one is complete. Prepare to discard secondary rockets. Congratulations, Captain, you are on your way to Planet #C-97Y0."

Cheering was heard echoing through the comms as the happiness poured through the speaker, noting the pride that was undoubtedly abundant back in mission control.

"Is there anything you need before we sign off, Captain?"

"Yeah, actually. I have two things. Can you send me a picture of the sky? Make sure it is a good one, though."

"Umm... Okay. It will be sent in a few minutes."

"Thanks, I forgot to take one before I left. I won't be able to see the sky in a few decades, and I don't want to forget what it looks like completely, ya know?"

"Yeah, I understand. What else do you need?"

"If Cynthia ever wakes up, can you tell her that I will love her forever, and she will be in my heart on this entire journey? I want her to know that I followed through with this mission for her, and that in 30 years, I'm expecting to see her waiting for me when I get back."

The radio was silent. The uneasy breathing of the Vice Admiral was the only thing that went through. The entire command room stopped dead in anticipation of what this conversation would become. The Vice Admiral, speechless, took a deep breath and started talking. His heavy sigh blew on the microphone, making it audible to the captain.

"Wallace, I... You got it." The charismatic admiral was at a loss for words.

"Thanks. See you all on the other side."

One button press was all that was needed to separate the pioneer from the rest of the world. Disabling the communication system, Captain Albedo sat in silence.

***

I'm so stupid. Why did I say that? His mind was racing as his face grew redder and redder. That was so embarrassing. Why did I do that to myself? Why did I do that to the Vice Admiral?

"You cut off communication, so an apology is not possible until you come back home." LYS' blank stare dug into the side of Wallace's head.

"Oh, so you're in my head now? Stay out and leave my business to me."

"I'm not in your head. I determined how you might be feeling based on the physical signs you were presenting. You started sweating as soon as you cut communication. The temperature in the cockpit has remained constant, and you haven't done any physical work since take off. You started grinding your teeth, and your heart rate increased drastically. Along with this, you're--"

"I get it, you can read me like a book. Now--"

"Captain, I suggest you listen to what I am saying."

Again, the ship was completely silent. Taken aback by the sudden interruption from the android, the captain decided to listen to what it had to say.

"Don't dwell on the past. The mission is here, and this is all that matters. My job on this ship is to keep you on task, and I can't do that job if every moment you get, you start thinking about your wife. Captain, the world needs you to start prioritizing the possibility of colonizing a new planet over your comatose wife."

The captain dropped his head to hide the rage induced tears that were balling up on his face. "You see, you may know every little thing there is to know about anything, but what separates you from me is empathy. I have feelings, and you fail to understand that. The reason I accepted this mission is for my wife. You wouldn't be here if we didn't choose to create you in our free time. Cynthia was my everything. She *is* my everything." Wallace's face grew pale as he got more and more frustrated with LYS. He sat up in his chair, and faced forward. Just looking at the robot made him angry. "We humans aren't just bodies. We are people. All with different perspectives on life and the universe. You are a program that runs tests and gives outcomes depending on the situation given, so the next time you try to tell me how I should feel, I will not hesitate to pull the plug on your operating system."

Stupid machine.

***

"Captain, whenever you are ready, I can initiate cryosleep for you. Just tell me when."

The captain nodded, making sure to not give the robot eye contact.

"Captain?"

"What is it, Lys?"

"Don't blame yourself for Dr. Cynthia's condition."

"Are you sure you want to talk about this, LYS?"

"Considering you need me to put you to sleep, yes, I am confident you are only threatening me. Anyway, It's not your fault."

"What are you getting on about?" His anger was growing. Offended that the robot he created is trying to comprehend his feelings again after his empty threats.

"I don't know any specifics of what happened, but I do know that the love you have for her is unparalleled. If you did cause it, there is no way it was on purpose."

There was no escaping it; she was right, he needed her, Wallace thought to himself. "Cynthia had a brain aneurysm shortly after finishing the code for your artificial intelligence. We worked for days together, but she refused to sleep but I didn't. I should have made her put her work down, but she was so determined to finish you as soon as possible. I just... I should have stopped her." His voice started to quiver. He took a breath and continued. "The nurses put her into a medically induced coma to save her. I should have stopped her. She's in a coma because I let her strain her body like that." Captain Albedo said shakily, as new tears flowed freely as his sobs reverberated against the metal walls.

The two sat in silence, once again, but this time, it wasn't due to disagreements. The captain understood that he was able to go into his cryogenic chamber at any time, but he wanted his mind to be at peace before falling asleep for a decade and a half. He pulled out his locket, and looked at it for one last time.

"Hey LYS?"

"Yes Captain?"

"Thank you."

"Oh I'm just following my programing. Are you ready to go to sleep?"

"Yes, I am ready."

"Alright. I will begin preparations. You need to change into your clothes, and get in the pod when you are ready. Then, you need to put on the harness. However, before you do anything, I have a message from your wife." It handed him a white undershirt and grey sweatpants. He took it from the robot before realizing what she said.

"You what?" He didn't believe her. "What did you just say?"

"I have a recorded message from your wife."

"Play it, then!" He would have been jumping out of his seat, had it not been for the seat restraints.

"Yes captain. Playing message…"

"Hi honey. This come to you as a surprise, but I thought you might need it going into the cryosleep. This mission has been our life for the past ten years. You are sailing away into space at the moment you are hearing this, but I just want you to know that-" the sound of sniffles broke the next words, "I don't know how to say this without crying." He could hear her as she took a pause, breathing in deep and started again. "I love you, and will forever look up at the sky and see you in the clouds. A ton of thoughts must be swimming through your head right now, but no matter what, continue with the mission. Follow through. Don't let our life's work go to waste. I love you. Good luck."

Wallace sat, speechless, taking in every word she had said. With a new look of confidence and determination, the captain changed into his new clothes, and drifted over to the pod in the corner of the ship. With the locket in one hand, he strapped himself in with the other. Slipping into the rough, straight-jacket-like suit inside the pod was uncomfortable, but necessary for the cryogenic freezing process.

"LYS, I'm ready."

"Are you sure? There is no turning back once I turn it on."

"I am sure. Fire it up."

The once dark cylinder flickered to life with bright, white lights. A low buzzing noise could be heard from all the inner components booting up.

"Ok Captain, I need you to relax. It won't work properly otherwise."

Breathe, Wallace. Breathe, he concentrated on calming his nerves to ensure a safe transition to his long sleep.

"Your vital signs are normalizing. Commencing startup in 10 seconds. 10… 9…"

The captain held onto his locket, taking deep inhales followed by deep exhales.

"8… 7…6…"

I got this, he heard the doors of the chamber seal shut.

"5…4…"

Just breathe.

"3…2…1…"

"I love you Cynthia."

"0…"

✳✳✳

"Hi, I've come to see Dr. Cynthia Albedo. I heard her condition is improving, and I have a message from her husband."

"Oh, hello there."

The admiral's overpowering size and his military uniform caught the secretary off guard.

"She hasn't gotten many visitors lately, but I'll have someone take you to her room." The man sat down in an uncomfortable waiting chair that was extremely small for his immense size.

A few minutes later, a nurse entered and guided the admiral to Cynthia's room. On the way, he noticed many of the rooms were filled with families and other loved ones, all either visibly happy, or crying and mourning. "We are almost there, sir. Are you aware of the state of Dr. Albedo's condition? Or were you just told she was awake?"

"All I know is that she is up. As soon as I got the news, I rushed here. Her husband gave me a message before he left, and it is my duty to fulfill his request." As he said that, his chin rose with pride. Knowing that he was about to carry out what Wallace sent him to do made him feel a sense of accomplishment.

I've been waiting six months for this, he thought to himself, I know what to say, but how am I going to tell her?

"I'm sorry to inform you, but in her state right now, Dr. Albedo is awake, but remembers very little of her life. She barely remembers Wallace and her parents, but apart from that, her mind is basically a blank slate." She sighed. "It's such a shame. On the bright side, she is recovering, and we will soon start to help her recall all those lost memories."

"Well, progress is progress!" The admiral covered his disappointment with a quote his past military higher-up said all the time. Since Wallace's mission started, he was promoted one rank higher, and given more medals of service.

"Here we go. She's right inside. I'll be right out here if you need me." The nurse gestured to the final door of the long hallway. The door had a shelf of vases next to it, all filled to the top with an assortment of beautiful roses.

The admiral slowly walked into the room, each step feeling like they took forever. If only Wallace was here, he thought, he would have killed to talk to his wife before he left. After hesitating for a few seconds, he went to start the conversation he had been thinking about since Wallace left.

"Cynthia? Hi. I'm Admiral Mathews. I have something that your husband, Wallace, wanted me to tell you."

After a minute of silence, he decided to try again.

"Cynthia?" His voice filled with worry and guilt. "I have something I need to tell you."

All of her attention was out the window. She watched the clouds with a look of envy, almost if she knew that was where her husband was.

The admiral sat down on one of the chairs next to the bed, facing the window with Cynthia.

11

Minutes of complete silence passed, the two of them looking up at the sky through the bedside window.

"Wallace," She muttered under her breath.

"I'm not Wallace, but I need to tell you that he loves you with all his heart and will remember you forever and ever." The sentence jumped out of his mouth involuntarily. He had it prepared after the long wait in silence.

"Where is he?" Her voice was extremely soft and gentle, very quiet, but still audible.

The admiral froze up completely, unaware of how he was going to answer the heavy question.

"Ummm," the solution rushed to his head. Pointing to the clouds, he waved his hand across the sky. "Somewhere up there. He's going on a big mission, and won't be able to see you for a while. He loves you with all his heart and will always be with you" He started sweating profusely. His only prepared line not seeming to have any effect on her.

She gave no response, only staring up at the clouds. Every plane that passed over head seemed to fascinate her.

In the doorway, the nurse stood watching and waiting for a good moment to interrupt.

"Ever since waking up, she's been obsessed with that window. We open the blinds for her every morning, and whenever we ask her if she wants anything else, she pushes us away. She's just content with the sky" The Admiral joined her in the doorway. "You tried your best. She just needs time."

As they were walking out of the room, they heard Cynthia start whispering.

"He's up there." A small tear falling down her face. "He's up in the clouds."

✳✳✳

Odd Bond

"**A**ngelo."

"Here."

The teacher looked back down at his attendance sheet, marking the student present. Angelo fixed his eyes on his desk, patiently waiting for roll call to end. The rapid tapping of his right foot on the floor occupied the short pauses between each name. So far, the names down the roster were students that Angelo did not mind. His eyes followed the light lines and marks that other students had sketched on the desk.

Clearing his throat, the teacher announced, "Eugene—"

"It's Gene," a student from the far corner of the room interrupted. "Gene is fine."

The name struck a bell within the class. All the students but Angelo turned their heads in unison, glaring at Eugene. Some smirked and snickered at the sound of his name, and others groaned lowly at the sound of his voice. The teacher carried on down the list, exhaling loudly through his nose, and the class returned to face the front.

"Alright, that's enough," the teacher said. "We greet each other with smiles and friendly faces." Angelo wondered if that was possible for the class. He shrugged the thought off, however, knowing he was not part of the problem.

Angelo turned slightly, straining his eyes just to look at Eugene with his peripheral vision. Oh, it's him, he thought. Angelo felt indifferent towards Eugene. To him, Eugene was another speck of dust in his universe. Another student, Angelo mused, that he would come across,

15

yet add no significance to his school life. What the other students thought did not matter; they were all one and the same, and it was of no concern to him. Suddenly, Eugene jerked his head up and met Angelo's eyes. Angelo felt the gaze pierce into his own head. Feeling his stomach weaken and his breath stop short, Angelo averted his face from Eugene's line of sight. Thoughts punished his mind. I was staring too long, Angelo told himself. God, that was embarrassing.

Marking off the last box, the teacher peered at each student in the class and greeted, "Welcome to Algebra." The typical first-day-of-class introductions took the entire period. Every face rose to look at the clock as the bell above the doorway rang. Through the screeching of chairs across the floor and the rustle of backpacks being lifted, the teacher exclaimed, "Have a good rest of your day!" The students immediately paired with their friends as they exited the room, giggling and muttering to one another.

Angelo bent down to tighten the laces on his shoes. His movements were planned, each with the purpose to avoid the impression that he was stalling. Opening his bag, Angelo's hands fumbled inside, moving its contents meaninglessly. Everything was set in place, packed, and ready to go, but Angelo felt otherwise. He was desperately trying to think of something, anything, to do in his own seat till the cluster by the doorway diminished. As the last of the mass squeezed out, Angelo sighed with relief and prepared to leave. Upon grabbing his backpack, his ear picked up the clang of a chair against a desk. His eyes followed the source to one corner of the room. He assumed he was the last one to leave, with the exception of the teacher, scrolling through his emails. It was Eugene.

As the boy stood up from his seat, he faced Angelo and nodded upwards with his head as a greeting. Angelo lifted his left hand and gave a slow, awkward wave, as if he was wiping a foggy mirror. Eugene responded with a quizzical expression, his eyebrows perked upwards and his eyes squinted. Acknowledging the rising tension between the two, Angelo pivoted on his right heel and left the room.

✳✳✳

The next day in class, Angelo sat near the back of the room. He already knew that the students would become a distraction. The back was his comfort zone, an isolated dome that he was quite familiar with. Eugene rushed into the room and sat beside him. The bubble of space that enveloped Angelo popped, and the serenity he felt began to fade.

"Hey," Eugene said, looking briefly at Angelo. He settled down, threw his backpack to the side and scooted closer to his desk.

Angelo observed his actions before replying, "Uh, hello." His voice was tender and barely audible, untrained from being quiet throughout the day. Think, Angelo, think, he repeated to himself. In his caged mind, conversation was taboo. Talking meant gossip, and gossip meant drama. Rumors rapidly spread around the school, no matter where the person was. As word was passed down from person to person, it became increasingly exaggerated. It would evolve to such absurd levels, yet people gulfed it down, believing it to be true. Such was the case between Molly and Emma, and last year's incident in the cafeteria.

Molly's voice broke the usual noisy commotion of the lunch room, "That's not what I—"

"Shut it, Molly," Emma said. The room slowly hushed and heads turned to the source. The two girls were standing in front of each other. "You stole my boyfriend 'cause you were jealous I had it all."

And, with a spike of rage, Molly grabbed an opened milk carton and held the item above Emma's head. Emma gasped as Molly tipped the carton over, a wicked smile plastered on her face as she let the milk pour out. The entire grade screamed at the savagery. Molly threw the carton aside and stood victoriously with her hands on her hips. A custodian hurriedly wrapped a towel around Emma, escorting the drenched girl out of the cafeteria. The people chanted Molly's name, deeming her the heroine as she proudly left the room.

Angelo stared at Molly's gleaming expression as she made her exit. He scanned the cafeteria, trying to determine the source of the cheery uproar. Why? Angelo thought. Both of them had done things that had consequences. It was then, however, that Angelo understood Molly's gallant stature and the praise of her fellow students. He recognized the power of words; how it brought one to glory and one to ruin. One sentence from today could be the topic of tomorrow. Talking, he concluded, inevitably led to trouble. Fortunately, not one more word escaped his mouth as class began immediately.

The teacher was relentless in lecturing the students about the content. Each sentence that spewed from his mouth automatically silenced the hand that a student would hesitantly raise. One student looked at their friend, mouthed a "What?" and shook his head. Another student, sitting by the window, raised an eyebrow and shrugged in confusion. There was another, diligently taking notes, who breathed loudly out her nose expressing her distress. She put her pencil down and crossed her arms as a final act of surrender, but the teacher pelted words like bullets with no mercy.

But Angelo simply stared. The hieroglyphics etched into the whiteboard were native words that his mind had no difficulty in translating. While the teacher's words streamed through his head like a steady river, Angelo looked to his right to find a ravaging ocean. Eugene was fidgeting madly. His feet were rapidly tapping the floor, pencil striking the messily scribbled paper, one hand rubbing his temples. The boy was wearied, and the crinkles on his forehead became more apparent by the second.

Suddenly, the teacher turned around and pointed his marker at an unsuspecting student. The whole class sat up to attention, and their eyes darted to where the end was pointed.

The teacher asked, "Gene, what are the factors for this polynomial?" The problem on the board was fairly easy, at least to Angelo. He caught on, however, to the true purpose of the question. It was to determine whether anyone was paying attention, or falling behind.

First, a second of silence. Eugene cleared his throat and his voice cracked as he muttered, "Uh…"

Angelo surveyed the room and saw every pair of eyes glaring at the victim. Eugene was petrified, unable to form an answer. He just needs a bit of help, Angelo thought to himself. He clenched his teeth and took a deep breath. Keeping an impassive expression on his face, Angelo covered his mouth partially with the sleeves of his sweatshirt and whispered, "One and two."

"One and two," Eugene confidently repeated. The class returned their gaze at the teacher.

The teacher nodded in response, "That is correct." He wrote the numbers on the board and continued on with the lecture.

Eugene exhaled in relief. He lightly hit Angelo's shoulder with the back of his hand and said, "Thanks, dude."

***

That miniscule exchange was all that was necessary to start an odd bond. When Eugene sparked a conversation, it made Angelo feel relaxed, albeit, in the middle of class. It would begin with a random question that digressed from the lesson, and initially Angelo would shrug it off or nod nonchalantly. But as Angelo became more exposed to Eugene's train of thought, he began to search for an answer within his own head. It distracted him from the pressures of school that flooded his mind.

In the several days that they were beside each other in Algebra, Angelo grew more comfortable and found it easier to speak. When the class answered with silence, Angelo raised his hand with the correct answer.

"Let me ask again," the teacher announced. "Does anyone remember the sine of pi over three?" His eyes swept over the room, searching for one reckless soul to please his disappointment. Every head dangled over their notebooks, determined to be invisible. Come on, Angelo thought, you're their only saving grace.

"We went over this last—"

Angelo perked his head up and declared, "The square root of three over two."

"Thank you," the teacher exhaled, showing gratitude with a gentle bow. "Someone knows what they're doing."

Eugene, on the other hand, became more focused with Angelo around. Sitting next to the smartest kid meant there was hope that he would have help whenever it was needed. True to his wishes, Angelo would always answer Eugene's questions when a problem was too confusing. In return, he would say something ridiculous. There was a time when he was able to leech a chuckle out of Angelo, and Eugene never lived it down. Angelo would never admit it, but he was undoubtedly amused.

One day in particular, Eugene was a little too loose and cracked a joke loud enough for the teacher to hear. It was not any normal joke either, but one that was a bit out of bounds from what would be considered standard. Angelo was ready to laugh through pursed lips, but the teacher reacted instantly.

"Hey! We do *not* make those types of jokes in this classroom," the teacher said sternly. His eyes were fixated on Eugene and the class stopped to stare as well. Angelo clenched his teeth and fixed his expression, feeling every muscle in his body tense up, hoping that he was not caught. He kept his eyes low, reading the math on his notebook in an attempt to put up a facade. It did not take a genius to understand the situation Eugene was in, however.

Eugene gave a sheepish smile before saying, "Sorry, my bad." The teacher resumed his activities and the class returned to work. He let out a defeated sigh and whispered to Angelo, "Oops."

Angelo mumbled, "You really don't hesitate, do you?" His words were drowned by the overwhelming embarrassment that consumed him.

"What?" Eugene said.

Angelo turned his head so his voice could be heard more clearly. "You need to hesitate more. You speak whatever's on your mind."

Eugene did not know what the word 'hesitate' meant. He was about to ask, but he caught a glimpse of pain in Angelo's eyes. The look was too familiar to Eugene and he noticed the expression in a snap. It mimicked the same appearance people had when he would present his thoughts on a subject.

He muttered to Angelo, "Okay." For the rest of the class, the two stayed silent.

The starting bell for the next period already rang and Angelo was having trouble opening his locker. His fingers were shaking from the fear of being late to class. Just as he was able to successfully open the locker, Angelo heard someone speaking from around the corner. He slowed his movements and perked his ears in an attempt to listen.

"I don't get what's wrong with him," one student said, clearly exasperated. Their footsteps were nearing closer, and Angelo moved his head further into the locker to avoid being identified. The same voice, a girl's, continued, "It's like he's got a mental condition or something."

"Yeah, Gene's annoying as hell," another student said. Angelo surmised that they were two girls. His eyebrows furrowed upon hearing that name. "He literally doesn't know when to shut up."

"Right! And he's so stupid, like—" her voice cut off, followed by a frustrated sigh. They turned the corner and passed Angelo, now messing with the textbooks in the locker pretending to organize them. "God, I feel so bad for Angelo," the girl said as if she was giving her condolences.

As their footsteps became softer, Angelo sniffed the air around him. Nice perfume, he thought.

Eventually, Angelo began identifying the faults within Eugene's behavior. No longer did he snicker at Eugene's antics, but rather saw it as a distraction. Eugene was met with a blank face no matter what he did. He was beginning to become a burden.

The class had recently started a new unit, and they were in the midst of a fundamental concept. Angelo sensed Eugene lean over and whisper, "Dude." The boy kept his head stationed to face the whiteboard while his eyes looked at Eugene. "Why did the chicken cross—"

Angelo immediately shut him down with a gesture of his hand. Not one muscle on his face moved as Angelo told him sternly, "Focus." He directed Eugene's attention and pointed to the board.

Eugene was physically taken aback by Angelo's response. "Right, sorry," he apologized and proceeded to pay attention.

One particular day, an old woman ambled into the classroom with a yellow ID card strapped around her neck. She placed a beige file folder on the teacher's desk before introducing herself.

"Hello, class." Her voice shook with her frail age. "I will be your substitute teacher for today." With a shaky twig of a finger, she pointed at the file folder and said, "Your teacher has left some classwork for you to finish by the end of the period."

Immediately after the attendance, the class divided itself into its distinct friend groups. Angelo and Eugene stayed in their respective seats. Before Angelo could even begin to write his name down, Eugene began, "Why didn't the toilet paper cross the road?"

"Okay, let's tone it down," Angelo intercepted. His calm demeanor urged Eugene to listen. "You know that stuff can wait."

Eugene argued, "But we have a sub today."

"I have work to do," Angelo said steadily, "and you are a distraction." He rolled his eyes and tackled the assignment. Eugene felt the words sting his chest. It was quickly overshadowed by astonishment, however, as Angelo worked with unparalleled speed and efficiency.

Angelo finished with half an hour left in the period. The day had been relatively slow, and having nothing to do for the rest of the class was detrimental. With nothing to fill his head, Angelo would retract into the mess of fantasies that were his thoughts, often longing for the calmness that he created within them. It was a bit peculiar that Eugene had been silent since the class started. He seemed occupied in trying to finish the problems. Pride ignited within Angelo, feeling that he had some influence in Eugene's work ethic.

Taking out his notebook, Angelo flipped the pages. His eyes scanned over previous doodles from months past, a collection of his daydreams and fantasies. When he flipped to a fresh, blank page, Angelo began to sketch. Art was never his forte, but the artistry was present. The figure in his mind was translated onto the paper through light strokes, lines protruding from its general shape. It was traced with darker lines, adding pressure at the tip of the pencil. Its teeth and eyes followed; pointed fangs drawn through a technique in flicking the wrist, and menacing eyes with shrunken pupils that spewed hostility. The scales were intricate and tightly packed like chainmail. The final image was of a dragon, from its slender neck up, with its mouth agape like a viper preparing to strike.

As Angelo was drawing the final touches, Eugene was pulled away from the packet by the illustration that caught the corner of his eye. It was grand and detailed, nothing in which any other student has had the ability to present.

"Did you draw this?" Eugene asked, his admiration for the drawing apparent in his voice, varying in pitch with each word.

Angelo stared at him first. Are you stupid? He thought. The hand holding the pencil slightly twitched. Discarding the possible replies that were currently forming in his head, Angelo said, "Yes, Gene."

Eugene groaned in awe. "That's so cool," he said. Holding the page in his hand, he requested, "Yo, can I take this home with me?"

"Sure?" Angelo was taken aback by the question, but he was sure that Eugene had good intentions.

***

Class had started, but the teacher was busy talking to another faculty member. Eugene pulled out a piece of paper out of his backpack in a rush, the page slightly crumpled. He called out to Angelo, "Dude, look at what I drew."

Angelo analyzed the page. With the slightest hint of doubt, he asked, "You drew this?"

"Yeah," Eugene immediately answered. Angelo felt an aura of pride emanating from the boy. The drawing was another dragon, but of its full scale. It took up approximately two-thirds of the entire page. The dragon's pose was dynamic, wings folded and its arms tucked in while its neck curled. It was clear where the point of perspective was, but some parts did appear disproportionate from the rest. Huh, he thought.

As he continued to stare at the page, Angelo felt a rising suspicion. He looked at Eugene straight in the eyes and asked, "Why did you bring my drawing home?"

Eugene's face glowed with delight as he answered, "I wanted to draw something as cool as your dragon." Angelo returned his eyes to the paper, squinting as he scanned over every detail. Eugene watched intently, waiting for a response. As the silence extended, however, his patience began to falter. "So, what do you think—"

"So, you copied it?" Angelo said. His words turned a few nearby heads in the room. Eugene froze as the words penetrated his confidence.

"No! No, well," Eugene stumbled in his words. His eyes frantically looked in every direction, searching within his own head for an appropriate answer. The students in the vicinity nudged others to look and listen. "Well, yes, but—"

Angelo immediately blocked Eugene's rambling. As soon as his suspicions were confirmed to be true, Angelo felt no sympathy for the boy's futile excuses. They were right, he thought. His mind snapped back into the conversation when Eugene's mouth stopped moving.

Eugene could not break the impassive expression that Angelo had introduced him to early in the year. Even still, he needed to quench the underlying anger within Angelo. Attempting to shift the mood, Eugene retracted back into his ego and said, "It's pretty awesome, though, huh?" The class directed their eyes at Angelo, eagerly waiting for a response.

"It's pretty stupid," Angelo retaliated with astounding volume. The shockwave of frustration that burst out of him brought fiendish smiles to the surrounding students' faces. Stuck in his fit of rage, Angelo shoved the paper onto Eugene's chest. The words that formed in his head flowed directly out his mouth without obstruction. "You're stupid."

***

As days passed, the stalemate between the two did not waver. No one bothered to seek closure, going through the rest of the school year in their own way. Angelo began to talk. Although he involved himself in petty drama that he had attempted to avoid, talking about Eugene's incompetence put Angelo on the spotlight.

"Did you hear," the students began, "some stuff went on during algebra between Angelo and Gene."

Others spoke in disbelief. "No way," they said. "Angelo? That quiet kid?"

"Yeah, people saw him get pissed at Gene. Don't know why, though; must've been bad."

"Damn, well, if Gene could piss Angelo off then that just means Gene's the problem."

"I knew something was wrong with Gene."

Soon enough, they approached Angelo, searching for the need to satisfy their craving for conflict. They pestered him with no remorse for invading his privacy.

Slithering in with a tempting smile, they struck, "Yo, Angelo. We heard some things went down between you and Gene. What happened?"

Great, Angelo thought. Now, he had a swarm of vultures flocking around, waiting for their prey to make a move. Wishing to end things with one quick strike, Angelo blurted, "Nothing special. Told him to screw off."

Their faces were in shock as their breath escaped through their mouths. "Damn," they muttered. The words that left Angelo's mouth spread like wildfire. As more people discovered where those words originated, the more attention he attracted.

He tried to douse the flame, "Come on, guys. It's not that big of a deal."

The flame persisted, *"You* of all people told Gene to screw off."

Upon hearing them talk, something surged within Angelo. It was not clear at first, but it felt empowering. He was the talk of the town; the hero that brought the pest to its knees. For once, Angelo felt the power swell and he adored the newfound sensation. The superiority stirred Angelo to continue, and the cycle of rumors ensued.

Eugene grew quieter. As word circulated the grade, it persistently hacked away at his dignity. Walking through the hallways, Eugene's name was thrown around like a chunk of paper. It was not difficult for his ears to catch the ball as it always seemed to aim straight for the basket.

"You think he kept asking Angelo for the answers?"

"Probably. There's no way Gene could pass Algebra."

Something within Eugene dwindled as he collected each and every word. It added weight to what was once light. He wished that he had known sooner. Eugene simply wished he had realized that Angelo was no different from the rest.

A Scholar's Pawn

Everything around me fell into focus, my gaze distracted by the cold concrete walls covered in graffiti. The busted up couch I sat on was almost too uncomfortable today, springs poking into my back as the musky smell wafted from its fabric. Soft groans left the walls, the creeks of the abandoned building protesting as it settled in its foundation. My ears caught the sound of small clicks and flicks. I looked across the room to see DeAngelo, a lanky Italian boy, fiddling with a butterfly knife, his pale legs kicked up on a cement block as he leaned back into a disfigured chair. A jolt from my left made me turn to face the person next to me, Ray. My eyes looked first at the hand, then traced up the arm which had been covered in a faded denim jacket. Up from his hazel face, I glanced at his hair. It was made up in dreads, clean locks that fell over his green eyes. After finally catching my eye, he looked at me, not even saying a word. All he did was silently nod towards what lay in my hands. I finally looked down.

The envelope felt heavy as I held it. I couldn't, for the life of me, bare to rip it open. This was my future, this was my next four years, hell, this was the rest of my life. With the stark white envelope contrasting with my dark hands, I ran my thumb over the emblem in the top corner. Reading the words 'Admissions Office' almost made me nauseous.

"God, I feel like I'm gonna pass out." I muttered, using one hand to rub my forehead.

"Dude," Ray blurted out, clasping a hand around my shoulder, "you're gonna be alright! If anything, you should be excited about this."

His bright smile was nearly contagious, getting me to smirk a little through the sweat on my face.

"Yeah, man," DeAngelo jumped in, dropping the knife into his lap, "I'm not usually an optimist about this type of stuff, but my gut just tells me that there's no way there could be bad news in that letter." The two looked at me, faces lighting up with positivity. With a little more confidence than before, I nodded my head, looking back down at the envelope.

The paper felt like glass as I slipped my nail through the side, cutting it open. Biting my lip, I grasped the letter between my fingers, carefully sliding it out. My hands shook as I began to unfold the paper. The words blurred as my glazed pupils tried to adjust. Breathe, I tried to remind myself, just breathe. Closing my eyes, I took in air slowly through my mouth, letting it go out my nose with a soft 'huff'. Finally, I focused on the paper, reading the lines of words one after the other.

My face stayed neutral as I read, tears involuntarily welling up in my eyes, dripping down my cheeks. I could see the happiness in my friends' faces drop, worry slowly taking its place. Ray reached a hand out again.

"Jamal? Is… is everything-" I quickly cut Ray off.

"I got in. I got into Duke." My neutral face curled up into a smile. My anxieties were washed away as the realization hit. The paper shook in my hands out of pure excitement. The two boys went from worried, to shocked, to exhilarated in a matter of seconds. They yelled in joy, both of them standing up and grabbing me in order to pick me up and hurl me into the air. I didn't protest as they cheered, excitedly parading me around.

After their adrenaline settled, they finally put me down. DeAngelo smiled wide as he picked up the six-pack from behind his chair.

"Glad to know I didn't run a packy for nothing." He snorted, tossing Ray and I each a beer. We all cracked open our cans, raising them up, as if to make a toast.

"To the best friend I ever could've asked for." Ray beamed, smiling at me with pride.

"And to the smartest kid at Vincit High!" DeAngelo added, finally inniating us to clink our drinks together. The rest of the chilly January night was met with joyful laughing and spilled drinks as we did what any group of troublesome high schoolers would do. It was a wholesome celebration amongst close friends, a true feeling of happiness warming my chest. Indulging myself, I decided to let this feeling ride out for the rest of the night.

***

My body felt warm and fuzzy, the heat from the blankets tingling my skin as I came to my senses. Looking around, it was clear that I was in my own bed at home. Not certain how I had even managed to get there safely, I thanked whatever force had gotten me back home unscathed. It was probably sheer luck that the night prior had been a Friday without me even realizing. Adjusting myself upwards from my bed, shocks of pain shot through my body. I certainly wasn't used to that type of alcohol consumption, but, despite my aches and pains, the day's peaceful vibe left me feeling relaxed. It was a quiet Saturday morning, listening as my parents shuffled around in the adjacent rooms. My father shuffled around in the kitchen, preparing a sweet smelling breakfast; presumably pancakes since they were his favorite. I could hear the front door open up, my mother greeting him as she presumably walked in with fresh laundry.

Soon after stepping out of bed, I headed for the shower to wash the musk of yesterday off. I didn't expect a hand to jut out of nowhere, blocking my way to the bathroom.

"Oh, uh, good morning, mom," I said, yawning in the process. I stretched as she looked up at me, eyes going from soft and motherly to sad and concerned. It took me a moment to notice the already opened envelopes in her hand. One of them was easily recognizable, it being the acceptance letter I had already opened. The other, however, was something I hadn't seen before, something that obviously didn't make my mother happy. It was like she had been gripping onto them all morning, both papers covered in large creases and wrinkles from where she held them.

"Jamal…" She started in a soft voice, "we need to talk." My stomach twisted. Had she found out about last night? Was she going to punish me for drinking? I could take a slap on the wrist and a lecture from my mom any day, but with the look of worry on her face, I could tell it was more than that.

She led me into our small kitchen, sitting me at the dingy dining room table. My dad, still working at the stove, avoided looking at me. I began to nervously fiddle with the stained tablecloth, rubbing it between my thumb and index finger. All the thoughts of what they were going to tell me raced through my head. Were they not going to let me go because I was drinking? Were they too disappointed to let me go?

"Mom, what's going on?" I finally asked, heart racing. My eyes darted from my solemn mother to my father, slowing his movements as he turned to look at us. It was those moments- slow moments- that would let the actions of the world fall silent. There was a disappointment hanging in the room, the pressure becoming near unbearable.

"We saw your acceptance letter, and we are so very proud of you. We're so happy you got in, seriously." She gave me a flickering smile that soon turned back into a frown. She looked at the envelopes, picking up the unknown one and sliding it over to me.

"But, we got another letter today." I picked up the envelope, checking the return address.

"This... this is the scholarship I need." My heart pounded in my ears. I could already tell where this was going as I quickly pulled out the letter. My suspicions were proven correct as I read every word. My eyes became heavy with tears, but this time, I didn't have my friends there to comfort me. My grip tightened on the paper as my mother began to speak.

"Jamal, I... I know that we've talked about this before. We can barely support having a house as small as our own. How on Earth do you expect us to pay without a scholar-" I didn't even let her finish before I was already out the door. I didn't even bother grabbing my jacket, wiping my eyes as I stomped across the street. Ray's house, surprisingly smaller than my own, sat in a yard surrounded by a rusted chain link fence. Flinging the gate open, I stumbled through his yard towards his door, almost wading through the weeds.

I placed my forehead against the door, frantically knocking as I awaited my answer. The door gently swung open to reveal a groggy and confused Ray.

"Hey dude, how's it going?" Ray looked up to see my puffy eyes, worry immediately resurfacing on his face, "Jamal? What's wrong buddy?" He gestured to let me in, but I quickly refused.

"The three of us need to talk," I wiped my eyes once more, letting out a shiver, "is De with you?" Ray nodded in response, gesturing for me to come in. Looking into Ray's disheveled living room, I could see DeAngelo sprawled out on the couch, blankets strewn about. DeAngelo's eyes blinked open as we walked in, immediate confusion shown on his face as he saw me come into view.

"Jamal... what..." He slurred out sleepily, wincing a bit as he stretched.

"De, Jamal needs to talk to us, so up and at 'em bud." Ray went over to DeAngelo, helping him off the couch. Watching DeAngelo hobble around sleepily, my eyes also caught the sight of Ray's mom shuffling into the kitchen. She shared a warm smile with us as she made herself a cup of coffee, but nothing felt as warm as the sudden embarrassment of my situation as it washed over me.

"Can we not talk here? I... don't feel comfortable saying this with your family around." I whispered to Ray, shifting my weight around uncomfortably.

"It's fine man, I know where we can go to talk."

✳✳✳

It wasn't long before we all sat in the same spots as the night before. DeAngelo sat on the lopsided arm chair, as Ray and I sat across from him on the busted-up couch. Beer cans still littered the floor, a reminder of our past endeavor. The happiness of the night prior seemed wasted as I gazed at the remains. After filling the two in on my new conflict, I sighed, letting my face fall into my hands.

"Jamal... I don't know what to say." Ray said, looking away from me in disbelief. DeAngelo sat quiet, almost totally still. I looked up at him, but he lacked any emotion. If anything, it looked like he was deep in thought, trying to process what was happening.

"It's," I breathed heavily, "it's fine. I can probably just make my start at the local community college. I can get a job and maybe get my own money to pay for Duke. Then I'll apply again and hopefully-" DeAngelo began to interrupt me.

"Dude, screw that." DeAngelo blurted out, giving off a devious smile, "I have a much better plan." His voice was mischievous, giving me an instant bad vibe. DeAngelo didn't have a reputation for having very *legal* ideas.

"De, your plans always spell trouble." Ray said, mimicking my thoughts exactly.

"Hey, come on man! My plans are *always* foolproof." DeAngelo huffed.

"Uh huh, very foolproof. Remember your 'foolproof plan' from 8th grade?" Ray sneered, watching as DeAngelo just chuckled in response.

I could see the way DeAngelo smiled maliciously as he remembered his mischievous past. Around the time when Ray and I had first become friends with DeAngelo, he wanted us to get a taste of the troublemaker life. Although Ray and I certainly weren't angels when we were younger, we still managed to keep our heads out of any disciplinary trouble. DeAngelo, however, wanted to put a stop to our "goody two-shoe" facade and start a new beginning for us. With no reason attached besides getting us to "live a little," DeAngelo conjured up a plan to ruin the school's lunch. Since one of us mistakenly said "Only leeches would enjoy this sludge" during lunch, DeAngelo quickly knew what we needed to do. It took us weeks to get our supplies as we waded the water of the river, hunting for little blood suckers. When we had enough of the little slimy creatures, we put the plan into motion. Although it took a lot out of us, in the end, it was kind of hilarious to watch people freak out during lunch.

"How could I ever forget? People were picking leeches out of their lunch all afternoon!" DeAngelo continued to giggle as Ray just crossed his arms.

"Yeah, but do you remember which one of us got sent to the principal's office first?" Ray noted, pointing to himself in annoyance. DeAngelo only scoffed in response, deriving a couple more chuckles before I decided to speak up.

"Okay, okay, just tell us your 'oh so' great plan." Although the situation seemed to have turned lighthearted, I had to get to the point of it.

"Well, you see," DeAngelo began to fidget, "I can't actually tell you specifically. It's gotta be a surprise for it to, y'know, work." Ray and I both looked at each other with immediate worry, then back to DeAngelo.

"De, whatever you're conjuring up in that crazy head of yours, I would honestly like you to keep to yourself." I knew this was trouble, anything he calls a 'surprise' is worth worrying over.

"Aw c'mon, don't be so dramatic Jamal!" DeAngelo stood up, walking towards me.

"De's got a point, you do like to dramatize 'lil things with all your big and fancy words of yours. I bet it's not all that bad bud!" Ray said, almost reassuringly.

"Look, me and Ray will take care of all the dirty work. You just gotta go home and get some rest. Maybe try studying or something, keep on top of your classes and all that." The fact he described it as dirty work only added fuel to the fire, but he didn't let me interject any longer.

DeAngelo shooed me out of the room, getting the message across that he wanted me gone. Before finally forcing me out, DeAngelo said one last phrase.

"Things are gonna turn out well, just you wait."

After that, I decided to finally comply, sauntering out of the dark building back into the cold outdoors. Only prayers could help keep me content as I walked back home.

✷✷✷

Each page turn became more and more exasperated as I grazed over the text. The ripped edges curled in my fingers, the uncomfortable worn texture of the paper making my face scrunch up. Each calculus equation added to my ever growing headache. In a final act of frustration, I took the cover and slammed it shut, shoving it away in disgust. I wasn't normally like this, usually trucking through my studies with ease. But it was all too much to focus on. Studying only reminded me of the college I couldn't afford. But if I didn't focus on studying, then thoughts about

DeAngelo's plan would get to my head. It all just gave me a migraine, and I just wished my body would let me sleep. The dusty textbook did not help with my head either, the musty odor wafting back in my face as I slammed it shut. Trying to tire myself out, I decided to pace around. Step by step, I circled my room, letting my mind finally indulge in thoughts of what DeAngelo could be up to.

Was he planning on poisoning Duke's admission staff? No, I already got in. There's no point to that.

Was he going to counterfeit the money? Nah, he wasn't the brightest bulb in the chandelier, and I highly doubted he had the smarts nor the equipment to manage that.

Was he going to hack the school into believing my balance was already paid? Honestly, I wasn't even sure he owned a computer.

In the end, pacing around kinda worked, but it only ended up making me slightly anxious and tired. But all of a sudden, it hit me. I stopped in my tracks, letting my next thought sink in.

Was he planning on robbing someone? I tried to shake the thought away with no success.

DeAngelo had always been a troublemaker, plain and simple. He wasn't necessarily violent, but he was a huge fan of knives and was fascinated by any high-thrill heist movie. I couldn't even count on two hands the amount of times he made me watch Ocean's Eleven. It just made an uncomfortable amount of sense, leading me to pace out my door and back into the outdoors. There's only one person I knew who could put my thoughts to rest.

Trotting across the street for the second time that day, I rapped on the door again. This time, Ray's mom opened up.

"Oh, hi Jamal! What brings you here at this hour? Did you forget something here?" Ray's mom answered sweetly, her voice warm as usual.

"Hi Mrs. Risus, is Ray 'round?"

"He's home, but he's already in bed." In bed? It was only like 9:00. Ray never went to bed that early, especially on a weekend.

"Is he still awake?" I asked curiously.

"No. When I came home, he was already asleep. He seemed pretty exhausted, so I decided to not wake him. I thought he was tired because he's been with you and DeAngelo?" She questioned back.

"Ah, no. I had to go home early to study. Big test on Monday, y'know?" I semi-lied, not explaining that the two had literally forced me out of our get together. A better question came to mind as I thought of DeAngelo. "...did DeAngelo come home with Ray?"

"Oh, no actually. Ray said he was staying at someone else's house tonight."

"Mhm," I hummed, realizing that DeAngelo wouldn't have stayed the night with anyone besides Ray or me. Something definitely wasn't right, but all I could do now was turn to Mrs. Risus and say, "Well, thank you. I'm just gonna go home then."

"Alright, Jamal. Have a good night, now." She said with a wave.

Waving back, I walked back across the street. Unease sunk in as I entered back into my own home.

I lied flat on my bed, watching my hands as the fingers twitched and jumped. That surreal feeling when I'd drink too many caffeinated beverages suddenly coursed through me. My eyelids never stood still, blinking from opened to closed, opened to closed, over and over again. The silent room hurt my ears as all I could hear was my own heartbeat. Loud, uninterrupted pulses kept me from being able to sleep. Out of agony, I turned to face my wall, placing a hand on the cold surface. The icy touch almost soothed my overheating body. My head felt haunted as I forced my eyes shut. Sleep felt like a distant dream at this point.

✳✳✳

I could only thank God that the next day was a Sunday. My alarm clock blared as I slowly opened my eyes begrudgingly, dreading the coming day. Throwing my hand to the nightstand, my hands grazed the sides of the alarm clock, accidentally pushing it from the table top to the ground. With a loud bang, I let out a groan, turning over to reach underneath the bed to fish around for it. I didn't even remember setting the alarm the night prior, but my frustrated hand just grasped the body of it and shoved it back in its place. Cracking an eye open, I let the light from the window blind me for a split second before viewing my surroundings. Yup, still my room; a small nightstand adjacent to my bed lay cluttered with different papers and textbooks, while a hill of clothing piled high in the middle of the floor, waiting to be cleaned. The room, while a little messier than I would have liked it to be, still felt like my room in the end. Forcing my body up, my eyes squinted in pain. The lack of sleep I'd gotten the night before had really taken a toll on me, frustration becoming my key emotion. Eyeing the now silent alarm clock, I saw the time. The day still ticked in the A.M., which meant I had a chance to catch Ray before he decided to leave. Grabbing a random pair of shoes from the floor, I laced them up sloppily, forgetting to double knot. My body shook with questions, leading me to ignore my parents as I bolted out the door, marching on over to Ray's.

By coincidence, I managed to walk over in time to find Ray leaving his own home.

"Hey-" My eyes drifted down to what Ray was hauling. A duffle bag? "...Ray."

"Hm?" Ray looked up, nervously eyeing me. "Oh, oh, hey, Jamal." His eyes quickly averted mine as he adjusted the strap on his shoulder.

"Yeah, hey..." Before I began questioning him, I pointed to the bag.

"Whatcha got there?" I squinted with suspicion as he nervously reached to scratch his neck.

"Yeah, this. This is just some stuff De needed for... y'know."

Glaring at him, I started my barrage of questions.

"Actually Ray, I don't know. I don't know and I really think I should. What the hell are you two up to? Why are you guys being so suspicious?" Ray looked down at his feet, as if he was a child being scolded.

"Listen, I- I wanna tell you. Honest, I do," Fidgeting with the button on his denim jacket, he continued, "but De said that if I told you, the plan would most likely be a flop."

"But why hide stuff about me... from me?" I objected, stepping forward assertively.

"This- this needs to work! If I tell you, it just won't work!" He started to become defensive, stepping back in return.

"Why does it have to work, Ray? What about me knowing is so

detrimental towards this plan?" Turning his head away, Ray clasped his hand to his mouth, as if he was stopping himself from talking.

"We just wanna get you to where you wanna be," he inhaled, lip quivering, "You deserve to be doing what you wanna do, man. I just don't wanna see you stuck here when I know you could be doing what you love." My anger subsided for a second as I realized the pain in Ray's voice.

"You've been there for me so many times before, I just- I just wanted to help you out just once in return." Ray went silent after that, the sudden awkward despair of the situation setting in. I reached out in compulsion, only for Ray to jut back in protest.

"I gotta go, man." He said, adjusting the bag back onto his shoulder.

Instead of objecting any further, I just watched as he ambled off. As he went down the sidewalk, he let his head hang low, hands jammed far into his pockets. Something didn't sit right inside of me, as if I had done something wrong. A frustrated sigh left my throat, my conscious not even noticing my body move as I began walking in the same direction as Ray. If he wasn't going to tell me what was happening, I was just gonna have to figure it out myself.

Ray went from sullen to anxious, head jerking back and forth to look around himself, seemingly paranoid of his surroundings. Slinking behind to stay of sight, my eyes watched as Ray approached his destination. It wasn't exactly shocking watching as Ray slid himself through the hole-cut in the wire fence. He snooped his way onto the property, entering the door to the all-too-familiar abandoned building. As to not draw attention to myself, I waited a few moments before making my way over to the fence. Narrowly avoiding the edges of the cut wire, I tiptoed cautiously across the gravel. I set myself up below the room we would usually hang out in-- a smaller, almost office-like room, that stood only about a story above the entrance-- assuming that's actually where he was going. My ears quickly caught the sound of voices, causing me to go still.

There were the muffled sounds of my friends, listening as the two greeted each other. Hiding in the nearby overgrowth, I allowed my ears to perk up, straining them to listen into their conversation. Sounds of shuffling and rummaging could be heard, as DeAngelo verbally began an inventory of the things being reviewed. His words were unclear, but repetitive. Multiple times, I heard the word 'check' being uttered. It wasn't until a few 'check's in did I realize what they were listing.

"Gold watch?" Ray would say.

"Check." DeAngelo would utter back, a clank following afterwards.

"Gold necklace?" DeAngelo started.

"Check." Ray would then follow up, the sound of clattering chains in return.

The cycle continued on for awhile. My original suspicions began to smooth out as a new theory popped into my head. The two weren't actually about to plan some movie-fueled bank heist, to my relief. But obviously, they had been on the hunt for something entirely different.

"Hey, De?" My thoughts were interrupted as my ears pricked up to listen again.

"What's up?" De said in response, continuing to shuffle through their findings.

"I was just wondering," Ray had noticeable hesitation in his voice, "are we ever gonna tell Jamal about where we got the money from?" A hearty laugh erupted from DeAngelo, throwing me off as I listened.

"Come on dude, you really think Jamal would ever accept the money if we told him where it came from? He's too much of a goody 'lil two shoes, man. We'll just lie about where we got the money from" DeAngelo chuckled, a sort of menacing tone in his voice.

"But he's gonna ask. He already asked me what we were doing." Ray sounded nervous, which in return led DeAngelo's laughter to quiet.

"Well, you didn't tell him, right?" The intimidation rose in his voice, giving me goosebumps.

"Of course I didn't, dude. But," Ray paused anxiously, "he just seemed really upset. I think we've put more stress on him if anything, which right now probably isn't the best."

"Ray, he's gonna feel guilty if we tell him where the money came from. You know damn well we don't need this stuff, our families don't need this stuff, and the neighbors don't need it either. It's all just stuff, stuff without any use. It's like, what's that big word Jamal likes to use, 'materialistic'?" I sneered at the all-too edgy comment. It was a very DeAngelo thing to say, which led to more pieces of the puzzle coming together. But the sudden long pause that came from the two left a pit in my stomach.

"He deserves this more than we do." I barely heard DeAngelo say. For some reason, that statement made my body wrack with emotion. It never dawned on me that DeAngelo cared that much for me. Putting his own freedom at risk just so I could go to Duke?

"De, I want Jamal to go to college just as much as you do, but this," I could imagine Ray gesturing to the pile of goods they had, "it's just not right, and I know Jamal would never want this." The atmosphere was tense, even from where I hid. The sound of frustrated footsteps began, exiting the room and down the corridor.

"Hey, hey wait!" Ray's voice followed the footsteps, which led to me sinking deeper into the bush to further hide myself. I watched through the leaves as DeAngelo stomped out the entrance, rattling the fence as he tore his way through the hole. Ray followed shortly behind him, calling out his name as he expressed for them to just 'talk it out'. Watching as the two fled the property, I snuck my way out of hiding. I have to do this quick, I thought to myself as I dashed into the building.

The air felt colder than usual as I jogged up the steps towards our hangout. The door was left open, leaving light to flood into the hall. Peaking in, the sight that came into view made my stomach churn. A pool of jewelry, watches, and small antiques lay scattered about the wooden table. Small items I'd seen on shelves and through windows, on necks and wrists. I walked up to find Ray's infamous duffle bag, shiny contents spilling out from it. Disappointment swelling in my gut as I surveyed the scene in front of me. They stole stuff from not just anyone. These were definitely items from richer parts of the city. God, my head began to swim as I realized the extent of their endeavor. My thoughts rang out as my legs began to tremble. In a matter of seconds, I took the duffle bag and put it at the base of the table. Taking my arm from one end of the table to another, I swiped all the treasures back into it. Picking up Ray's stuff, my eyes didn't seem to notice the second bag slumped against the couch. The weight of it all made it harder to walk, my shoulder beginning to slump as it struggled to keep it balanced. Legs still trembling, I attempted to speed out the building.

My steps landed heavy on the sidewalk, ankles hobbling as I

attempted to carry the stolen treasures back to my house. Head hung low, I watched my feet land one after the other. It wasn't until my eyes looked back up did I notice the person watching me. One of my neighbors sat on his lawn, hovering above a rose bush. He stared at me, squinting his eyes in order to recognize me. Before long, he smiled in my direction, giving a wave to me. I gave a small, hesitant wave as my nerves started to tighten. He broke his eye contact in order to look down at what I was holding. Not long after, his smile began to drop, leading me to begin walking again. I gripped the bag tighter, sweat forming above my brow. It wasn't long before I was finally back home, nearly tripping up my front steps. Breathing a sigh of relief, I let my head rest against the door. Letting my hand go to the knob, I attempted to jiggle the door open. I froze, heart race increasing as the realization set in. The door was locked. My parents weren't home. Adrenaline began to kick in, my breath hitching as I tried to catch it. I could feel the weight begin to push down more and more on my shoulders, the stress making me give into the pressure. A familiar sound shocked me as the red and blue flashed the street once again. Turning around, my eyes made contact with a cop glaring at me as he stepped out of the car. Before I could say anything, he began to speak, tone harsh and stern.

"What's in the bag?" He snapped at me as he began to approach.

"Nothing, I-" I inhaled sharply, "It's not mine-"

"Not yours, huh?" Bad answer. "Show me what's in the bag."

"I- I'm not," My voice trembled in fear as I began to hesitate, "I can't-"

"Show me what's in the bag, now!" He shouted as he hovered his hand over his holster. Panic overtook me, pushing the bag open and out of my hands so it lay flat on the ground. Before the officer could say anymore, I was already on the ground, knees against the sidewalk and hands behind my head. Watching the officer advance towards the bag, he began to shuffle through, pulling out handfuls of jewelry. My face dropped, a hot feeling of shame overtaking me. Looking up once more, I could see two figures down the street onlooking the situation. The familiar bystanders stayed at a distance, watching as the officer forced me into the back of his cruiser. I could tell, even from afar, the faces of panic they wore as they realized they couldn't do anything in the moment. All they could do was watch their best friend get taken away by the cops.

***

Fiddling my thumbs anxiously, I watched the people in the station walk by my cell. It was a timeless place, time almost stood still inside it as everything on the outside continued on. It all felt surreal, especially due to the deafening silence that hung low within the building. People would pass by without a word, officers would go into other rooms in order to speak. From the amount of time I sat there, it almost left my mind why I was even there in the first place. Closing my eyes, I let my head lean against the cold stone wall.

Almost as soon as I tried to relax, the door to the cell flung open. An officer stood at the entrance, bluntly gesturing for me to get out. Before I could even mouth out a 'what', the officer pointed more firmly.

"Just get out." He exclaimed in the process.

Deciding not to question any further, my body stretched up from where it sat, hurriedly walking out of the cell. The officer turned, leading me through the station. My first thought was that I was getting transferred to a different cell, and my irrational side kept thinking this was my beginning steps to *prison*. But, to my surprise, he led me to the lobby of the station, where a familiar face greeted me.

"Jesus Christ, you're actually okay!" Ray said as his face lit up, grappling me into a hug.

"What's going on-" I muffled into Ray's shoulder as he squeezed me tighter.

"I'll explain when we get home, just enjoy the freedom you got man."

***

The concrete room was almost the same from where this started. Same ragged couch, same empty beer cans, same busted-up arm chair. Only thing that was missing was the small Italian boy who would sit in that chair, fiddling around with a pocket knife. The absence of his ambience, the absence of his voice was almost heartbreaking.

"So, he really just turned himself in." With my eyes were glued to the floor, my body wasn't even capable of forming tears anymore. Out of anything that had happened the past couple of fever dream-esc days, this had been the most shocking.

"Look, he... He couldn't handle the guilt. I tried to stop him, but he thought it was the best way to get you out of their." Ray tried to get me to look at him, but to no avail.

"I just- I just don't understand. I don't even know what I'm not understanding. I just..." Without finishing my statement, I curled up and leaned further into the couch, away from Ray. All was quiet for a moment, the silence of the room shaking me only further as I continued to live out the repercussions of my friends' actions.

"This-" Ray cleared his throat, turning over to grab something from beside the couch, "This is probably not a good time, but..." Turning over to see what Ray had grabbed, my eyes widened.

"You still have a whole other bag of stuff?" I questioned, watching as Ray peeled open the bag to reveal the contents.

"Yeah, this was DeAngelo's bag. He got a lot, certainly a lot more than I did. I'm not sure what we're going to do with this, considering turning it in doesn't seem like the best plan of action right now-"

"No," Ray looked up at me with surprise, "I know exactly what we're going to do with this." Ray looked at me quizzically.

"If DeAngelo really planned to pawn this stuff just to give it to me for college tuition, then there's only one way to repay him for doing something so... Hazardous." I stood up, grabbing the bag.

"Whoa whoa, hold it bud! What exactly do you think you're gonna do to *repay* him?"

"Isn't it obvious? There's only one thing we can do to help him right now." I breathed for a second, clearing my head as I seriously began to think this through. Holding up the bag, I pointed to it as I spoke.

"We're going to bail him out."

✳✳✳

Patiently Waiting

I raced around the wide open rooms, exploring every new nook and cranny. Everything was new to me, the amazing smells of different foods, the open spaces filled with furniture, and the humans who loved to follow me around. Strange objects surrounded me that were nearly double my size and sections of the ground were covered in a soft material that warmed my paws from the cold floor. My nose guided me to an open room at the end of my new home, there was the smell of someone else that definitely wasn't human. I rounded the corner of a large cushioned object to find an older looking dog sleeping on a mat. Looking up at me with hesitance, he slowly got up and walked over. White hairs all around his face came into view as he approached me. My body was shaking uncontrollably, a little at first, the shaking grew up through my whole body and I felt the uncontrollable urge to talk to him. A suppressed yelp left my throat as I looked at him eagerly. Walking towards him, my nose seemed to have a mind of its own as it began to sniff everything- how excellent, a new friend!

"Why are you in my home?" The dog eyed me with suspicion

I began to run circles around him; I always wanted to meet another dog- who knew it would happen today?!

"Hi! I'm new! Who are you? What is this place? Why am-" the dog cut me off with a loud bark to keep me from continuing on with my long list of questions. I came to an abrupt stop in front of the other dog as he let out a long yawn. There was an awkward moment of silence as I waited for him to finish. The older dog began looking me up and down as his nose guided him around me. I figured it was better to stay quiet; I didn't want to annoy my soon to be best friend.

"The humans call me Tico. You will eventually get a name from them. I hope you won't be here long. I don't want you to disturb any more of my naps" As he mumbled this out, he slowly walked over to his mat and collapsed back into his previous spot. I stood in place, frozen in confusion, did I say something wrong? I mumbled to myself. My gaze fell back onto Tico who was snoring loudly. I began to notice the immense amount of wrinkles across his face. He was obviously much older than I was. I looked towards his tail which seemed to curl around itself. Something must have been wrong with it since mine was just a stub.

Why wasn't he excited to see me? Didn't he see how awesome this was?! There were two of us-*two!* He was the first dog I ever met and he seemed to hate me. I couldn't wrap my head around it.

As I watched his chest slowly rise and fall, the humans stood behind us making strange noises. Turning, I saw that they were staring at me, repeating words that just didn't make any sense. Curiosity got the best of me as I walked towards them, wondering what they kept repeating. After my first two steps, their teeth became much more visible and their voices became so much higher. My eyes darted back towards Tico, hoping he would wake up so he could tell me what was going on.

As my back began turning away from the humans, they started saying it again,

"Lincoln! Lincoln!" I walked back over and the same eruption happened. Suddenly, it clicked. The humans were now all sitting on the floor with their arms open wide. A smile crept onto my face as I walked towards them. The closer I got, their voices somehow grew higher and higher pitched. With each step, I became more and more excited until I was sprinting into their arms. As the four humans began petting me I thought, Lincoln, it had a nice ring to it. Maybe this wouldn't so bad after all.

✳✳✳

To Tico's dismay, I stuck around for much longer than he had liked. Everyday he would try to keep his distance from me, but that didn't stop me from still trying to hang out with him. If Tico heard me run into the same room as him, he would get up and leave before I could even speak. Also, when the humans gave us food, it was almost as if Tico inhaled his food and left before I could finish my first bite. It started making me really annoyed, what was up with him?! All he ever wanted to do was sleep, eat, and avoid me! My anger got the best of me one night as Tico tried to slip past me again.

"What is your problem?!" Tico turned to me as a low growl began to grow in my throat. Facing me, it was clear he had no sense of urgency in his calm movements. It made my blood boil as he responded with slight yawn.

"No problems here, if anyone seems to have a problem, it's you." I could have sworn a smile began to form on his face.

"Wha- What is my problem?! You leave the room anytime I walk in! And you never want to talk to me! You scarf down your food so fast that you are gone before I have a chance to follow! And you are asking me what my problem is?!" We faced each other, not saying anything, just waiting for something to happen. Tico's smile had turned back into its usual annoyed frown as he let out a low sigh.

"So you aren't leaving?" My body grew stiff as he spoke. He was just making me more annoyed with each word. None of this made sense, I had just gotten here, there would be no point in me leaving.

"Why would I be leaving?" Tico seemed to notice how lost I was since he let out a short chuckle. I watched as his eyes could no longer meet mine and as he began to talk, there was a shift in his voice.

"I kinda thought I was alone." Before I had a chance to question him, one of the humans called us outside, by instinct we turned around and walked into the warm air. Tico strolled over to the edge of the landing and sat down. As my legs carried me next to him, Tico began to speak, but he seemed to be lost in thought as he looked out to the grass below us.

"All of this was mine, I could sleep whenever I wanted to, eat at my own pace..." Tico's eyes began to scan over everything on the ground below us as a low growl began rising in his throat. I waited to see if he was going to keep talking as my head tilted up towards the sky. It was pretty dark out, but the sky was filled tons of shimmering lights. There was just enough light to illuminate the ground below us so that we wouldn't get lost in the dark. Out of the corner of my eye, Tico's teeth became more and more visible as his growl grew louder and louder. In almost a whisper I spoke up,

"What's wrong?" Tico suddenly went silent, the only sound left came from the occasional rustling of leaves. Our eyes met and in that moment I wish I hadn't said anything. He opened his mouth, revealing every single tooth while also barking in my face. Each growl and bark sent a shiver down my spine. I had no idea what to do or say except to wait for him to stop and make the first move. After what felt like forever, he yelled at me,

"This was all mine...All of it! And then you showed up." He quickly turned away from me and stormed the stairs into the yard, leaving me behind in utter shock. As I watched him leave, I said the only thing I could muster out.

"I just wanted to be friends."

✳✳✳

Saying things were awkward between Tico and I was a major understatement. I had no idea how to act around him anymore, it was kinda scary. Our relationship was already pretty shaky, I didn't want to miss out on us becoming friends. Spending some times with the humans was really the only option left. The major downside was I couldn't understand what they were saying most of the time. I remember just walking aimlessly around the house when all of a sudden, something whizzed by my face. Turning, I saw the little girl jumping up and down and pointing in the direction of the object. My eyes darted from her, back to the object, and back to her. Suddenly, there was a low groan from across the room.

"Bring it back." I slowly looked back at Tico who was watching me from another one of our mats. I was still so confused, why would she throw it if she wanted it? Tico immediately picked up on my hesitance and barked back in annoyance.

"Oh my gosh, Chloe wants you to bring it back to her so she can throw it again!" I went to get the object before coming to a halt.

"Chloe? Wait does she have a name too?!" Tico began laughing so hard at my question, I wasn't sure if I should be relieved or annoyed. After catching his breath he continued.

"What else would it be, did you really think none of the humans had names?" My tail began to shaking like crazy. This was so exciting!

"What! How was I supposed to know they had names? Wait can you tell me all of their names?!" I had completely forgotten about whatever Chloe had thrown at me as I walked towards Tico. Tico pushed himself up, sitting on the floor, as I took my spot right in front of him, eager to learn as much as possible.

"So that one is Chloe," he said as he looked over to her before she stormed out of the room, "the other kid is Joseph. And the big one with short fur is Patrick, and the one with the long fur is Mary." There was a huge smile across my face as I repeated each of the humans' names.

"Chloe, Joseph, Patrick, Mary, Chloe Josep-"

"Ok that's enough Lincoln." Tico let out with a slight chuckle as he pushed himself up off the mat and started walking out of the room. I followed not far behind him, quietly muttering the names over and over again, the smile never leave my face with each name.

***

The more time I spent with Tico, the more I noticed little things about him. Without fail, Tico would always sit by the humans whenever they ate together, waiting for anything to fall. I think he sat near them because he liked being around them, but he would never admit that to me. Tico would also spin in two circles before finally laying down to sleep. He must have had some method to his madness because I have never seen him forget to do his little spins. I usually noticed his little quirks whenever I was waiting for him. Waiting for Tico was one of my favorite things to do, even when Tico would go as slow as possible just trying to annoy me! The best times to wait was before heading doing into the grass, we usually raced each other down and around the entire yard- it was so fun! One night in particular, as we walked outside there was water falling from the sky. I stood by the edge of the landing where the water didn't hit us, looking up in awe. Tico was right behind me, staying very far from the edge. There was a constant pitter-patter sound as the water hit the ground, the sound instantly calming me down. My nose couldn't get enough of the refreshing smell as I waited for Tico to come up beside me. Moments passed by before realizing Tico hadn't come up beside me. My head turned at the sound of him quietly mumbling to himself.

"Nope, nope, not doing it, no." I started laughing at him. I could barely breathe as the supposedly 'tough dog' glared back at me.

"What's wrong? Afraid to get a little wet?" I stifled through fits of laughter. Tico just glared at me before walking back into the house, his back legs slipping on the wet ground. My eyes glanced up towards Mary, who kept her eyes fixed on Tico as he slipped. Her face seemed to grow more tight with each slip and her voice had lost its usual chime . Before I had time to question it, she slammed the door abruptly behind him. My ears perked up again at the sound of the water hitting the ground. As my body turned back towards the yard, my mind kept replaying Tico slipping and Mary's low voice. That wasn't normal, right? It was probably nothing, just human issues, I told myself as I began my descent towards the wet ground.

✳✳✳

Tico and I sat by the back door of the house, watching as white puffs began to fall from the sky. Tico sat there gazing back at the humans, not as excited about this odd stuff. I was jumping at the door, hoping to run outside. I had never seen anything like that before and I wanted to take it all in. I mean come on! There was white puffs falling from the sky! He finally got fed up with me jumping around him as he barked out,

"Can you calm down, Lincoln?" Despite the anger in his voice, I couldn't stop leaping around him. My legs seemed to have a mind of their own, pushing back off the ground every time I landed back down.

"Are you kidding! This is so cool! What is that? Can I eat it?" Before I could let out the millions of other questions on my mind, one of the humans opened the door. In an instant, I sprinted to the edge of the long descent down to the ground, my body skidding to a halt before going over the edge. It was like nothing I had ever seen before, the entire yard was covered in the puffs. As I leaned out, one landed on my nose, there was a shock from the coldness which quickly went away as it turned into water- so cool! I turned around and watched as Tico slowly made his way out the door. My body shook uncontrollably as he slowly made his way over next to me.

"Could you hurry up? I'm dying to get down there!" Suddenly, I noticed how much he struggled to maintain his balance on the cold ground. His back legs slipped on almost every step and his face was tight with concentration as he slowly placed each down. Mary's low voice popped back into my mind. I shook my head, trying to get rid of the thought, but as I looked behind Tico, I could see Mary and Patrick watching him. They kept muttering back and forth, and never looking away from Tico. My body tensed up and all I could think was this isn't right. Tico finally made it by my side, he stared out at the open area, I figured it wouldn't be bad to bring it up.

"Tico, are you-"

"Don't." His sudden anger shocked me. I realized this was a line Tico wouldn't let me cross. We stood in silence, the cold breeze causing me to shiver. All the excitement from only moments earlier was gone. My eyes drifted back to Tico, waiting to see what he wanted to do. He finally pushed himself up and slowly made his way back inside. I watched as he hopped into the house, but I couldn't get myself to follow. I looked up and locked eyes with Patrick, neither of us turning away. His mouth opened as if to say something but he stopped, and instead let out a long sigh before closing the door. A chilling breeze caused me to look back out at the yard to see the white puffs fall more slowly to the ground. Another speck landed on my nose which I quickly shook away to avoid the chill. My paws began to sting against the cold ground, which I tried to shake away with no luck. Tico was right, I shouldn't have been so excited, I thought to myself. I backed away from the ledge and made my way to the door as my mind repeated the same line over and over again. Don't worry about it, it's Tico, he's going to be fine was all I could say.

✳✳✳

As it became warmer out, the humans began taking me on "walks." It was the one time I could explore the world around me. Even Tico would get excited for walks, but quick into our adventure he usually regretted the extra exercise. I watched Tico as we descended down a large hill, his back legs were basically dragging against the rough ground. I knew better than to bring it up with him, it would only ruin the walk. As we walked, large vehicles would occasionally drive by, leaving behind an awful smell. The smell was quickly overpowered by the mark of previous dogs who were there before us. Tico made sure to teach me to leave a mark behind whenever we came across something left behind by another dog. We stood by a tree, there must have been at least three other dogs there before us. Tico demonstrated what to do, I didn't understand why we had to leave our mark behind for other dogs. As if he somehow read my mind, Tico turned back to me.

"This area is ours, we need everyone to know," he said in a confident voice while he circled back around to mark the spot one more time. Patrick pulled us along before I even had a chance to try. I tried to tug back against the rope, but Patrick was much stronger and pulled me forward. Tico looked back and saw me pulling back against Patrick. I expected him to be aggravated or annoyed, but the kindness in his voice took me off guard.

"Don't worry, you will have plenty of more opportunities." He kept walking, trying to find a new spot for us. I couldn't help but smile, Tico was not one to show positivity too often. Soon enough Patrick let us stop for another moment, Tico turned around and waited for me to walk over next to him. He didn't say anything, but he gestured for me to leave my mark. I assumed I did it right since Tico didn't say anything. We continued on our walk, waiting for each other every time the other stopped. I noticed a smile that grew on Tico's face that stayed for the entire time. I couldn't stop the smile from creeping onto my face as well.

***

As much as I enjoyed the walks, the humans slowly stopped bringing Tico. I was rather annoyed, it wasn't as fun without my friend by my side. It didn't make any sense, it wasn't like Tico was a bad dog. I assumed Tico didn't care because it meant less exercise for him and more sleep time. It also seemed like the humans were always watching us, and more specifically Tico.

When ever they would let us outside, one of them would carry him up and down the stairs to the grass. They were giving him all there attention and giving me almost none. What was the big deal? Most of the time he was sleeping, what could possibly happen to him? One night I walked into one of the rooms thinking about how annoying the humans were being, but that annoyance was quickly replaced with worry. The humans were sitting together and talking in hushed tones. Tears streamed down their faces and their bodies were shaking. The only person that talked was Patrick, but even his words came out in stutters. I stood in the entrance of the room just watching the scene unfold with no idea what to do. After a few moments, Chloe stood up and stormed out of the room, Joseph not far behind her. Once the kids had left the room, Mary almost immediately began to shake more as Patrick rubbed her back. I couldn't stand being in the room any longer so I ran. I didn't care where in the house I ended, it just had to be away from any of the humans. I skidded my way to Tico, who was spinning in his circles to lay down to sleep. My quick entrance startled him.

"Is everything ok?" his voice seemed to have no emotion to it. No annoyance, no anger, no happiness or exhaustion, nothing. I tried responding without sounding too shaken up.

"Oh, me? Totally fine...yeah... What about you?" He gave a solemn smile, something definitely wasn't right.

"Never been better." There was a long pause, the silence was painful. I made my way next to Tico as he finally collapsed into his spot, our bodies huddled close together for warmth. We sat there for a minute, neither of us saying a word.

"Lincoln," Tico said quietly, "You're a good friend." I shifted my eyes towards him, but he wouldn't meet my gaze. I wanted so badly to just catch eyes, as if seeing his face would help get rid of the knot in my stomach. Instead, he shifted his body away from me. I had to stop myself from getting up and sitting right in front of his face. Tico's words should have made me happy, I should have been saying how great of a friend he is too, but the sadness in his voice stopped any words from leaving my mouth.

"I just thought you should know that...Good night Lincoln." With that, Tico shut his eyes, a slight snore began soon after that. My body felt numb, nothing made sense. Questions flooded my mind. What was happening with the humans? What was Tico not telling me? I forced my eyes closed to try to get some sleep. I would just ask Tico in the morning.

✳✳✳

I woke up to find myself alone, the humans and Tico had already left. I thought it was strange, Tico normally waited for me or at least woke me up. I made my way around the house, searching for anyone. Then I heard it, the sound of gasps of breath. I followed the sound into what I assumed was Chloe's room, where the whole family sat together with Tico in the middle. Chloe and Joseph were hugging Tico, a constant stream of tears running down. Mary and Patrick sat beside them, rubbing their kids backs, the same tears running down their faces. I watched Tico, he leaned into every pet, every hug, giving more kisses than I had ever seen him give. As everyone pet him, there was the quiet sound of gasps for air between their tears. Nothing made sense, the question of why was screaming in my head. I couldn't stand to watch, but my feet felt glued to the floor. Being in the room made my fur stand up against my skin, I hated every bit of it. Tico finally looked over at me and in that moment I wish I never left the mat. There was so much pain in his eyes and yet there was a smile across his face. My legs wouldn't move despite my brain yelling to go over to Tico or to at least speak up. There were thousands of things I could be saying to him, like what was happening, are you okay, can we please just go back to sleep, but I couldn't. Patrick finally stood up, in his hand was Tico's old gear from our walks. My heart skipped a beat, we hadn't been on a walk together in ages! I began circling Patrick in anticipation as he put Tico's gear on, waiting for it to be my turn. As I ran around him, I tried to ignore the voice in the back of my mind reminding me continuously, something isn't right. Suddenly, Mary picked me up off the ground and held me. The tears hadn't stopped coming down her face. I had been waiting so long to go out with Tico and now she was stopping me? I watched as

Tico and Patrick began leaving the room. My body began to squirm in her arms while I began barking at Mary. I had to know where Patrick was going with my friend. I finally leapt out of her arms and raced towards Tico yelling.

"Wait! Don't leave!" Tico turned around for a moment, I could have sworn I saw a tear in his eye. He smiled at me as Patrick began pulling him out the front of the house. Why wasn't he fighting back? I raced towards Tico, but no matter how fast I ran I couldn't make it to him in time.

"Goodbye friend." That was the last thing he said before the door closed in my face. I quickly turned around, hoping the humans were playing some sick joke, but the rest of the humans dispersed around the house, each going into their own room and closing the door behind them. The house was suddenly way too quiet and I realized how alone I was.

"Fine," I blurted out, "I'll just sit here and wait for them to come back." I positioned myself right in front of the door so when Patrick walked in, there was no way to avoid me. My eyes were fixed on the handle, I was ready to show them that this was the last time they would leave for a walk without me. Every now and then one of the humans would pass by, not paying any attention to me. There faces still held the same somber expression. Maybe this isn't a joke, I thought as I watched Mary pace around the house, and occasional tear streaming down her face. No, it has to be a joke, what else would be happening? My mind began racing to all the times Tico slipped around the house, when he walked outside, how he slowly began sleeping whenever possible instead of moving. I forced myself to be positive, the humans were probably just going to get him some help, that's all this was. My body finally collapsed to the floor from all my stress, my eyes never leaving the door.

"Tico is going to to be fine, I just need to wait for him." I mumbled before a wave of exhaustion came over me.

***

There was a sound of jingling at the door that startled me awake. The were finally home! I jumped back onto my paws as Patrick walked in, Tico's gear in hand. My entire body froze as my eyes fell to his hand.

"No, this can't be happening." My mouth kept repeating over and over again. I had waited for my friend to come back, why wasn't he here? Patrick looked down at me, a slight smile on his face as a single tear fell to the ground. He reached down to pet me, but I backed away from his hand. Tico's scent was all over him. A growl left my lips as Patrick tried to pet me a second time. Where is my friend? I heard the sound of the back door opening and before I could make up my mind, my legs were already moving. I zoomed between furniture until I made it outside. I forced myself to stop at the edge of the steps. My eyes examined the ground below me. Nothing moved, it was if there was no life. My head fell down to the steps, my eyes looking down to the grass at the bottom. I couldn't get my legs to move, the only thing that seemed to be functioning was my thoughts as my brain filled with too many things to count. My vision became blurry as tears began to well up in my eyes. I didn't know what to do, all I knew to do was wait for Tico. I heard one of the humans call my name, but I didn't listen. They kept calling,

"Lincoln! Come on!" I ignored every word. I stood my ground at the end of the steps, not without Tico. After a while their calls faded away until everything was silent again. My legs gave out from under me and I fell with a thud. I tried to stand back up but my legs would not stop shaking so instead I put my head between my paws in hopes to make everything go away. Mary finally came and grabbed me and carried me inside. As we walked, I leaned into her arms, everything felt empty inside me. She placed me down on my mat. I looked to my right where there was an indent where Tico would sleep. He will be back, everything is going to be fine, it's Tico, your best friend, nothing bad would ever happen to him. As these words flooded my mind, our first encounter replayed in my mind. The pure rage Tico gave out when he saw me. Then his goodbye, how much love he put into his words. There was a pounding in my head felt like it was about to explode as more thoughts of Tico kept popping up. I pushed myself up from my spot and began to walk away before unintentionally looking back at the mat. My paws guided me back over, but over to Tico's spot instead. Once I stepped over his spot and then found myself spinning in two circles before plopping back down. There was an overwhelming gust of his scent, causing my mind to slow down before getting hit with a wave of exhaustion. I almost forgot that Tico wasn't next to me before my body finally relaxed and peacefully began to fall asleep.

✳✳✳

You Got the Job

Tarah took a deep breath in as she went to place her hand against the door knob, her palms cold and clammy, and her foot tapping repeatedly against the floor. She didn't completely understand why she had been called back in to meet with the hiring manager after having already gone through her interview. Whatever the reason, it must have been important enough that they had to meet in person, and she didn't want to risk losing the position. It doesn't matter now, she thought to herself; she wanted the job, and she was willing to meet as many times as they needed her to in order to ensure she got it. Being a recent college graduate, she didn't always get a reply back when she applied for jobs in other places. It was the first real shot she had at getting a stable job.

While attempting to clear her mind and relax her shoulders to calm her nerves, which were currently making her stomach do somersaults, she wondered if the woman she met before, Kristin, would also be called in to have a meeting since they were going after the same position. She knocked on the door, waited till she heard a faint 'come in,' and turned the knob.

Her eyes gazed over the familiar surroundings of the office, first looking at the large glass windows on the opposite wall that separated the room from the bright, sunny day outside, to the flourishing green plants and comfy blue chairs near the employer's desk.

However, something was different; out of place.

Gazing over at the chairs again, she realized there was someone already sitting there. Taking a closer look, she noticed the person's short, dark brown bob haircut, the back of their navy blue blazer, and their tan suede heels. She remembered seeing a woman wear those exact heels the last time she was here. She couldn't help but wonder to herself if it might be Kristin. Sure enough, as she walked toward the chairs to sit down, the person turned around, and her eyes slowly met Kristin's. As they held each other's gaze, she couldn't help but internally lose her calm. Clenching her fists in a subtle way, digging her fingernails into her palms which had begun to sweat, she forced a smile to form on her lips as she tried to exchange pleasantries with Kristin.

When they first met last week, while waiting to be interviewed, Kristin really confused her. She started off friendly - initiating a conversation and smiling a lot - but towards the end, she became irritated by abruptly ending their conversation when Tarah mentioned the job position she was after. Tarah didn't know if that was just how she always was or how she acted in that moment, but she was still somewhat weary to be around her as she could potentially act like she did then. She must've been called in too. Ms. Warrick must have wanted us to all meet together, Tarah reasoned.

She couldn't help but fumble with the hem of her sweater when she moved to sit down in the only available chair; right next to Kristin. As she sat down, they caught each other's glances for a brief moment before Kristin turned her head away and nervously shuffled in her seat, as there was nothing they could do to fill the awkward silence that had followed their quick exchange. While they waited, Tarah thought back to their first encounter once again.

She had just applied for the position and couldn't believe how fast she heard back from the company. After clicking submit for the application on the computer and heading to bed, she was awoken the next morning by the sound of her phone ringing; it had been Miss. Warrick asking her to come in for an interview. She had continued on with Tarah, telling her that her resume looked to be in line with the position's qualifications, and that they wanted her to come in for an interview. Fighting the urge to yawn while simultaneously attempting to sound put together despite the disheveled bed that she was laying in while taking the call, Tarah mulled it over, thinking it a bit odd that they had gotten back to her so quickly and had wanted an interview face to face and not on the phone, as many of the other places she'd applied to had wanted. Swallowing hard, Tarah thanked Ms. Warrick, telling her she'd love to interview for the position.

A few days later, Tarah found herself waiting in the main office of the company for her interview, worrying that something was going to go wrong and she wouldn't get the position. While sitting there, she noticed another woman smiling and chatting with some other people across the room; they looked to be having a funny conversation as they were all laughing with each other. Accidentally, Tarah and the woman ended up making eye contact, which made Tarah turn her head quickly in the other direction. It wasn't long after that she felt the presence of someone sitting down next to her.

"Hello, my name is Kristin Sawyer, what's yours?"

Turning her head back around, she shook hands with the woman, "Ah, nice to meet you. My name is Tarah McGinty." Noticing her professional attire, Tarah forced a smiled. The woman in front of her was dressed like an executive and it took all of her willpower to not let her voice waiver, "Judging by your attire, I would assume you are here for an interview as well?"

Kristin nodded her head, "Oh you're applying too? Which position are you here to interview for?"

Tarah had no idea what to say, she didn't know there were multiple positions open. It certainly did make her feel better though. This meant that, there was a good chance not everyone in that room was there for the same position as her. "Oh, I'm here to apply for planning and advertising consultant position."

No sooner had the words left her mouth than she saw Kristin's face change; she was no longer smiling. Instead her lips formed into a small frown and her eyes held a look of frustration and annoyance. "What? Is something wrong?"

"No," she replied, "Just that I was pretty much told, by the person who works with the one conducting the interviews, that I would get that position because I was the only one who applied for it."

There was now a look of pity on Tarah's face as her acquaintance explained how she was lied to, but, in the back of her head, she knew that Kristin shouldn't have believed the person in the first place. When she went to console her though, Kristin didn't act the way she thought she would.

"Well may-"

Kristin didn't give her a chance to finish before she stood up, glaring at her, and walked away.

Next thing Tarah knew, she was once again sitting alone by the front desk, still a little confused as to what just happened. She didn't have much time to think about it however, because just after Kristin left, the door to the manager's office opened and a woman with blonde hair stood in the doorway, "Tarah McGinty," she got up and walked towards the woman, shaking her hand. "Hello, please follow me."

Reminiscing about those memories made her feel a bit more comfortable with her surroundings, but it did nothing to help with the awkwardness that still lay between her and Kristin.

Nonetheless, she was able to refocus her attention when she heard the door open and saw the manager's assistant walk in. "Hello ladies, Ms. Warrick will be with you in soon, she's in a meeting upstairs and won't be done for another ten or fifteen minutes. If you need anything while you wait, feel free to use the vending machine down the hall and she will be with you when she's done." They both nodded, and the assistant hurried out of the room.

Being left alone in the room once again, they both let their eyes wander around the office so the time would go by faster. After eyeing all the artwork that lined the conference room and a gorgeous blue vase, the seconds seemed to grow longer, dragging almost, and the silence did nothing to help the time pass. In an attempt to break the silence, Tarah turned to the other girl and began.

"Hey, Kristin, right? How have you been?"

She turned her head to meet her gaze, "Fine, why are you asking?" There was almost no tone to her voice, causing Tarah to flinch a little.

"Just trying to make small talk while we wait." Kristin nodded her head in understanding.

"Well in that case, how are you?"

"I've been good. I've just been wondering, what about this position makes it so interesting to you?"

"Well, I've always had a knack for advertising, and I believe that can help this company's sales increase a lot with my ideas. What about you?"

Tarah began to feel a little bit more comfortable and, in turn, was able to relax more, "I've always liked game design, and I've always been able to make up games that my younger cousins and siblings love."

Tarah couldn't help but smile, thinking of how much better the interaction was going compared to their last discussion which had ended so abruptly. Little by little, she could almost feel Kristin's guard beginning to drop.

A few minutes later, the door to the office opened again, and in walked Ms. Warrick, "Hello Mrs. Sawyer, Ms. McGinty, sorry I kept you both waiting so long," Tarah and Kristin both shook their heads and told her there was no harm done, "at any rate, I called you two back in to talk about the planning and advertising consultant position you both interviewed for."

Immediately, Tarah felt the temperature in the room drop as the tension rose back up between the two and she shuffled back and forth in her seat while fidgeting her fingers.

"Looking over my records of what you both submitted, it seems you two are the most qualified out of the people I interviewed. It also seems that you both are especially skilled in one of the skill requirements-"

While Ms.Warrick spoke, Tarah was trying to see if she could figure out where the conversation was going. Confused about why Ms. Warrick would call them both in and interview them together, Tarah's eyebrow raised a bit as she tried to reason with herself what was happening.

"Since you two are proficient in two different skills that the position will require, to go hand in hand so to speak, I want to see how well you two work on your own versus when you partner up, seeing that teamwork will be especially important for the position." Ms. Warrick pushed her glasses up with her index finger and smiled at the two, "I would like you both to come back tomorrow so I can see how well you work in these situations. If you have no questions, that is all I have to say, and I look forward to seeing you both tomorrow."

Getting up and walking towards the door, Tarah and Kristin were still in a small amount of shock as to what they had just heard. She wanted to see how well they worked together? Did she think they were friends? That they've known each other for a long time? Because they weren't, and they hadn't. They just met a week ago, and had only conversed twice and one of those wasn't very professional.

Tarah, who was deep in thought, absentmindedly followed Kristin until they both exited the building, but not realizing Kristin had stopped, Tarah bumped into her back, which snapped her out of her thoughts. She could see the confusion and frustration Kristin was feeling as she watched her scrunch up her nose and let out a deep breath.

"So," Tarah fumbled, "what do you think her aim is?"

There was no response. Tarah could sense that Kristin was upset, and like last time, she tried to comfort her. "Hey, I'm sure it's nothing detrimental. I'm sure you are still being considered for the position; she wouldn't have asked us to both come in tomorrow if that wasn't the case."

Kristin turned around to look at her, glowering; her eyebrows lowered and a frown more than present on her face. "So you think that's supposed to make me happy. Only one of us can be hired, one! I mean, looking between the two of us I can tell that I'm older so I've obviously had more wok experience than you, I can probably handle professional situations better than you, and I'm most likely more qualified than you for this position!"

Tarah didn't know what to do; Kristin's outburst had surprised her and, though she was used to arguing with people in a similar mindset, she had never expected to experience that type of situation with someone who acted in such a professional manner. Still though, she couldn't stand the way Kristin was acting.

"I get that this job means a lot to you, but just for a moment, forget the requirements, forget that only one of us can be hired, forget what Ms. Warrick was saying." Kristin went to butt in, but Tarah didn't let her. "No matter what happens, you are a highly skilled person, and from what I've seen, when you aren't arguing with me, you have a very personable attitude. There are other jobs out there and I'm sure you could get any one of them!" Kristin just stood there, staring at her in shock.

"Thank you for your encouragement. I just have so much riding on this opportunity, and I guess it's getting the best of me. I've been turned down for so many other jobs because I always end up being as they put it 'not what they're looking for.'"

"Well, I'm willing to come in tomorrow and work my way through whatever this company has in store, and I suggest that you do the same. Opportunities like this don't happen all the time, and they seem interested in hiring you, so just give it a chance and show up tomorrow."

That night, before going to bed, all Tarah could do was think about what could be instore for her tomorrow. She wasn't sure what the end game was for Ms. Warrick; did she think they would make a good team? Could they possibly work together without arguing? Tarah took a deep break as she turned over, hugging the pillow.

She knew she was probably stressing herself out more than she needed to, but she wanted to make sure everything would go smoothly. Deciding there was nothing more that she could do, she set her alarm and went to sleep.

Tarah woke up early the next morning to allow herself extra time to get ready. She had no idea what Ms. Warrick was expecting of her but was determined to impress. Making her way to her closet, she pulled a new pant suit and rolled a lint roller over the jacket, ensuring it looked as neat as possible. Looking at herself in the mirror as she put the clothes on, she grabbed the bottom of either side of the jacket and gave a short swift tug. She couldn't help but smile as she looked at herself; she was nervous, but the professional clothes gave her a new burst of confidence she was unaccustomed to. While eating her breakfast, she couldn't stop thinking about Kristin and how they seemed to get along well until they were reminded that they were fighting for the same job. The more Tarah thought about it, the more she was finding the commonalities that might make her and Kristin a good team. She just hoped that Kristin would feel the same.

Leaving at 7:35, she was able to arrive to the company with seven minutes to spare. Entering the lobby, she knew exactly where to go as she strolled past the front desk and said good morning to the secretary. She got onto the elevator and pressed the third floor button. On the short trip up, she could only think of how she hoped Kristin would show up. Even though it was a job opportunity and her closest chance at getting a job this soon out of college, she was glad that Ms. Warrick was willing to give them both a shot. From everything that Tarah had heard from Ms. Warrick, they were both good fits for the position.

The elevator dinged as it reached Tarah's recommended floor, and she got out. Arriving at the familiar blue door, she looked at the plaque that read *Warrick, Claire; Hiring & Management Supervisor* before she knocked and entered. As she walked into the room, she saw Ms. Warrick and her assistant by the windows.

"Come in, come in, Ms. McGinty, you're the last one to arrive." Hearing her say that made Tarah perk her head up as she turned to face the chairs only to find Kristin sitting there. They smiled at one another as Tarah sat down and Ms. Warrick cleared her throat. "Okay ladies, to start off the day, I am going to put you each in separate rooms to work. You will both have one hour to create a pitch idea for a new toy our company's kid's department can sell, as well as sketch out an advertising campaign for it."

She paused to glance at both of them to see what their reaction would be. Not noticing much more than a nod of their heads, she continued, "Once you have completed that task, you will then get another hour to complete the same task, only this time you will be working together. Are we clear?"

"Yes ma'am," they answered in unison.

"Then get to it. Follow my assistant and she will show you the rooms you will be in."

Both Tarah and Kristin immediately followed the assistant out the door and down the hall to two quiet conference rooms where they were then left alone to work. For Tarah, creating the toy was no problem as that was something she did often with her little siblings growing up; the advertising, however, was a different story.

It took her twenty-five minutes to come up with her toy. Drawing out her sketch, she created a board game that was a mix between a puzzle creation and and trivia questions. But now that the idea was done, she was starting to struggle on how to create an outline for her advertising campaign. She wondered if Kristin was having the same problem as her, but quickly put it out of her head to focus on her own task.

"Maybe I can try showing how much fun puzzles or academics can be," she mumbled to herself. Settling on that idea, she got to writing.

Almost ten minutes before the assistant came in to tell her time was up, she was finally able to finish her campaign, including a commercial idea. It might not have sold the most toys off the shelves, but it was decent enough that she could see it making a good profit. As she put the pencil down and pushed her chair to get up to leave, Tarah let out a breath of relief she didn't realize she had been holding, "Wow, that didn't feel like an hour at all," she murmured.

The assistant chuckled, "Please, follow me to the other room for your next assignment."

Tarah got up, stretched, and followed her down the hall to the other room, seeing Kristin already waiting there for them. "Okay you two, your hour starts now."

The two sat down got to work.

"Okay, what's a good toy that we could create that would be versatile for kids of many ages?"

Tarah lightly tapped her pen against her head, "How about a new board game? Even adults play them." She quickly began to sketch a rough outline of the idea in her head, "We can combine a logic or math based premise to help teach young kids while at the same time time coming up with characters and an adventure for them to go on."

Kristin nodded her head excitedly, "That's a great idea! It's better than anything I could come up with, especially so quick!"

The two sat for the next ten minutes working out the little details of the pitch until they couldn't think of anything to add. Kristin stretched in her chair, "There, now on to the advertising campaign."

"I don't exactly know what to do for this, what are your ideas?" Tarah rubbed her neck sheepishly.

Kristin thought for a minute, "How about a slogan along the lines of 'You never know where the learning ends and the fun begins'? Then in the commercial for it, we can have two little kids playing the game with their grandparents, all laughing and having fun, and the girls demonstrating how much they're learning." Tarah agreed, absolutely loving the idea.

They had just finished writing out the last details of the commercial when the assistant walked in and to tell them the time was up. However, they weren't expecting Ms. Warrick to walk in too, "Congratulations you two! You're both hired."

They stared at her in shock, not knowing what to say. Tarah looked on quizzically, unsure of what was going on. Ms. Warrick hadn't even reviewed the work they had done yet, how could she have made a decision. As if Ms. Warrick was able to read her mind, the woman let out a chuckle.

"The whole point of this was to see how well you two could work together, and you did it flawlessly. I knew from the start it was going to be at least one of you two, since you were the only ones who were well qualified for the position. So, congratulations. I expect to see you both tomorrow at 8:30 sharp."

The Waiting Game

It was a rainy day in late October, the changing leaves stood out so starkly against the gray of the early morning sky. I was on my way to the café when I ran into her. She was in a rush, messy hair, and the buttons of her sweater were unaligned. She held something in her hand, green and folded but I couldn't get a sense of what the object was before she had turned away from my view.

"Sorry sir!" She called over her shoulder before turning a corner and disappearing from view. I stood there for a moment, taking a second to process what had happened before subtly brushing off my shoulder and continuing to walk. It had been an odd encounter, but still normal enough in a day to day. At least this interaction had not been long enough to drive me into an awkward silence. Still, the girl that had bumped into me seemed troubled and I couldn't help but to wonder about what this stranger could be in such a rush over.

Walking into the café, I was greeted with the familiar scent of coffee and a multitude of unnatural flavorings and syrups. The space was largely unoccupied, but eyeing the counter, I noticed the girl from before, although now it seemed that she had taken the time to adjust her shirt and to put on the previously folded green apron, which was likely what she had held in her hands when she had run into me.

"Hello there! What can I get for you toda- Oh! You're that guy I ran into! Listen, I'm so sorry about that; I didn't even see you there, are you alright?" She asked in a rushed jumble of words.

"Oh, I'm alright, but thank you for the concern. I wasn't following you to get an apology, just wanted a coffee," I reassured her with a smile, and was greeted in response with an awkward chuckle.

"Right, so what can I get for you?"

"Just a medium white chocolate mocha."

"Coming right up, you can take a seat if you want. There isn't really anyone in here, so I'll bring it to you when it's done."

I nodded, moving to a seat. Within minutes, the girl returned holding a steaming cup in her hands. "Here you go, sorry for the wait."

"It's no problem, you're very kind..." I looked to her name tag, reading what was engraved quickly "*Paige*" She shifted, and nodded.

"Thanks sir, just doing my job."

"Henry," I offered in response. "My name is Henry."

I left not too long after that, my drink half gone and a skip in my step.

***

I kept coming back to the cafe, making a routine of it to come at exactly the same time, I had practically memorized Paige's schedule within that short period. I knew when she would be in and which days she usually had off. Today however, was a bit different. I held within my hands a single daisy, an innocent flower, to thank her for the work she did. When I got there, I greeted her with a wave and a smile.

"My usual please, and one more thing, I found this on the way here, it's a little busted up but the woman said it's one of the last of the season. I wanted to thank you, you've always been so attentive."

"Thank you, Henry. It's a nice gesture, but you really didn't have to. I'm just doing my job."

"Nonsense, a pretty girl like you deserves flowers. I won't take no for an answer." I retorted, holding the bloom closer to her, completely unaware of what to do next if she refused again.

It was frustrating how difficult she was being over a simple flower. She must have realized the inner turmoil she was causing me because she finally took hold of the stem, thanking me again before setting it on the counter with a smile that seemed a bit strained. If I had to wager a guess, I would say that the stress of the days of working were getting to her. Nonetheless, I retrieved my usual order and sat down at my normal table.

Days like this passed quickly enough. I had begun to spend more and more of my time within the cafe, lingering to watch the happenings of the space for as long as I could. There was only so much else a recently retired man such as myself could do throughout the day. So I kept an eye on Paige, distantly wondering if our exchanges had any difference than the interactions she had between her and her other customers. As it was, I certainly tipped more, and she offered me much more small talk. What could I take that as? Could it have been a sign for something more?

She looked up as I thought to myself, our eyes locking before she darted her gaze away, focusing on the ground and hugging her arms close to herself. That had to have meant something. She must have been embarrassed that I was watching, but she must have liked it. There couldn't have been another explanation for her actions. This was it, I needed to speak with her, but here was too crowded.

It took some time. Her shift had been another three hours, but I was patient. I was fully capable of waiting for her. When she disappeared into the back of the building, I moved towards the back of the little shop. I walked briskly, seeing a door open as I approached. Paige held her arms close to her, gaze held steadily to the floor. She looked so worried, she had to have had a bad day at work. I wanted to ease her worries, to help her dismiss all the negative thoughts she seemed to have had swimming in her mind.

"Paige!" I called, hoping to not startle her, but she all but leapt when I did so.

"Henry, what are you doing here?" She asked, eyes darting in what must have been embarrassment. There was a catch in her voice, longing, most likely.

"I need to talk to you, it's important, please just hear me out."

"You can't be here, I need to leave," Paige said, watching me closely, her eyes darting between me and the street.

"Just listen to me!" I had been advancing on her as she tried to take a step back, but the hand I placed upon her shoulder held her where she stood. I needed her to listen, I had to be sure.

"That look, our talks, please tell me that what I'm seeing is real,

Paige, we have a connection, I don't want to be in the dark anymore." I watched as she processed the information, watched as her face turned sour.

"Henry whatever you think you're seeing, isn't true. I don't like you, I'm doing my job. Nothing more, nothing less." She stated plainly before ducking under my grasp and walking off.

I watched her go, confused. It couldn't be, the signs were all there, she might just not know what they are yet. But I knew, and I had to make her realize what she was brushing off. I'd make her want to be with me.

***

I took a break from the cafe for a few days, wanting Paige to know just how bad her days would be without me. It was hard though, I found myself longing to return to the cafe, longing to be in her presence. Just the thought of not seeing her each day sent an ache through my chest, not actually being able to see her turned the ache into a sharp knife that felt as if it was being shoved into my ribcage.

On the fourth day, I couldn't take it anymore. I had to see her. I would put in a bit of effort too, I owed her that much after being so distant. As I walked, I passed by a flower shop. I entered, wanting to pick out something for her. I emerged with a small gathering of pink carnations to offer. The rest of my walk proved uneventful, and I strode into the cafe, my mind raced far ahead of my feet. I could practically see me and her together when we met after my absence.

I strode through the door, making a beeline straight for the counter. There she was, looking perfect with her green apron and messy hair.

"Paige! I'm here to apologize, I stayed away for selfish reasons, but do you understand now?" I asked, putting the flowers on the counter.

Staying away from the cafe, and in turn, from Paige, had been one of the hardest things I had experienced, so surely she must have felt the same agony I had inflicted upon myself.

There was a change in her expression when I advanced, her eyes grew wide and she took in a sharp breath.

"Please just order and leave Henry, there's nothing for me to understand other than that you're seeing things that aren't there, and that you're making me uncomfortable, so if you aren't ordering, then please leave."

"Paige, you can't seriously mean that, let me win you over, I brought you flowers to show you I'm being sincere."

"Flowers I never wanted and that I don't accept. You need to leave now, you're making everyone else here uncomfortable as well and I will call the cops." She retorted, no remorse in her voice as she stared at me. A shiver ran up my spine; she was gorgeous even when she was angry. I just had to do more. She would see; she had to.

Taking hold of the thrown aside blooms, my knuckles were white as I gripped them. I stormed towards the door, shoving the flowers into the trash as I walked out of the cafe. I shook with the force of my irritation, my fists clenched and my teeth were grit to the point of numbness. I didn't know what I was going to do yet, but I had to do something. I had no clue she was that far into her denial. Now, more than ever, she had to realize just how strongly I knew she felt for me.

***

Hours passed as I walked, wanting to clear my mind and to pass time before I returned. I was persistent, I had to be. I had to make her see how wrong she was. She needed to see the signs that I saw. There was no way that they weren't there, I didn't want them to not be there. I wasn't going to let them not be there.

Going back to the cafe was innocent enough. It was growing dark, the sun already trying to dip below the horizon. Lumbering along, my hands in my pockets, my gaze not drifting from its place on the ground. I didn't enter the cafe; it would have done me no good regardless. My only reason for even being there was to watch Paige, and follow her to a more secluded spot where she would have no choice but to actually talk with me. Paige emerged looking frazzled, her hair even messier than when we had spoken earlier that day. Her cheeks were red, and her eyes were puffy. I could see her gaze darting to and fro, as if she herself was searching for something. Could she have been searching for me? I longed for that to be the answer, but I couldn't possibly find out now. Patrons were still walking around, some that had left the cafe minutes before were still loitering around the space so I had no choice but to bide my time until there was no one else. When she began to walk, I followed, keeping my distance. I couldn't risk a confrontation out in the open like this, not here. This was a private matter, between me and her. I couldn't let anyone else interfere.

Paige began walking quicker, holding her arms across her chest, staring at the ground. Suddenly she pulled out her phone, dialing something I was too far away from to see before placing the device to her head. She spoke in a low tone, I couldn't make out the words and I wasn't about to risk getting caught yet. It wasn't the right time. Paige made odd turns as she walked, cutting across the road and making circles with the streets she took. Just the task of keeping up with her caused my breath to quicken. Following her had become a challenge and I was getting increasingly winded. Her pace slowed as she put the phone I had forgotten she was holding into her pocket before ducking across the road at a full sprint, grabbing a set of keys from seemingly out of the blue and shoving one of them into the door of the home she ran up to. I watched her enter the house, the door audibly slamming shut before I began to approach slowly, trying to calm my racing heart not just from the walking that we did, but also from the nerves. This was it, she had to talk to me now, I wasn't going to take no for an answer. Scaling the steps easily enough before bringing a clenched fist to the door, rapping loudly upon the wood. There was no response from within, even though I knew she was in the house.

"Paige! Open up, I need to speak with you!" I yelled, banging on the door once more. Again, there was no answer. I wiggled the handle, my knuckles white as I held tight to the handle. "I know you're in there Paige! You can't hide from me forever, just open the door I only want to talk tonight!" I could have sworn to have been able to hear a muffled sobbing at that moment, so I slowed in my approach. "Paige, just open up. I'm sorry to upset you, but we need to talk."

"Leave me alone, you creep!" Was the only response I received? The voice was shaky, but undeniably Paige's. Her request fell on deaf ears. She simply didn't understand what I would do for her, what I would take for her, and what I could do to her if I didn't get my way.

It was then that I heard sirens, they were close, a street or two at the most. I looked back to the closed door in shock, banging on the door with a new intensity.

"You called the police on me!? I just wanted to talk to you!" The desire to insult her, to call her whatever came to my mind rose within me, but I couldn't do that. I wouldn't leave either. I would rather be dragged away than to leave her willingly. I needed her, I yearned for her approval, for the love that had to have been there whenever I saw her.

I kept slamming on the door, yelling for her to open up. I could see the troopers speeding in the distance, gaining quickly and it only served to increase my insistence. I forwent my hands in turn trying to force the locked door ajar. Using my entire body to slam up against the frame. The sound of screeching rubber filled my ears a mere second after the door buckled, the lock giving way to my insistent slamming. Nearly falling into the doorway, I slipped inside to get out of sight of the police that were sure to have been rushing forwards towards where I had stood just seconds before.

My gaze drifted, having clearly been let into the living room I needed to find Paige quickly, before the only one that was found was me. I caught sight of a small area rug, crumpled and pushed away from what I assumed to be where it originally sat. As if the person that had stepped on it last tripped on it and simply left it wrinkled in their haste. My feet moved much before my mind did, following the sound of muffled, hiccupping sobs. They brought me to what looked to be a coat closet offset from the main entrance, which was good for me as the cops were not halfway across the lawn and gaining fast.

My usually unending patience had begun to grow thin. Paige had made a scene when all I wished to do was to talk, so instead of turning the handle gently I rammed into it, feeling it slam up against the opposite wall. This door was considerably thinner than the one at the entrance of the home, the force of my body physically splintering much of the wood from the frame as it swung open. Paige had curled into herself, a whimper escaping her lips as her body trembled in the corner. Even terrified, she was beautiful.

"Get away from me!" She screamed, her back turned to me as she tried to keep me from having any point in which to grab her. Reaching out, I went to pull her up by the only thing I could grab hold of, the bun she had her long locks in each day. My actions however, were stopped by the sound of boots slamming against hardwood, and a deep voice yelling.

"Step away from the woman, turn around, and put your hands in the air where I can see them."

Being a sensible man, I followed the officer's orders. My hands were held upright in plain sight as I turned away from Paige to face the officer.

"This is all a misunderstanding officer, we're simply having a chat, isn't that right, Paige." My words held a grit of irritation, and as they escaped my mouth I looked over my shoulder, just in time to see Paige staring at the officer holding me at gunpoint, mouthing the words "help me" before a sharp bark forced me to face him once more.

The officer said nothing to Paige as I stood there, my arms growing tired and my side beginning to ache with the trauma it received when I broke the doors down. The officer, still holding his gun on me, advanced. Only dropping the firearm once he had grabbed hold of me. The handcuffs that were tightened around my wrist were cold with the night air, and they jangled on the joint painfully.

"You have the right to remain silent. Anything you say can and will be used against you in a court of law. You have the right to an attorney. If you cannot afford an attorney, one will be provided for you. Do you understand the rights I have just read to you? Now, with these rights in mind, do you wish to speak to me?" I nodded in response to him asking if I understood my rights, however I stayed silent. It was over, I was reasonable enough to realize that as I was dragged from the coat closet, my arms cuffed behind my back.

"Lets go, get moving." The officer sad, grabbing my shoulder roughly, dragging me towards one of the cop cars parked outside. I kept silent, as I was thrown into the backseat, leaning against my arms. Watching as the cop moved back towards the door, I glared at him as he stepped up to the door. When Paige emerged in the doorway, my teeth ground against each other, my fists clenched. How dare she run away from me but be so willing to meet the officer halfway.

"You're all set now ma'am, we're taking him back to the station. He won't be bothering you any time soon." She nodded in response. Even with the physical distance, the tear stains on her face were glaringly visible. She still shook with fright. My body shook too, but fear was not the cause for my tremors. Silent anger was the only thing I registered in that moment, the desire I had to ease her worries was buried in the pit of my most negative emotions.

My teeth ached with the force of my silent anger, watching as Paige retreated into the depths of her home. My mind instantly raced once she was removed from my line of sight, ideas churning in the deepest corners of my brain all on what I would do once I was free from my restraints. But I know how to play the waiting game. She won't be able to resist me for long. I'll make her want to be with me.

Benevolence

Adappled light reached the deck where I sat silently upon a rickety old porch swing, a thick blanket draped across my shoulders to keep away the deep chill of the late morning. A breeze carried to me the scent of the forest and snow, a comforting smell that held hints of the earth and the foliage it supported. Adjusting the reading glasses that sat loosely on my face, I looked away from the tree line and directed my attention to the thick-spined book that was held in my wrinkled hands. I tried my best to hold back a yawn, not having slept well the night before. It wasn't often that the woods were too loud for me to sleep, but last night was the exception. The creatures of the forest had been particularly active.

I found myself lost in the well-worn cover of my copy of a book well past its prime, the spine held together just barely with a few pieces of tape and a small prayer for the objects integrity. Most of my mornings were spent this way, thankful that the overhang of my porch offered a fair amount of coverage from the elements.

A rustle was heard from the bushes, a muffled cry coming from the shifting foliage and a single eye could be seen peering from the edge of the forest. Squinting heavily, I tried to make out the shape, the distance too great to see much of anything clearly. My reading glasses had been taken off to let dangle loosely around my neck and I stood, wondering vaguely if I would be able to get a better look at what was causing the disturbance by change in angle. It was to no avail, because by the time I got myself out of my porch swing the rustling had stopped and any signs of the creature that had been there moments before had ceased. Leaving my book upon the swing, I took hold instead to the cane I had previously propped against the side of my home when I first sat down. I walked slowly to the stairs leading to my yard. Curiosity may have killed the cat, but it was satisfaction that brought that silly lad back.

Hobbling up to the tree line, it was clear that whatever had been there before wasn't there anymore. Though it was clear that I definitely wasn't going senile, the footprints in the snow and a small patch of fuzz confirmed that there was something there only moments before. Using my cane as a prop, I lowered myself to examine the paw prints left behind. It was easy enough to recognize that they weren't from a coyote or a wolf, they were too small, and those creatures were much too shy to come so close to my home. I pulled myself up, shrugging slightly. Whatever had been there likely wouldn't be back, and I had to start my day. I walked back into my home, grabbing my book on the way inside and effectively forgetting about the encounter.

***

Going about my normal routine for the week, I would catch little glimpses of the creature from time to time, reminding me of its presence. It had been strange the first few days. Between hearing it trudge through the snow sometimes, to catching little views of it on the edge of the tree line. I had yet to see it clearly, and having my suspicions as to what it was, I set out to make some accommodations for what I dubbed my new guest.

I had set up a small shelter after gathering a multitude of items from my weekly trip into the closest town set about an hour's drive down a small dirt road that had largely frozen over in the cold winter months. I had grown to worry over the small creature that I only ever caught glimpses of. It couldn't have been any of the normal animals I usually saw in the forest, the markings I caught glimpses of told me that this was no bobcat.

***

Night fell quickly upon my little house, the shadows of the trees stretched until it seemed as though they would engorge the small accommodation. I stood within my kitchen, preparing a serving and a half's worth of dinner set onto two separate plates. I shrugged on a loose, but thick, shawl and made my way towards my porch with one of the plates. I took it out to the small shelter I had set about a foot away from the porch steps and left it outside of the opening for the creature that I had come to provide for.

Turning, I began to walk back to the warmth of my home when I heard it, a raspy breath followed by a subtle scratching from behind me. I turned, searching for the source of the disturbance and found my gaze connecting with that of a yellowed eyes wrought with the passing of hard times. He held my gaze for what felt like an eternity, but was only just a moment before he sauntered up to the plate that I had left only minutes prior. The begrimed tabby snatched the morsels I had left for him quickly, before turning back to the trees his scarred form had emerged from and trotted back into the undergrowth to enjoy his meal in peace.

I watched him retreat into the woods, hobbling into my home with the use of my cane. I felt eyes peering into my soul as I stepped through the doorway, but I ignored the gaze in favor of returning to my home to rest for the night as the temperature began to drop further, and the night wore on. Catching a glimpse of the small shelter from the window, I watched a small shadow lurk quietly inside of it as a small smile set upon my features.

As the night passed, it was hard for me to sleep; the forest was active that night, with the screams of coyotes drawing closer to the house than was normal for the shy creatures, and worry that set in for the scarred tabby that I had resigned to dub as Jack for the time being. As day broke, I set out to greet the newly-named Jack, and to grab the now empty plate from beside his shelter. I heard the screams as I opened the porch door, and jolted, fingers gripping the handle of my cane tightly pushing the door completely open, unsure as to what I would be met with.

Jack stood between the tree line and the porch, back arched and tail puffed up three times its normal size. Just behind the line of trunks stood a canid twice the size of the disgruntled feline. Its jaws hung open, and a terrifying gleam was held in its eyes. I held in a gasp, instead raising my cane and shook it about.

"Leave him alone you mangy mutt!" I yelled, marching to the edge of my porch as quickly as possible, having to bring my cane down to hobble down the stairs "get away from here!" I shouted, getting steadily closer to the conflict in the space between the forest and my home. The coyote shifted its attention from the scruffy tabby and instead growled at me, its ears flicked back against its scalp as it watched me with horrifying intent. I was back to swinging my cane in the air, trying to seem as big as I could while Jack's back flattened out, his tail slowly returning to normal from it's incredibly poufy state as I stood between him and the coyote. The unusually bold creature's eyes were an unnatural green, its gaze never wavering as I marched forwards still waving my cane around as if it was a sword and I wasn't an old lady. The beast growled at me, opening its toothy maw with a threatening bellow before being matched with a low growl from the tabby cat behind me. It was then that the coyote turned and fled into the woods, but not before stopping just at the tree line and looking over its shoulder once more at both me and Jack.

Once the mutt was out of sight, I returned my cane to the ground, leaning on the tool with a huff before I felt pressure on my leg, and heard a gruff chirp. Looking down, I was met with the sight of Jack head-butting my calf gently before the tabby turned away, and fled back into the shelter that I had provided for him.

***

Days past that were much of the same, me going about my routines while also accommodating the house cat that now lived right beside my porch. I had yet to see another run in with the coyotes that I now knew lurked in the woods a bit closer to my home than comfort.

A new occurrence that I'd grown accustomed to was the gifts that had started appearing on my porch swing each morning. As I stepped out onto the porch, I found a patch of fabric sitting upon the swing. Footprints lead from the porch steps to the woods, the only telltale sign I had that it was Jack leaving the gifts for me.

I made my way slowly towards the steps, a small plate held in my hands as I whistled a soft tune to announce that I had breakfast. I watched as Jack peered at me from within the small shelter I had provided, a single yellow eye watching as I hobbled down the stairs, leaning heavily on my cane before I felt the object's grip on the weathered wood slip, the pole shoving itself backwards as I flung forwards. My grip on it dropped as I put out my arms in a desperate attempt to catch myself before I felt my hand slam against the last step, a crunch sounded from the impact and I felt myself pitch completely off the stairs, head slamming against the snow covered ground before my world went completely black.

***

Waking again was quite possibly my worst experience. My wrist felt as though it had been cast in molten iron, but strangely enough a deep chill had not set into my bones. In fact, my body was in so much pain, but I wasn't cold. Not in the least, I wasn't wet either, strange since I remembered falling outside. I should very well be dead or dying of hypothermia, but I wasn't. Looking around, I took account of the well-worn couch that sat faithfully within my living room. My head pounding with an aching persistence, there was no way that I would have found my own way into my home. Who brought me here? My mind raced with dozens of unanswered questions, all more distressing then the last.

My instant panic was disrupted by a disturbance in the kitchen, and my attention was drawn instantly from the pain of my painfully obviously fractured wrist, to the very real possibility that there was a stranger in my home and being so far away from any civilization I would have no way of getting help. Panic flared once more, outweighing any reason that sat in the deepest pits of my mind as a figure peered out from the kitchen, a single yellow eye peered at me from the doorway, a strange man looking to me from within the seclusion of the room.

I drew my injured wrist to my chest, cradling it with my other hand, doing my best attempt at a threatening glare that a 76-year-old injured woman could manage. The man put up a single hand, a wordless signal that he would present no harm. In his other hand he held a small plate of what could only just be made out as leftovers from the night before.

He didn't otherwise move, instead just standing there with the plate held in his hands.

"Why are you here? Are you the one who brought me inside?" I asked, watching as the man took walked forward. He knelt down when he got close, producing the plate for me.

"Eat, you need to heal. You saved my life, and fae don't like to be indebted to anyone."

* * *

A Ring Worth a
Thousand Wishes

"**M**y wish, for you, is that this life becomes all that you want it to. Your dreams stay big; your worries stay small. You never need to carry more than you can hold." The alarm clock sounded as it played mine and my grandma's song.

It was going to be the first day back since it happened; school was the last place on my mind.

"Peyton are you up?" My mom said, shouting as her footsteps came up the stairs.

"Yes, but please let me stay home, mom." My voice was raspy from just waking up. I began pulling my blanket over my head as I tried to escape the world.

"No. You have been out for almost a week you need to go, sorry honey." My mom said back to me as she entered my room, reaching to rub my back.

"But mom, it's going to be so hard," was all I could groan out back to her. Couldn't she just understand that I just needed to be home?

"You'll be okay, she will always look over you and be with you. Now go shower, please."

Getting up from my bed, I grabbed my clothes and a towel as I made my way down the hall. With a loud yawn, I began the long trek down the hallway before stopping and turning into the bathroom. Stepping into the shower, my body began shivering as the cold water began pouring down. As it began to heat up, I put my head back, letting the stream run through my hair in an effort to calm my nerves and take my mind off the endless worries and concerns that had flooded my head since the alarm rang.

"Peyton, it's 7:20, you have to get out soon." My mom said while knocking on the bathroom door.

"Almost done!" I rolled my eyes as I let out an exacerbated breath, turning the faucet off. After changing into my clothes, I turned the knob on the door, causing a creaking sound that echoed throughout the entire upstairs. As if she had bionic hearing, my mom yelled from downstairs something about hurrying up. Running a quick brush through my hair, I looked in the mirror at my finger, which typically had a gold ring on it but today it wasn't there. I reached for my shirt. Nothing there. Worry flooded my mind. Where could it be? I knew my mom would be mad if I was late but I needed the ring; it was something I always had with me.

"Mom the ring, it's gone!" My voice echoed throughout the house as I was trying to stay calm.

"What do you mean?" My mom yelled back from downstairs with a puzzled tone to her voice.

"It's not on my finger. I can't go without it."

"Take a deep breath, we will find it. Finish getting ready for school and I'll look for it."

"Mom, we need to find Grammy's ring." Looking at my mom's face, my eyes began filling with tears.

While finishing getting ready for school, my mom rummaged through the house. Trying to retrace my steps while throwing things into my backpack was no use; the ring was nowhere to be found. A pit grew in my stomach over the thought of going to school without it. I promised my grandma the day she gave it to me that the ring would always be on my finger.

✳✳✳

A knock came from the door as my mom slowly slid the door open, a big smile formed on her face.

"Hi Grammy!" I said, walking over to my Grammy in excitement.

"Oh hi sweetheart, who are you with?" Grammy asking with a confused look on her face, staring at my mom as if she had never seen her before.

"Mom, it's me, your daughter, Jen." My mom replied, trying to reassure her as she began walking over to her.

"No you're not! Give me her daughter." Grammy screaming, shaking in fear while reaching out to me.

"Grammy it's okay, that's your daughter, Jen."

Sitting next to Grammy while talking to her, my eyes kept staring at her ring. It was so pretty and always caught my eyes. It was the prettiest ring I have ever seen, a gold band with blue and white diamonds.

"Grammy, your ring is so pretty!" Wishing the ring was mine, my blue eyes lit up at the sight of it.

"I was going to wait till right before you left but since you said something, I'll say it now. This ring is not mine anymore, it is now yours. I've always seen you looking at it and remember when you were little you used to always want to try it on," she said to me, while taking the ring off her finger. In a fleeting moment of clarity for her, she continued, "Wear this always and remember that I'm always going to love you and the band is our bond together and the diamonds are…"

"The happiness and all our memories since they're sparkly!" I interrupted, knowing the words that followed. "Thank you, Grammy!"

"I'm happy to finally give it to you." She smiled, going into hug me tighter than she ever had while kissing my forehead.

"I promise to wear it everyday, love you, Grammy." I said, throwing my arms around her, a smile plastered across my face.

"Love you, Peyton."

***

As I was leaving for my bus, my mom was screaming, "Peyton wait, the ring! It was on your floor."

A flash of energy was going through my body while sprinting up the stairs, eager to get my grandma's ring. A big smile formed across my face as I let out a deep breath, feeling relieved that it wasn't lost forever.

"Thank you, Mom," I said to her, a feeling of relief falling over me.

"Now go catch your bus." My mom began saying as she hugged me back.

My excitement took over and said a little too loudly, "Her ring is never coming off again!"

"You can take it off, just remember where you put it." My mom said as she was kissing me goodbye.

"I guess."

It was the first day back since the worst day of my life. I really hoped nobody would hug me or say they're sorry or anything because tears would start coming out of my eyes. As the bus arrived, I began wishing it was dropping me home not taking me from it. The bus felt like it was taking forever, with everyone screaming and jumping. Staring out the window, I noticed the trees all changing colors. Fall was Grammy's favorite season, it's the first one without her here. Some trees were green, brown, yellow, orange and red, they are all so pretty. Stepping out of the bus, I took a deep breath and said to myself, "You can do it Peyton, Grammy will always be with you."

An hour left then I'll be home, now it's time to go to health class. Sitting down in the back of the room, crouching down in the seat my mind couldn't stop thinking about grammy. We were working on our family tree projects, but now having to redo it. How am I going to bring myself to take her out of it? Sitting there just staring at my poster the teacher came over to me, she told me she is sorry for my loss of my grandma and I don't need to remove her if it will make me more sad. Once she left, I was still doodling on a piece of paper thinking about removing grammy from the family tree or not. The night everything happened just kept replaying in my head, I just wanted a redo of it.

ring ring, it was finally time for me to go home. Throwing my backpack on while rushing to the door, eager to get on the bus. Sitting by myself in the back corner of the bus, staring out the window for what felt like hours. Finally, it was my stop.

"Hi mom, I'm home." Throwing my backpack down as soon as I walked in the front door, taking a deep breath of relief.

"How was school?"

"Boring and long."

"I'm sorry honey, do you have homework?" My mom said while she looked up from her laptop as I was walking through the doorway to the kitchen.

"Yes, but not a lot." I mumbled while walking over to hug my mom.

"Go get a snack and start it, let me know if you need help." My mom said while squeezing me tight.

"Can I take a nap first, please? I'll set an alarm for 30 minutes."

"Yes, then you need to start your homework." My mom reached for her laptop as she went to finish her work.

***

"Peyton do you want to come visit grandma with me or are you still going to your friends?" My mom yelled as she grabbed her car keys.

"My friends, I'm going to walk there now." I put my arm through my coat jacket.

"Okay, have fun, I love you."

"Love you, give Grammy a hug and kiss from me and tell her I'll see her tomorrow."

The fresh breeze of fall blew onto my face while opening the front door. The trees were finally changing colors, Grammy must be so happy. As I began walking to my friend's house, I wondered how Grammy was doing today, will she remember her daughter today? It was slowly killing all of us seeing Grammy losing herself more and more everyday.

Walking up to the door, I let out a long sigh as I put a smile on my face and pulled the screen door open. Bringing my hand up, I rapped on the door.

"Hi Peyton, the girls are having snacks in the kitchen." Kristen's mom greeted me at the front door.

"Okay, thank you." I took my shoes off before walking around the house.

"Peyton!" My two friends shouted while running over to me, knocking me to the ground.

They were watching High School Musical, so I sat down and finished watching it with them. It was nice and relaxing not having to worry about anything. We belted out the words to every song, not caring about who heard us. Once we finished the movie, we ran upstairs eager to hangout longer. Laughter filled the room as we exchanged stories and jokes; this was just what I needed. My stomach ached from laughing so hard. After we all finally caught our breath, we huddled on the floor and began watching YouTube videos. Time seemed to fly as we aimlessly picked video after video, just looking for anything interesting to watch. We probably watched about 15 videos before my phone started ringing.

"Hi mom, I'm leaving soon."

"I will be there in two minutes to get you." My mom's voice shook as she began talking to me, sounding like she was crying.

"Mom what happened?"

"Peyton, I'll tell you when your with me just say goodbye and thank you."

"Okay." Replying in a quiet voice, my heart dropping. What happened, was it Grammy?

Hanging up the phone and grabbing my things, I headed downstairs to say goodbye. As the door opened, tears filled my eyes, why couldn't my mom tell me on the phone, it has to be really bad. As the car was pulling into the driveway, my mom was wiping her eyes.

"Mom, what's wrong?" I said, asking while opening the passenger door, my heart beginning to race.

"We are going to go for a drive first." My mom's eyes were bright red from crying.

As she pulled out of the driveway, all that went through my head is what could've happened. Maybe it was happy tears, but maybe it was sad tears. Five minutes into the drive, noticing this wasn't just a random drive, it was Grammy and I's drive. Something happened to Grammy but what? I couldn't wait any longer.

The words just came out of my mouth, "Mom, what happened to Grammy? Is she okay?"

"Peyton, I am so sorry, but Grammy passed away tonight." My mom announced, pulling into a parking spot, her voice trembled while talking to me.

"No she didn't, she's okay. Go to the nursing home, she's alive. You guys probably didn't realize that it was just her sleeping, she always forgot people were there and would fall asleep." I said in complete shock, trying to deny her passing.

"Peyton it's hard, but she's gone. She told me to tell you to keep bringing happiness into everyone's life and that she will always love you."

"No mom, I didn't get to say goodbye. I should've been there with her!" I screamed while tears filled my eyes.

"She always wanted you to have fun and be happy." My mom tried to reassure me as she rubbed my back.

"No it is not okay, I am selfish..."

My body shook as the alarm sounded, waking me up as tears poured down my face. I took a deep breath and realized it was just a nightmare.

***

I rummaged through my junk drawer, ignoring the various bobby pins and hair ties, I felt a prick on my finger. As I quickly drew my finger back, my eyes caught sight of a thumbtack. Still going through the drawer searching for the ring box so I wouldn't lose the ring again, my fingers finally felt it as they glided across the soft and smooth material. Popping it open, my eyes went to what seemed like a piece of paper. What could this be, why haven't I seen it before? My heart raced as my tiny fingers reached for this strange white object. Without thinking anymore, my body took over and slowly unrolled the piece of paper. Why was this in here, did Grammy forget to take it out? My pulse quickened as my eyes scanned the piece of paper, catching sight of the words, "Dear Peyton." My fingers unrolled the paper faster, eager to finish reading what it said. It was a letter from Grammy, how did I never notice this? I laid in my bed with the letter in my hands, reading it as tears of joy rolled my face.

Dear Peyton,

Hi P, its Grammy. I am writing to you to remind you that I will be okay so don't worry about me. I am sure I've passed away since you have the ring and found this letter. I am in a happy place now with a full memory! I will miss making new memories together and reliving our old ones but now they will never be forgotten. My favorite ones with you will always be our Sunday's together when we would go shopping and get our nails done or just stay at the house, it was always just the two of us. You always had the biggest smile on your face with your eyes wide open when you looked at my ring and it brought me so much happiness. Our memories could go on forever so I'm not going to say them all. Don't worry, I will always be looking over you, my beautiful granddaughter and the rest of our family. Always remember our song is my wish. This is my wish (my wish, for you). I hope you know somebody loves you (my wish, for you). May all your dreams stay big (my wish, for you). I love you P.

Love,
Grammy

***

Gratitude

"Honey, the bills came in the mail today. Come look at this." Sam's mom had a worried look.

"What's wrong?" Sam's dad took off his coat and put in on the chair, letting out a sigh. "It keeps piling up on us, huh. It's now three times more than we usually pay. We can only afford that price for so long before something happens."

"Mom, can I use the TV to play my new video game? I finished my homework." Sam ran down the stairs from his room.

"Okay, only until dinner is ready." Sam's mom stirred the soup on the stove.

Sam grabbed the remote that was sitting on the couch and turned on the TV. He reached into the cracks of the couch to find the controller to start the game.

Looking out across the room, he thought to himself, Hmm, why is the box for the pool table out here? Dad is always playing it with his friends. And why is the ping pong table folded up and in the corner? Sam started to get curious.

"The food's ready! Come upstairs."

Sam placed his controller on the couch and ran to the dinner table while making race car sounds. The fresh smell of spaghetti rushed through his nostrils, making his stomach grumble. Once he sat down at the dinner table, the family held their hands together for a short prayer. He was breathing heavily while his heart was racing.

"Amen. Remember to be thankful for everything you have." Sam's mom reassured.

"I'm thankful for my game and my computer. Oh yeah, my tablet too." Sam dug his face into the plate, inhaling the food.

"Well, I'm thankful for our family being safe and healthy." Dad said as he took a sip of wine.

Throughout the meal, Sam's mom and dad exchanged stories from their day, looking across at one another. But the only thing on Sam's mind was finishing as quickly as possible to get back to the games that illuminated the otherwise dark basement.

"That was good, Mom. Thanks for the delicious dinner!" Sam left his plate on the dinner table and ran back down to the basement.

Running past the living room, Sam overheard the news playing from the TV. He heard a woman crying and quickly stopped to look at the screen. In the background, there were dozens of photos of 'for sale' signs on houses. The news reporter droned on about how people were losing their homes as quickly as they lost their jobs. Panning out, the camera moved from the woman and the screen split to a street which had six houses, all lined with the signs that read foreclosure sale in big red letters. As the segment continued, analysts mentioned how long the problem could last and their predictions of what would happen next. Sam's mom shook her head as she grabbed a towel from the kitchen.

"Can you believe this?" Sam's mom said, starting to wipe the table, looking over to her husband who was watching the news.

"The economy is going to hell-even at our job. It gets really hot in factory, especially standing for 12 hours with machines that rattle the building all day. Not many people are showing up anymore." Dad poured himself another glass of wine.

"Numbers are still going down?" She let out a sigh. "What are we gonna do?" Mom took a seat with a concerned look.

"Nothing much. It might be too late to do anything now."

"You think Sam would care?"

"I don't know. He probably wouldn't understand what is going on. We don't have many choices." Sam's dad leaned back on his chair.

***

Sam and Mason got out of the bus stop on the last day of school and walked together back home. They were ecstatic and overjoyed about their summer break and how they could play video games all day long. With new game releases, the boys would be busy all summer long. As they walked to the front door of Sam's house, they were ready to rush down to the basement.

"Oh, hey Mom. I thought you were working?" Sam said in a surprised tone.

"I took a day off today. Oh, hey Mas-"

"Can he come over today?" Sam cut off his mom. "He wants to play the new game with me."

"Sorry honey, maybe another time. You can go to his house if you want to though. Make sure his mom is okay with having you over alright? Also, don't come back too late."

"Mason, lets go to your house then."

Sam and Mason walked across the street and entered the house. They dropped their bags by the garage and proceeded to go to the backyard. The summer heat struck them like a desert wind. Mason walked to the bin and took out a beach ball to throw around. Sam took his shirt off and jumped into the deep end of the pool. The radio blasted through the speaker as the kids had fun in the pool. There were bags of chips and pizza boxes on the table for them to eat.

After hours of playing in the backyard, the boys headed inside the house. They dried themselves with a towel and played hide and seek throughout the house. Since school was over, it meant that Sam and Mason can go over each other's houses to play everyday. They celebrated for completing elementary school and getting ready for middle school. They knew that middle school would shorten their time of hanging out, so they planned to spend the most time with each other over the summer as possible.

"Sam, your mother just called me and said that you can stay over for the night. You can sleep in Mason's room."

"Yay!" The boys jumped in excitement.

Across the street, Sam's mom started to clean out her cabinets and closet. She took a portrait of her family three years ago and stared at it. A rush of emotions left Sam's mom with her heart sinking to her stomach. She couldn't understand why it was happening to them. What had they done wrong; how would they be able to move somewhere else? Sam's mom sat down on the bed with her hands on her knees. Staring at the ground, she thought about all of the great moments her family had within their home as tears started to well up in her eyes as she remembered the time when she and her husband bought their big home together. Being able to upgrade from their previous houses made them happy since they were able to afford the high price. Sam's mom stood up and wiped her tears as she heard the garage door open.

Sam's dad took off his jacket and placed it on the rack as his wife greeted him by he door. "Hey honey, how has your day been?"

"Typical. It's been slow for a while now. I'm trying my best to give the money to the workers but that means there's little left to bring home for us. I know that everyone is struggling too, but it's my business and I need to be able to support them as well. Why are your eyes red? Are you okay?"

"Yeah, I was thinking about the day we moved here and how happy we were. I was just having a moment, but I'm fine now."

"Are you sure?" He placed his hand on her shoulder as she nodded. "Okay, well lets keep going, we still have a lot to pack. What time are they coming tomorrow?"

"Around 1. We'll have to get Sam from Mason's house a little before that. He's not going to take this well."

✳✳✳

"Oh my, there is so much to pack in Sam's room. He has a lot of stuff." Sam's mom brought boxes into the room.

"If you didn't buy him everything he wanted, then maybe there wouldn't be so much to pack. Look at all of these toys he never even looks at. What a waste." Sam's dad was frustrated.

"I want him to be happy though. I want-"

"You spoiled him to the point where the money we had was blown away with all of these toys that Sam doesn't even play with anymore. All of these figures and cards have dust gathered on them." Sam's dad yelled and walked away.

Sam's mom sat down on one of the dinner chairs that was left by the front door. She looked down on the ground in silence. It felt like her whole world was collapsing in an instant. Drops of tears splashed onto the ground as her heart felt like it was melting. She heard her husband angrily storming around the house as he ruffled through boxes. All of the happiness and peace her family had a week ago fell apart, almost immediately.

"Mom, I'm home!" Sam took his shoes off and threw his bag on the ground. Then he came at a full stop with a shocked look on his face. "W-what happened?" The house was filled with boxes that were labeled and taped. It looked like the house was full of nothing. No desk, no couch, no dinner table.

"Oh, h-hey Sam. What are you doing here so early? Don't you want to be at Mason's house?" Sam's mom rubbed her eyes.

"His mom said that he had a doctor's appointment early in the morning today, so she sent me back home. She said she called you but you didn't pick up."

"Umm, okay then. Well, here is your tablet. Keep yourself occupied."

"Mom, Mason has the new console at his house and I want one too. Can you please buy it for me? Please? We can play online together." Sam had his hands closed together while looking up to his mom.

"Dad and I are really busy right now. Plus, you already have the new game and a tablet. That's enough."

"Humph, *not fair*! I want the new console now! Or else I'm going to be mad." Sam crossed his arms and started to stomp on the ground.

"Do that and then watch your Dad get mad at you. You don't want to deal with Dad, especially now. Go sit in that chair and play on your tablet."

Sam's mom started to think about how her husband might've been right about spoiling her son. Sam's tantrum and complaining made the situation even worse for her. She looked at all of the boxes by the front door and saw six labeled boxes that said *Sam's toys*. She walked upstairs to finish packing the leftover clothes in her closet. Only depression filled her mind as she wiped more tears off of her face.

"Why is everything packed away? Wait, are we moving, Mom?"

Placing the box in her hand on the ground, Sam's mom looked up at him and walked over to where he was sitting. "Yes, honey. We found another home that has a better education system than here, so we're moving to a different town. It's going to be really nice there."

"But why? I love living here, though."

"We do too, but it is something you wouldn't understand. All of your stuff are in boxes that say your name on it, but don't open them." Sam's mom pointed at the boxes near the front door. The sound of large trucks was heard outside of the house.

"Honey, they're here! Come downstairs." Sam's mom yelled across the house.

4 large men entered the house with gloves and boots. They greeted the parents and walked around the house to see all of the boxes and heavy items. Sam had no other choice but to sit silently and play on his tablet. Hours went by as the men walked back and forth, in and out of the front door. Sam had to stand up and sit on the stairs since the men had to bring the rolling chair into the trucks too. Sam had his earbuds in, staring into blank space while listening to music.

Confused still by what was going on, Sam couldn't understand why they were moving-his school was a good one. Didn't his parents understand that he loved his friends and his teachers and the school he went to? Trying to stay optimistic, Sam thought of how his life was going to be better when they move. He imagined himself having a big bedroom and the basement all to himself. His stomach started to flutter with excitement thinking about having big birthday parties and 3 couches for all his friends to sit on. They would be playing on his brand new console and sleeping over often throughout summer break. A grin started to form on Sam's face.

"Sammy, lets go buddy. Hop into my car." Sam's dad glanced around the house for any missing items before they locked the door.

✳✳✳

"Hey Mr. Luck, how are you?" Sam's parents shook their lawyer's hand.

"Very well. Please have a seat. What brings you here today?"

Sam's dad looked down and took a big sigh. "As you probably know, the situations that are going on currently are affecting our family pretty badly. We won't be able to sufficiently pay off the bills we owe in the upcoming months. What can we do?"

"Let me see the papers you have today," he said, reaching his hand out. "Hmm, so it seems like you own four houses that are still being paid off. I suppose you're currently living in one and three are used for others to rent?"

"Correct, but you probably already know why I came here today then. I'm not getting the monthly payments from the tenants mainly because they can't afford to pay it. The eviction process takes too long to file since many other home owners are trying to do it too. Our money is drowning away fast now since we're the ones mainly paying for these bills now."

The lawyer took a moment to read all of their bills and the current finances for the family. While he was going through the files, Sam's dad leaned his head on his hand that was on the arm rest. He started to think about how his family would be able to regain their happy relationship. He recalled the best moments in his life such as having his son enter the world. The happiness of him and his wife was something he wanted to feel again. He wanted to bring back joy instead of the restless fighting that he had been dealing with.

"I'm sorry to hear that. Everyone is suffering from this and I've had many clients these past few days come to me with the same situations. Unfortunately, I was only able to offer one decision to them, since there weren't many choices."

"Whatever we have to do, we'll do it. We're desperate at this point."

"You'll have to file for a default and give up your homes to the bank. You can still keep one house that you're able to pay the mortgage for. Based on your current finances, I think it is best to give up the house you live in now and move to a smaller one. Other than that, the rest will be given to the bank."

"Alright, we'll do that."

"I would recommend that you start packing your belongings as soon as you can. I advise that you don't make it too obvious since your son may start questioning what is happening. It is best to not inform your son about everything since his lifestyle might completely change. I'm sorry that your family is going through this. Like I said, there are many other families who are going through this too. I hope for the best." The lawyer placed the paperwork into a folder and put it in the cabinet.

"Thank you, have a good day."

**

As the car pulled out of the driveway, Sam looked around the neighborhood and glanced at the houses around. He looked at Mason's house and thought about the memories they had together. The pool, the basement, the sleepovers. Signals of anxiety and sadness sizzled through his veins and down to his stomach. He put his earbuds on and played sad music to block out the outside sounds. He took a moment to himself and tried to figure out why his life is changing all of a sudden.

He could remember the first time that he walked home from the bus stop and how Mason had greeted him. Mason was his first friend that actually talked to him and had told him all the things that he liked to do. Their connection, it seemed, was as natural as they came. Tears started to well up in Sam's eyes as he passed the bus stop at the end of the street. The only thing that he could think of was the memories, as well as the anxiety of where he was moving to. Sam raised the volume on his tablet and fell asleep to ease up the negative thoughts.

Your destination is on your left, The GPS rang out as it was hanging on the front mirror of the car. Sam took a look at the houses around the car. To his surprise, the houses were very small. Looking out, he saw many houses the size of what had been their sun room.

"Alright Sam, here we are. You can go inside and have a look around. Pick what room you want to be yours." Sam's dad opened up the car door.

"T-this is our house? It's so small though."

"I know, but we live here now. I have to help the other men unpack and locate where all the stuff is going. Go inside and have a look."

Sam unplugged his earbuds out of his tablet and walked slowly towards the front of the house. As he approached the front door, he saw the wooden frames being skinned from the bright blue color that was painted over it. There were many spider webs in the corners of the house and the doorknob was rusty. He took a step into the house and saw a lot of dust hanging on the window sill and on the floor. He walked to the kitchen and saw that the fridge was small and old fashioned. The refrigerator didn't have an automatic water and ice dispenser on the exterior, which showed that Sam wasn't really "upgrading" from his previous home.

After the moving company finished bringing the boxes into the house, Sam's parents bought fast food and ate on the dinner table. His parents were exhausted with moving boxes into different rooms and gave a big sigh of relief as they sat down.

"Mom, why is this house like, smaller? I thought we were moving to a nicer one."

"I wish we did honey, but it's something that you wouldn't under-."

"Mom, I'm not a baby anymore. I want to know why we're here in a small house and why you didn't tell me." Sam's words became abrupt.

"Sorry, Sammy, I didn't mean to hurt you. I don't think you would know what is going on right now. I unpacked your stuff upstairs and plugged your console into the TV. On your computer, I wrote down the website of your new school on the post-it note. Check to see if there are any summer assignments you need to do."

"Ugh, fine. Don't come in my room." Sam stood up and slammed his chair back into the dinner table. He shut his door so hard that it echoed throughout the house.

He looked around his small room, with dozens of boxes riddling the floor. Sam struggled to understand why his parents were hiding something from him. Why were they treating him as if he was five? He could not understand. Sam opened up his laptop and typed in the link to the name of his new school. He looked at the 6th grade section of summer assignments. He clicked "History Class" and opened up a link of the document. It said:

Hello upcoming 6th graders! My name is Mr. Pin and I will be your History teacher next year! For your summer work, I would like you to write about what is currently happening in the news. I want 3 articles with 3 paragraph summaries each. Make sure you post the website with the summary. See you soon!

Sam typed in "current events" in the search bar and clicked the first link that showed up. As he scanned the titles, he noticed that they all relatively had the same names. The word "recession" was on every title. *More than 3 million have lost their jobs and about 2 million people had to close their homes. The numbers are still climbing as we speak. This may as well be the biggest recession America has ever faced. It might surpass the Great Depression. We will consistently post articles about any further upcoming news.*

Sam sat in his chair in silence. A rush of thoughts entered his brain as he thought about his parents and the "problems" he was facing weren't near to the conflicts his parents were dealing with. He began to think about what he was complaining about such as the new console and moving to a smaller house. Sam closed his laptop, placed his head on top of it, and teared up thinking about the stress he put on his parents. But he realized how grateful he should be to have a home and not suffer from his parents losing their jobs, let alone a roof over their heads.

＊＊＊

Size 7

Music blared through my speakers, sitting cross legged on the hardwood floor of my closet, surrounded by cardboard boxes. There's was still so much packing to get done by Sunday, I thought to myself. Everything in my apartment had been packed up, except for my clothes.

Already Friday, my stomach began filling with butterflies as I thought about my flight to Chicago, set to leave at 8:00am on Monday morning. The daunting task of packing my life into boxes seemed impossible. I'd been in New York for five years; that was a lot of time to accumulate a lot of stuff. As I thought more about it, coupled with the actual move to a new place I knew very little about, my hands grew clammy. The questioning thought, continually entering my mind made me second guess my decision. I struggled with figuring out if the move was a good one or if it was in fact a horrible mistake. What if the new job wasn't a good fit? The new job, at Urban Styles magazine, was something I'd dreamed about since I was 12. But now that it was finally here, I recognized how much harder getting there would be than I initially thought.

With the weather at a balmy 85 degrees, I was lucky that a portion of my wardrobe wasn't being used. I was able to quickly pack away three boxes with winter clothes.

As I taped up the last of the winter boxes, I turned and let out a sigh as I looked over the rest of my closet, debating what would go into the boxes next. Maybe the red dress I'd gotten on 5th Ave? Or maybe, the all the skirts? I shook my head, as I realized just how many clothes I'd accumulated over the years working as a fashion consultant at Pop Clothing magazine in the city.

Pulling myself from my daze, I raised my hand and wrapped it around eight hangers holding blouses and tossed them into a box with little care. A few more trips back and forth to the box, and it was full. Taping them shut, this went on for hours, in a mindless routine- grab clothes, toss in a box, tape it up, stack it. Glancing up at the clock, the red numbers read out 11:30 and I still had to go into work tomorrow to collect my things from my desk. Letting out a groan, I flopped down on my bed, almost instantly falling asleep.

***

The sounds of my alarm going off woke me up. Picking up my phone, I struggled to open my eyes, since it was only 6:30 and I didn't want to leave the warmth of my bed. Flinging the sheets off and sitting up, I stretched my arms up to the ceiling, almost knocking my wrist on my ceiling fan. My feet, almost as if on auto pilot, dragged myself into the kitchen as I reached over and pressed the button on the coffee maker as I waited for the only thing that mattered in those next few minutes, caffeine. Turning, I grabbed my favorite maroon mug which rested on the shelf. Placing it down, I waited for it to fill as the aroma filled the whole room, overtaking my senses. As coffee finished sputtering out of the machine, I grabbed my mug walking back over to my room and into my closet. Glancing around at the boxes and piles of clothes, I sighed and grabbed a pair of jeans and my favorite maroon long sleeve shirt, peeking my eyes over at my shoes waiting to be packed. Picking up my pair of black keds, I laughed thinking of my first day of work two years ago...

Light shined into my eyes as I sat up. Glancing over at my phone and sighing, I had woken up 15 minutes before my alarm. Angry at myself for losing 15 minutes of sleep, I said to myself, "Well there's no use trying to fall back asleep now," as I sat up and begrudgingly got out of bed. Walking over to my closet, I slid on my dark navy jeans and a lavender blouse. Walking over to my brand new box of keds, I pulled them out of the box and inhaled "ahhh the smell of new shoes, my favorite." I said, putting my black keds onto my feet and heading into my bathroom to get ready for the day. Taking one final glance at myself, I turned, heading for the door, smiling. I hopped into my car and zoomed off to my first day at Pop Clothing.

Squealing to myself with excitement, all I have ever wanted to be since I was a little girl was a fashion consultant; clothes and shoes have always been my favorite things in the world, but shoes, well, those were the most important. Walking into the office, my jaw hung open, as I gazed at the brick walls lined with fashion posters adorned with famous models on each one. I was in awe as I walked past each one, thinking to myself how lucky I was to be working there. Walking over to the receptionist, sticking out my hand "Hi, my name's Brooke and today is my first day here!" The gray haired lady smiled up at me, shaking my hand. "Nice to meet you darling, my name's Jan; I'll show you over to your desk." I followed Jan down the hall, passing offices with what looked like important people in each. At the end of the hallway, we reached an opening that expanded into a spread out area containing rows of cubicles.

"Here you are, if you have any questions, just ask me, here is your computer, password, and login, there should be an email on there telling you what tasks you need to complete today." She smiled as she walked back to her desk at the front. Smiling at my reflection in the computer I squealed, not being able to believe my new job.

✳✳✳

"Oh shoot, I'm going to be late," I yelled, looking down at my watch, coming out of my trance. Running into the kitchen feverishly pulling my jacket on, I grabbed my keys and purse and ran out of the apartment, slamming the door shut. Running down the stairs, I found myself swerving in and out of people talking and going up the stairs. Finally reaching my car, I raced off to work.

I sat down at my chair as the clock changed to 8:00. I let out a big breath I didn't know I had held in as the stress left my body-I'd made it on time. Even if it was my last day and I was just clearing out my desk, I didn't want to be late. Taking in my surrounding and sighing, I glanced around at all the brick walls with posters of famous models hanging on the walls, and it felt like I was just looking at all of this for the first time.

It was 12:00 by the time I had finished putting away all of my things, and began saying goodbye to my coworkers. Getting up from my chair carrying my two boxes of things, I walked out to my car. Opening my trunk, I placed the boxes down and slammed it shut. Glancing at my former workplace, I sighed, ready to move on to the next chapter of my life. Sitting back in my car, I drove off back towards my apartment to finishing packing.

Opening the door to my apartment, I walked over to my closet. Looking up at my shelves filled with my favorite pairs of shoes sighing, I didn't want to pack away my most precious possessions. Each set of shoes owned were special and unique. Laughing, I was not able to remember the last time I actually threw away a pair of shoes. No matter how old or ratty they got, or even if they didn't fit on my feet anymore, I refused to get rid of them.

As I looked up to the seemingly endless wall of shoes, I picked up my phone and opened the music app, selecting 'Today's Hits.' Pressing play, I began the arduous task of packing away each pair of my beloved shoes. As I picked up each pair, I couldn't help but laugh or smile, thinking about the first time they were worn. One specific pair caught my eye- the nude suede heels. I remembered buying those last year for my sister's wedding. What a mess of day that had been.

"Deep breaths Liz, everything is going to be okay," I had said to her, trying to calm my sister down since we only had about an hour until she was going to walk down the aisle. Her shoes had gotten destroyed by a leak in the venue's ceiling that had ruined the carpet within the dressing room, and her hair was not styling correctly. "You will be okay we are trying to dry off your shoes right now." As more hairspray was added into her hair trying to get it to stay, she finally blurted out. "No, it's not, Brooke, I'm getting married in less than 45 minutes and I have no shoes, and my hair is barely staying in place," she said with aggravation laced in her voice. For the next 20 minutes, all of the bridesmaids ran around trying to figure out Liz's shoe situation. Finally, there was a knock on the door, saying that all the bridesmaids needed to start walking down the aisle. At that moment an idea popped into my head, I ran over to all of the bridesmaids and made them take off their shoes, and sent them on their way out.

"Liz, here take my heels, you need them more than I do," I said, smiling.

"Aw Brooke, your shoes, are you sure? I know how much they mean to you," Liz said, a hint of hope in her voice.

"Yes, of course, don't worry about me; this is your big day."

We both walked out of the room and out to the altar with our bouquets of flowers in our hands.

As the song switched on the speaker, my mind pulled itself back as I looked down at the shoes in my hand. I should really give Liz a call, I thought to myself. Gently placing the shoes in the box, carefully making sure that they did not get squished by the other shoes, I continued packing. Hours passed by in what felt like minutes, I had already packed up out of the boxes of shoes. I knew I needed to hurry-the moving truck would be there in no time.

Walking down the hall with it's stark white walls, from the fresh coat of paint, that was put on last Saturday, I couldn't help but be happy that I was moving; this place didn't feel like home anymore. Making my way into the kitchen over to the fridge to grab a bottle of water, I sauntered back into my bedroom. Plopping down on my bed, needing rest, I couldn't pack any more shoes. Slowly my eyes began to flutter shut as I fell into a deep sleep.

✳✳✳

The sound of my phone blaring woke me up, glancing over at the red numbers on my clock, they read 5:00. Jolting out of bed, "Oh crap! I overslept again," I yelled out. I only had 45 minutes until the moving company would bring their truck and start to haul my stuff to my new apartment in Chicago.

Speed packing all of my shoes, barely taking a second glance to reminisce with them. Finally finished, I should probably label these so they don't get mixed up with all the other boxes, I thought to myself. Quickly grabbing a marker and scribbling on the word FRAGILE, I lifted up each box, inhaling the smell from the sharpie on the cardboard. I began to carry the boxes over to the door so they were all set and would not be forgotten.

About an hour later, the doorbell sounded. As I unbolted the door and opened it, the movers smiled as I stepped aside, allowing them to come in, showing them over to my boxes of clothes and telling them what has to be taken. After an hour of the two big burly movers, coming back and forth, they finally finished. Locking the deadbolt after saying goodbye, and heading over to the microwave, I heated up my cup of ramen.

The microwave sounded signaling to me that my dinner was done. Heading off to my bedroom to watch Netflix on my laptop and eat my food until passing out on the air mattress that was now on my floor. The next morning, I woke up and got ready. Slipping on my jacket I wheeled my carry on over to the door. Turning around, I took one last glance at my now empty apartment and walked out, slamming the big wooden oak door shut. The last thing I saw before heading down the hall was the number 342 on my door. "Goodbye" I muttered, heading off to start my new journey.

✳✳✳

Paws for Hearing

My eyes opened slowly to the far away, low buzzing of my alarm. 6:00 am, I thought looking over at the clock, time to get up and start another day. Tossing off the covers, my feet hit the cold, wooden floor of my bedroom and it made me shiver. Groggily, I walked down the hall towards the bathroom to get ready. There was no 'splosh' when the faucet turned on, just silence; though it was cut short when I was startled by the sudden, unmistakable, high-pitched squeaking of my drawer as it opened. Though I'd almost grown accustomed to not being able to hear lower pitched noises, since it's been happening for a little while now, it still startled me, however, when noises suddenly occurred after it was silent. I'd hear nothing but silence for a few minutes, or maybe even half an hour, and then everything would go back to normal. Sometimes, though, a lot of sounds were muffled and I had to listen to something multiple times or ask someone to repeat what they were saying to understand what was going on.

Walking back to my room, I passed my dog, Mason, who sat outside my door waiting for me to get his morning meal. "Hold on, I'll be out in a second." With a flick of my wrist, he walked away to the kitchen.

I decided it would be a good idea to also make breakfast for myself once I was done getting ready. Grabbing out a pan so I could make an omelet, I went to reach for a spatula but the pan slipped out of my grip and fell to the floor with a moderately soft clang; yet again, making it sound as if I was in a tunnel. Frustrated, I let out a long sigh thinking

119

that I couldn't take it much longer. It was just getting worse. Thankfully, later that day, I had scheduled an appointment with the audiologist.

Feeling something brush up against my leg, I looked down only to be met with the expectant eyes of Mason. He stood there with the pan's handle in his mouth as he waited patiently for me to take it from him; he'd done that many times before when I was unable to hear something fall or when the doorbell or phone rang, though, he wasn't the best at it yet.

"Thanks bud." He wagged his tail as if he understood what I was saying.

Then, following my hand signals, he sat down so I could grab the pan and wash it in the sink.

Once again, though, when the water turned on, it made no sound and everything around me was unbelievably quiet; it was like someone had put the whole world on mute.

Looking into the sink, I was beginning to stress out now, and also a little scared. I knew Mason could tell as well when I felt him lean against my leg. Patting his head, I knelt down next to him and sighed, "I'm alright buddy, everything's okay."

I sat there for a few minutes petting his head trying to calm myself down, the thought of breakfast now far from my mind; and slowly but surely, my hearing returned to hear Mason's soft whimpering as he waited for me to get up. I will admit, it was not fun, but at least Mason was with me and he is trained to help in these types of situations. He was given to me by my mom once my father was put into an assisted living home to help him with his hearing problems, once she could no longer deal with helping him herself. I always had a nagging feeling in the back of my mind that that is how I would end up.

Shaking my head to clear my thoughts, my body subconsciously stood up. "Well, Mason, I'm not going to get anything done if I keep sitting around," I steadily rose to my feet and walked to the counter to get my dog's food. He came jogging over wagging his tail and staring up at his dish in anticipation. "Geez, Mason," I said, "I get that you're hungry, but don't you have to crowd me." Laughing as I set the dish down, he barked as if to answer my question. I loved hearing him bark; when and if my hearing gets worse, that will probably be one of the things I will miss the most. Then, grabbing an apple, I checked the calendar to confirm that I remembered the time I had to be at my appointment by. Noticing I had just about half an hour and that there was no time to make any breakfast, I grabbed an apple and my car keys, said goodbye to Mason, and walked out to my car.

***

When I reached the audiologist's office and signed in, I sat down to wait. As I looked around, the only thing that came to my mind was the first time I sat in a waiting room like this when I first started experiencing my hearing problems. Remembering back to that day, I couldn't help but smile; my hearing had certainly been a lot better back then. I was frustrated by the fact that the doctor had given my false information that day and had not recommended me to see a specialist. Picking up a magazine, I only had time to skim the front cover before I heard my name being called by one of the assistants. As I strode towards her she smiled and motioned for me to follow her down the hall and into a blue room. There were ear dioramas all over the place, not to mention a few computers and what looked to be something like a recording booth minus the padding on the walls.

"The audiologist will be here in a few minutes, in the meantime, I'm going to ask a few preliminary questions." I nodded letting her know she could continue.

"When did your hearing problems start?"

"About four or five months ago."

"Is the first time you're seeking a professionalist's help? Or were you referred here by anyone?"

"Um, I saw two previous doctors before my second doctor referred me here," She shook her head in understanding, waiting for me to continue, "The first doctor I saw misdiagnosed me and basically told me that it was probably temporary hearing loss from being around loud noises for an extended period of time."

"Okay, what's your hearing like now?"

"Well, there are periods where everything sounds muffled or completely silent, and then everything will return to normal"

"How long do those periods typically last?"

"Sometimes anywhere from a few minutes to almost half an hour."

In between each question she asked she would type up what I could only assume were my responses, periodically pausing to think about something. It made me feel a bit anxious, like maybe I was overreacting and that it honestly wasn't as big of a deal as I was making it out to be.

"Alright," she chimed in, "the audiologist will be with you shortly."

She left the room, leaving me alone with my thoughts. I couldn't hear anything beyond the door - probably because it was too quiet for my ears to pick up on - and it was starting to scare me just a little bit because right now it really "sounds" as though I am completely deaf.

Not too long after the assistant left, the door opened and this time a man, seeming to be in his early thirties, entered the room. "Hello, I'm Mr. Blake, and I'll be helping you today." I nodded to him, not knowing what to say.

"You're nervous, right? Well you don't have to be. All I'm going to do today is examine your ears and put you through some tests to determine your hearing level and what the next step should be." He smiled at me as he spoke and I could tell he was trying his best to make me feel as comfortable as possible; the way he explained everything made me feel a bit more at ease too.

"Can you do me a favor and explain to me what happened between you and your original doctor, it says here on my sheet that he may have misdiagnosed you."

"Well back when I first started to experience some hearing loss I had waited about 3 or 4 days to go in and talk to a doctor-." As I began to explain what happened to Mr. Blake, I was reminded of the whole experience.

It was back in June when I found myself walking into my doctor's office. I had scheduled an appointment with him to talk about my recent hearing problems and hopefully figure out a solution.

"Hello Lisa, what seems to be the problem?"

"Well, sir, for the last few days I have been having a hard time hearing; there are times when everything will go silent for about ten minutes and then come back."

After listening to my response and asking me a few more questions, which in my mind didn't seem to be really effective in helping discover the problem, he used his otoscope to examine my ears. He said that he didn't really find anything wrong or concerning besides a buildup of wax in my ear; so he told me to try using ear drops or rinsing out my ear. That was literally the only thing he could recommend me, and it honestly didn't feel like it was helpful at all.

After I finished explaining what had happened with my first doctor's visit, Mr. Blake seemed like understood my situation a little more. "Okay, so it sounds like you were proactive with your situation, and didn't wait till it got really bad to seek help."

"Yeah, I tried following his advice, but nothing changed; I still experienced the same problems I did before I went to see him. Also, I figured he would recommend me to someone like you for a second opinion, but he didn't." I couldn't help but feel that maybe I should have done my own research and come here sooner.

***

"Yes, he should have given you some sort of recommendation; and that's what your last doctor did correct?" I nodded. Once he was done asking questions, Mr. Blake told me that he was going to re-examine my ears and put me through a few electronic hearing tests.

About a half hour later, I was waiting for Mr. Blake to come back with my test results and prognosis when everything around me went utterly silent again. This time it didn't sound like I had just walked into a tunnel or like someone had turned a stereo down; it was like I had genuinely gone completely deaf. Coincidentally, he did happen to come back just at that moment, and he could tell something was off. I looked at him and told him the I couldn't hear anything, hoping I wasn't screaming at him. He seemed to understand and I saw him mouth that he could wait.

It was about 15 minutes before my hearing came back, though it felt like forever, "Okay, everything seems to be back to normal."

He looked at me with a half-smile.

"Wish I could say the same thing. Unfortunately, it looks as though you have a disorder called otosclerosis, and the only way to get this is that you would have to have inherited it from a close familial relative. It is an abnormal growth of the stapes in the middle ear; and it looks to be in a pretty advanced stage. I'd say your only way of hearing normally again is to have surgery done."

I sat there gaping at him. "Wait what? So your saying that surgery is my only option or I'll go completely deaf permanently?"

"Yes, I'm not going to sugarcoat it, Ms. Bryn. Surgery is your only option now; that is, unless you would rather let it progress and go deaf. It is up to you to decide what you want to do, but I'd say, with this level of progression, you have about a month or two at most."

We talked for a bit about the surgery option, but I couldn't do it. I told him that I couldn't afford to have surgery done, not now, not even in a few months from now; I just didn't have that kind of cash and my insurance would never cover it. He also told me that, in choosing to go down the other road, he would help me in learning how to cope with it. "There are multiple ways to deal with deafness; you could learn sign language, have people write things down more often instead of speaking to you, or get a hearing aid dog."

"Actually, my dad had a hearing aid dog in training that helped him for about a year or so before my mom ended up handing him over to me. I guess the stress of having someone with a hearing impairment got too much for her and she just didn't want to keep the dog. So I've had the hearing aid dog for a few months now and I work on training him every day; helping him to follow my hand cues." He seemed genuinely impressed with my response.

"That's great," he laughed, "I don't know of many people I've come across who would actually take that responsibility on. Normally, if they were to get a hearing aid dog, they would want it to be fully trained already, so they wouldn't have to do it themselves; but that wouldn't help them in the long run. If you would like though, I could recommend you to someone that can give you more pointers on dog training."

"Really? That would be perfect."

He nodded, "Yes. Actually, there are multiple specialists here in this building that could help you with everything you need. We could schedule some appointments with them for you right now even. How does that sound?"

I couldn't help but smile. I didn't expect him to offer so much help, especially after my first experience, but it was definitely welcomed. "Yes please, that would be great; you have no idea how much this means to me."

It made me happy that I could end that visit on a positive note, and he told me that he'd contact me shortly with any helpful information regarding my treatment. Talking with him certainly did ease my mind in the sense that I was no longer as afraid of what will happen in the future. Though I still have doubts, I know he is offering his best recommendations and, at this point, anything will help. Thanking him, I turned and left.

Upon arriving home, Mason was waiting patiently by the door as if ready to assist me at the drop of a hat. Unable to contain a chuckle, my lips curved upward into a smile, "Hey puppy. Thanks for the warm welcome."

His tail wagged repeatedly, showing his excitement. It was as if he wanted to start a conversation with me, "Alright, let's get to training. We have a lot of things to work on if you're going to help me, successfully, in the future."

✳✳✳

After about a half hour or so of running drills over and over, it was clear that Mason was getting tired, and I wasn't exactly the most upbeat person either; so we ended his training for the time being.

Falling onto the couch, my eyes wandered to the ceiling. Slowly, I could feel myself starting to relax and it wasn't until there was a repeated tapping on my knee that it registered that my hearing had tuned out again. Looking down at Mason, he was swiping his ear with his paw and then he turned and walked over to where my phone sat on the table. While walking over, my hearing slowly returned and I heard my ringtone playing and I was able to answer it right before it went to voicemail.

"Hello?"

"Hi sweetie, how are you?"

"Oh, hey mom, I'm good. Hey, I went to my audiologist appointment this morning."

"Oh really, how did it go?"

Since my volume was all the way up, I could hear the change in her voice. She sounded almost distressed. "What's wrong, mom? You knew that I was going to have this appointment."

"Yes, but I just don't want you to end up like your father. Tell me, is it good news? It's good news, right?"

"Unfortunately not. Turns out the condition I have is actually inherited from dad; so it's the same hearing problem."

When she hesitated to answer I knew she had gotten upset, "Oh."

"Good news is, though, that my audiologist is recommending some specialists to help me learn sign language and to provide further training tips for Mason. I'm sure that, with their help, I'll be better prepared to face what is to come. You don't have to worry mom, I'll be alright."

"Okay sweetie, if you really believe in this that much, I'm with you; I'll try my best to be there every step of the way."

Ending the phone call, I looked down at Mason and pet his head, "You'll definitely be the key to my success now buddy. Good thing you adapt to new things quickly, that will definitely come in handy."

＊＊＊

Tails of the Underground

Standing on the dirty platform, I counted the metal steps, trying not to fall as I followed my outstretched hand. Quickly, being pulled without much force, my dad's scarf tickled my hand as it blew behind him in the hot train air. We entered the bottom tunnel, our destination, and finally got to take a break from running as the one with the blue stripe had not arrived yet. There's a blue one, a green one, and many more, but my favorite is the red one because I like the color red, and it stops at the museum with the dinosaurs. But we're not going to the museum today because dad had briefly mentioned having to make the blue train before grabbing my hand and buzzing off. Yet there was no blue train in sight and dad was beginning to look impatient and angry so I do not think now it is a good time to ask him.

A guy with large headphones passed us and was quickly replaced by a big, rugged looking man, he approached the two of us.

"Hey man, I need a little bit of help, I lost my wallet. I'll pay you back as soon as I can."

He was scary looking and I started to freeze, but dad pointed up at two balloons lodged into the beams of the ceiling.

"Look at those balloons!" He said to me.

"Common man, I'm sick, I have the flu, pneumonia, heartburn, pink eye, and the plague!"

Sometimes I wonder what the kids who lost balloons look like; I try to imagine their faces, solely on the features of the balloon. You can tell a lot about a person based on the type of balloon they buy, thinking to myself about the complex relationship between a child and their balloon. What if the balloon purposely left the child, balloons undoubtedly like to be in large groups, a school of balloons if you will. In their natural habitat, they cling together in large bunches, only to be sold separately. Maybe balloons fear isolation and that's why balloons seem to deflate hours after possession, but are always fully inflated at the cart.

"Sorry buddy, I don't have any money," dad said as we walked around the big guy. The big guy rolled his eyes and walked away begrudgingly, murmuring words I'm not supposed to say.

I like to keep an eye out for people playing the guitar in the subway, imagining the crowds they will one day gather. We keep walking and see an old man with a big beard that looked like he could play guitar, but was sleeping instead. My dad told me not to look at sleeping bearded men on the subway. We had to walk very close to him as I grabbed my dad's hand tighter, but dad pointed to the subway floor and said I should play the gum game. There were tons of gum on the grey floor to look at. Some were pink, some were green, but most were black. One of my favorite things to do was look for all the colors in the rainbow, but, I guess New Yorkers do not like grape gum because I have not once seen purple. After spending a brief moment gazing around the terminal, I found seven pieces of green gum, two white, four pink, and eleven black.

"Oh look, the train has arrived!" As the blue train pulled up, I saw one of its advertisements was a whole constellation of stars. I'm often confused about the stars in the sky, since I have never seen an actual star. Part of me believes they are just made up like the tooth fairy or kangaroos. Dad says the city lights are too bright, I do not know why the stars are shy to talk to the lights; I know plenty of kids who are not very bright. I have seen stars dozens of times in Grand Central, but even I have a hard time believing bulls and gladiators fight in the sky each night, but dad says they do. They are definitely real, it is just that it would become boring to fight with the same person all night, every night, yet the upstairs neighbors certainly seem to do so, so it could be possible.

"What's your main mission?" Oh no, I almost forgot dad's one rule! He is in charge of everything underground at the subway, reading the confusing map, talking to strangers, and finding the train (even when he appears to be lost). The only job I have is to watch the gap when entering the train. It is a very difficult job because if you fall in the crocodiles under the trains will eat you or the corrupt NYC politicians will kidnap you and force you to work in Times Square as Mickey Mouse. Ever since I was little, I had feared the dreadful sewer crocodiles most of all. Rumor has it that some kids won a regular sized lizard at the Coney Island Fair and brought it home. The boy also coincidentally bought one of those little toy animals that grows when you put them in water, the lizard ended up eating the toy and quickly began to grow. The lizard grew to the size of a cat before the boy was forced to flush him down the toilet. The crocodile still lives in the sewer to this day, growing each time he has a glass of water. At least that's what my dad tells me. I use to be afraid when crossing the gap, but as long as I do not look into the dark abyss that lies between the platform and train, I'm fine.

Luckily it was not too busy on the train. There were usually three different crowd levels. The first is when we both got seats, the second is we both have to stand, and the last is I get a seat and dad stands. I do not like the last one because that means two strangers have to sit on either side of me and they usually smell or play bad music loudly. But today we both got seats, which was a good sign because then dad usually tells me a story instead of spending the trip searching for free seats or looking over his shoulder for pickpockets.

"Look over at that train car." He said gesturing towards the green train on the other side of the platform. The train was extremely crowded and some people were even trying to squeeze in but were quickly giving up.

"Do you notice anything weird about it?" I shrugged my shoulders; it looked like a normal train to me.

"One of the cars is completely empty, why would a perfectly normal train car be empty at rush hour while all the others are packed?" I stared back at him, hoping for a good story.

"There's something wrong with it, like a broken air conditioner, a sewage leak or a loose dragon. Never get on an empty train car during rush hour."

Luckily our train was fine. Sitting down, I began to prepare myself for a train ride. One time, the train broke down and as we walked a long way out of the subway, dad told me the tale of the evil walking trees. He said that the trees in Central Park walk around at night and sometimes they step on people. That's why you can never go into the park at night. But the laws against trees are very strict and the punishment for stepping on a human is several years in jail, that's why if you see one tree isolated on the side of the sidewalk it is encased in a little cage.

As I began to look at the different pieces of gum, my eyes quickly fixated on a new color, one that I had never seen before. Under the adjacent bench laid a tiny small morsel of brown gum, retracing my mind I tried to recall ever seeing brown gum in any store. As I searched my memory I noticed the brown speck begin to twitch, sprouting six legs, and two long antennae. This was no piece of gum, it was a cockroach!

My body tensed up as my eyes stayed focused on the bug invading the safe person spot that is the train. I am supposed to watch out for spilt coffee and crazed axe murderers, not cockroaches. This is a spot to listen to my dad's stories, this roach was going to throw my entire trip off. Roaches and I cannot coexist.

My family was staying at my uncle's house in Queens, I had woken up first and made myself at home in front of the small tv-table. After spending about an hour flipping through news stations and looking out the window, I decided I was hungry, grabbing the foot stool from the bathroom I placed it on top of the tallest chair and climbed my makeshift tower to reach the old wooden cabinets. Eagerly anticipating to have a gander of what lay behind the closed doors, I grabbed both knobs and flung the two doors wide open. I was in luck, sitting in the middle was the lovable, Saturday morning making, blue and pink box of super dooper Berry Munchy O's, my favorite cereal.

My parents did not want me to have the delicious cereal, saying it was pure poison and consisted of my daily sugar intake for the entire year. But they would not be awake for hours, and I am sure my uncle would not miss one, or five, bowls of cereal. Moving the chair over to reach the bowls, I assembled all the necessary ingredients for the perfect bowl of cereal. Placing my bowl front and center, lining the box over it, I carefully poured the perfect bowl of cereal. I looked down at the bowl in all its glory and those tasty little blue and pink O's looked back up, and for a brief moment, I was in pure bliss.

That's when it happened. Out of the center of the heavily bowl, a small quiver emerged. At first, I was convinced it was my imagination, but as the motion became more vigorous, I knew it was not my imagination. I had to see what it was. Lifting my spoon, I flipped over the first layer of delicious O's to uncover the worst surprise. In the middle of my bowl was a hairy, dirty, wriggly roach. His legs spread over every piece of cereal as he munched on one of my O's. But, the worst was not over, I had to look into the box to see where the vile creature had come from. Inspecting the box, I found myself gazing into the labyrinth of dozens of the nasty creatures, who had made a home in my cereal.

I don't remember much after besides waking up hours later in a drowsy sickening daze and a strong distaste for O-shaped cereal. Ever since that infamous day, I have never laid hands on a single box of my uncle's cereal, cover my eyes when the commercials come on, and of course, I've developed a irrational hatred for roaches.

Seeing the wriggly putrid creature invading my personal space of the clean and friendly New York subway, I lose it. Immediately I bunch my knees into my chest so that there is no way of any foreign invaders crawling up my light up shoes. Next I begin to wriggle around ironically like my arch nemesis. Finally my head becomes buried into the safeness of my dad's wooly coat, much like those funny birds in Australia.

"What's wrong?" he asks me.

"I'm afraid it's going to eat my soul!"

"Well, it's only a tiny bug," he begins to say as he carefully balances his coffee on the infested floor, "There's only one of them, look I'll go kill it."

But as he stands up he pauses, and suddenly sits back down, continuing to stare at the putrid creature.

"That's no cockroach," He says in amazement, "That's a cop roach! It's illegal to kill a cop roach."

"A cop roach?"

"Yeah, you've never heard of a cop roach? Who do you think has to clean up the mean street of New York's microscopic world, all those crocodiles and cat burglars. You've heard of cop roaches right?"

He turned to a guy with large headphones on who was humming the words to a popular song right on beat the guy let out a overly passionate musically influences "Oh Yeah, Baby!"

"See, everyone has heard of it, in fact, I think I read about this one in the papers, he's on a special mission." He starts gesturing to his papers as he gets that long stare that indicates he's about to go into a long story.

"This no ordinary cop roach this is detective Flinsect of the NYBD (New York Bug Department) he played a major role in the crackdown during the pesticide epidemic of the 80s, but got out of the game after a bird bit off one of his legs, see how one is missing? He retired and lives a regularly normal roach life, you know, eating the frosting off donuts from those restaurants that leave them out behind glass, sleeping in the insect diagrams at the museum pretending to be made of plastic. Until one day, he got a call from his old boss, saying his partner Doug the bug had been murdered. If detective Flincest came back one last time to solve the mystery of the murder, he'd avenge his old partner and the commissioner would raise his pension by two rotten tomatoes."

Flinsect thought long and hard about this crazy situation, the tomatoes would be good, but his wings are not what they used to be. After a long and thoughtful three foot walk, Detective Flincest had an answer, he would do it for Doug the bug!"

My face lit up with excitement; I had no idea I was in the presence of a hero. I eagerly await in anticipation of the rest of the story.

"The first thing detective Flinsect had to do was get back into shape. After a quick Rocky-like montage with lots of inspiring music and stair-climbing, Flinsect was back in prime shape. He headed over to the NYBD HQ to get his first lead on the case from the commissioner. The office was built into a little match box under the Brooklyn Bridge, it was the staple of all thing good for the bug world, the red of the matches allowed all bug to see it from either side of the river. As officer Flinsect followed the all too familiar path up to the office years of memories flooded back to him. His first day on the job, being partnered with Doug, even the kiss he shared with the beautiful lady Earwig on that fateful summer night. But the path looked different now, it was littered with broken glass, graffiti, and jaywalkers. As he flew into the office he was met with a horrific sight. Someone had just lit the whole match box on fire. Before he could act, the entire box went up in flames, the commissioner and all the NYBD officers perished."

He continued on, continually eyeing the bug.

Detective Flincest was the only bug left on the job. He had to solve the case, for Doug the bug, the commissioner, for the liberty and justice for all. He flew around the area combing it for clues, but he couldn't find any. He knew he had to talk to someone with an ear to the ground, and he knew just the person. Detective Flincest headed to the grand NYC library.

He made his way to the great building that had meticulously detailed decor and beautiful ancient art. Approaching the gatekeepers, the two stone lions, he knew the answers would be inside. He painfully walked up the steps that towered over him putting all his training from the montage to work.

He finally reached the top and stared up at the large wooden doors that hid the answer to his questions. But, instead he turned left and entered the small half crumpled knocked over solo cup. The library did not allow bugs, obviously, instead he was looking for the bookworm.

He met the small worm that lived inside the cup and told him about the murders.

"Ah yes!" the worm murmured, "I've heard of these murders. I don't know who did it but I know who WILL know. The rats! You have to go see the rats!"

Flinsect, the cop roach made his way to the closest sewer entrance. Staring into the large metal grate that opened up to the ominous abyss below, cop roach's wings began to twitch as he balanced himself over the grate, hoping he did not get too nervous causing him to levitate and then fall into the darkness. Bending around the long metal bars, he slowly lowered himself down making sure his legs tightly clung to the putrid slimy walls.

"You didn't hear? There's been some murders! Somebody's been killing roaches. We're all getting out of here!"

Dad interrupted his story to tell me an important message,

"This is Mr. Moon's stop, keep your eyes peeled for him."

As Dad spoke, the train quietly rolled upon one of the least busy stops, in between the creepy and smelly stops. In the hot summer months, when the trains were empty, we liked to get out to stretch our legs and escape the hot stuffy car. A familiar man lived in the area and often played harmonica or guitar or both to passengers. Dad said he had always been there, even when he was a little kid. The man had a big scraggly black beard and wore loose fitting colorful clothing, often singing little poems and philosophical ditties. Dad said while most of the mysterious men of the subway were not to be trusted, Mr. Moon was different, and could be approached as a last result if no police officers were around. Dad had met him when he once got lost and the man lead him to the exit, since then the two had spent the years greeting each other, even going to buy a coffee and hotdog once in a blue moon.

"There he is!" I shouted spotting the colorful man wander about the terminal with his large sticker covered guitar case.

"Hey it's Mr. Man and his little dude, hey little dude." Mr. Moon waved at us smiling through his big goofy smile.

The train was too busy that day to get out an greet him without the chance of losing our seats. Instead, we shouted to him from the doorway of the train.

"Hey Mr. Moon, be careful out there, didn't you hear? There's been some murders! Somebody's been killing cop roaches."

"Oh man, not cop roaches." He said, easily picking up on what Dad was trying to do.

"I'll keep my eye out for him, I run these subways, he won't get away on my watch." He says winking at us, "I better get to lookin', stay safe guys and see ya soon."

With that, Mr. Moon waved us off as the doors closed and the train began to roll again, just before entering the tunnel he stopped, began to wise a merry tune and walked off to do Mr. Moon things.

As the train left the light terminal and into the dark tunnels that connected each stop, he noticed my eyes fixated on the wriggly bug slowly making its way along the underside of the opposite bench.

Seeing my nervousness had began to grow, he jumped back into his story. Flinsect kept moving down to the second layer of the sewer. This layer belonged to the rats of the most fearsome city in the underground world. As he make contact with the ground, he looked around to see no rats in sight. That was not uncommon, however. Rats lay in the darkness and prey on the clumsy ruffian or spray painter that decides to be adventurous and accepted the triple dog dare to enter the sewer. As Flinsect made his way along the eerily quiet path, he knew he was being followed, each one of his little legs left creepy crawly sounds that echoed down the long empty tunnel. It wasn't until he passed another grate up above that he saw them, off in the distance of the shadows, reflecting the sunlight, thousands of angry looking eyes.

Being spotted by the rats, he knew he had to act fast, cop roach heard a blood curdling screech and the pitter patter of crawling feet hustling towards him. He turned to run, even try to fly, but he could not get more than a few high jumps off the ground. His tiny legs were no match for the rats, even if he did have more than they did. The rats surrounded cop roach, looking dirty and slimy from dwelling in the darkness of the sewer. Cop roach would have thought it was the end for him if it was not for the card up his sleeve. As the rats began to lick their lips, he opened his mouth.

"I am a friend of the Rat King!" He delivered through his terrified, quivering voice.

"The Rat King?" One rat questioned in an eardrum twisting high-pitched snarling voice, as his mouth foamed. "How do you know him? Hmm?

"I am no sewer dwelling roach, I knew the Rat King when he was still a normal man!"

The rats stretched in shock, as no one knew the Rat King was human besides them, ever since his retreat to the blackness of the underworld.

The Rat King was a normal man, homeless but happy, a friend of Mr. Moon's but did not want to live in the subway underground anymore, wanting fresh air he moved into the topside living a luxurious life in the dumpster behind one of New York's fanciest restaurants. When cop roach was still just a larva, he discovered the dumpster as well. The generous man decided to share a delicious half-eaten goulash and savory rotten scallops. They soon became the best of friends. An unlikely duo, but when you live in a dumpster together, you make it work. They got over their arguments, whether they were pertaining to cop roach leaving the trash can seat up, or the Rat King eating the last piece of month-old steak, even if he was specifically told not to. Sadly, all good things end, and cop roach found a job, moved out of the dumpster, and left the Rat King to be by himself. Later on, he went back to visit but it turned out, a busboy from the restaurant went out to sneak a cigarette and caught the Rat King bathing in his back alley troth. The Rat King was arrested, but managed to escape after telling the cop, "Hey what's over there!" and ran away when the cop was distracted. He made his way down to the sewer and legend says he slowly climbed the ranks of the rat hierarchy, and with his superior human strength, and defeated the previous Rat King, since he had just been a normal rat. But, this was all legend, cop roach had no proof he was still alive.

The rats decided to take him to the Rat King to prove it, they restrained him tightly as they walked, making sure he could not wriggle away. Along the way, one of the rats stared him in the eye, gave off a big smile, and then kicked him on the back saying he wanted a sneak peak of tonight's feast. Sitting in the middle of the room, surrounded by rats and generic Chinese food boxes, layed a man. Dirty, with a long gray beard, with aged and tired eyes, was the Rat King. As they met eyes, the man's face slowly formed a smile, cracking the years of dried dirt that had caked on his cheeks.

In a raspy old voice that heard clearly not been used for anything, besides rat noise in years, fell upon Cop Roach's ears, "My oldest friend. It is good to see you again.... I thought you had been squashed or exterminated years ago."

Cop roach told the Rat King about his quest to find the murderer. The Rat King, his old friend, gestured to his guards to let cop roach go.

"Yes, we know of these murders, friend. He's been killing roaches all over the city. Rats too! We've been looking for him but we can't track him down."

"I'll find him." Flinsect said, "I'll find him if it's the last thing I do! I will avenge Doug and all the other roaches and rats he has killed!"

"If you can find him, we'll do the rest my friend. We found one clue that might help you. At the scene of the last murder, he left behind... this!" Next to the Rat King, two rats held up an old battered and torn wallet.

"A wallet," Flinsect said, "A human wallet! The murderer is a human! I will find him…"

Dad's story snapped in two by the entrance of the strong tough guy from the train platform. The same man who had claimed to have the common cold and the plague once again had began giving his spiel about his misfortune. Until he reached Dad, "Hey man, I need a little bit of help. I lost my wallet..."

The man, who was not wearing shoes, lumbered down the subway aisle, then noticed the small piece of brown gum on the floor. One that had legs and antenna. One who had a background and story true and clear to a young child. With one look the man screamed, "Ah! A cockroach! I hate cockroaches!" and squished the bug.

"Wow, Dad says, "The cop roach did it! He had to sacrifice himself, but he solved the crime. That guy was the murderer. Now he is marked on his foot so all the other roaches will know." Dad leaned in real close and whispered to me "Mr. Moon is on the case, he'll spot the guy and inform the rat king. He'll take care of that guy real soon."

Dad sat back on his subway seat. I glanced around and saw many of the other riders looking at us, listening to the story. As soon as they saw me look at them, they quickly looked away, not making any eye contact. Dad told me that sometimes Medusa rides the subway, so you never want to look anyone in the eye on the train, just in case it's Medusa. Just then, the train came into a station. Dad jumped up.

"This is our stop."

Ante Up

"**L**et's play a game." The voice is sultry in the black; familiar, but foreign all the same. She squinted her eyes a bit as she blinked them open, looking up from her slumped state. She sat high on a barstool surrounded by a dimly lit bar. Looking around her, she could see wafts of smoke followed by inky blackness, dark figures holding drinks and cueing up their game of pool. Confused, she turned her head forward, eyes meeting the deadpan gaze of the man in front of her.

"Wha-" She jumped, unable to finish her sentence as the glass hit the table. Looking down, a row of glasses sat neatly lined up in front of her. The man held up a bottle, caramel colored liquid sloshing around inside.

"This has always been a favorite of yours, hasn't it?" He chuckled, his voice playing out like a recording, like she's heard that voice say that before. It felt like a shock of déjà vu. The features of his face made her shudder, the memories of his dimples and his weird little nose scar made it hard to forget. She licked her chapped lips, mouth painfully dry.

"What do you- wait, what kind of game?" She scowled, confused and frightened as to what was going on. Her eyes were glued to the bottle as soon as it was brought out, heart dropping as she gripped her seat. He smiled deviously at the question, unscrewing the cap off in one swift motion. "What-" with a smooth wrist flick, he cleanly filled each glass, "what exactly is the rule of this game?"

"It's easy," he chuckled, gesturing out to the hundreds of shot glasses that stood lined up on the bar. "Drink up for every regret you've ever had. Starting with me."

***

Lynnie's body flung forward from her sleeping state, a sharp gasp escaping her lips. Heavily breathing, she curled up into a ball. She choked back tears, shuddering in exasperation. Another nightmare, she thought. Just another nightmare, you're okay. She slowly looked up and into the darkness of her room, eyes sliding over towards the bright red numbers at her bedside. 6:00 AM. Two hours before Olivia had to go to school, one hour before she had to wake up and get her ready, which meant no more left over time for another chance to sleep. Her head felt heavy, sagging down as she tried to push out the memory of the dream. Just thinking about it made her restless.

Lynnie breathed, reached out to flick on her lamp, and then swung her legs over the side of her bed onto the floor. Sliding on a pair of slippers, she groggily staggered out her room and down the hall. She stops in front of a door farther down the hall, the door covered in pink and purple stickers, crudely drawn crayon drawings taped on over one another. Gently pushing open the door, Lynnie eye's carefully surveyed the room. Her eyes met the body of her daughter, sound asleep with her back turned towards the door. Lynnie smiled, but didn't let it linger as she closed the door back up.

She stumbled out the hall and into the main room of the apartment. To her right was a small living room, an old box-shaped television adjacent to the wall accompanied by a small, blue loveseat. To her left sat a small kitchen, a coffee Keurig sitting neatly next to the sink. The Keurig called her name, mechanically starting her routine as she turned the machine on. She slid up behind the bar where her laptop already sat, pushing in the stool as she cracked her knuckles. Stretching a bit to fully wake herself up, she blinked as her computer booted up.

The first thing to pop up on the screen was the document she left open from her last writing session. The paragraph she'd been working on for the past few days lay open ended, the frustration building up as she read and reread the paragraph over and over again.

"It felt like her journey came to a halting stop. Everything around her continued as she watched it all fade away. No more music, no more concerts, no more of him. Maybe it all hadn't been real, she was just a roadie anyways. She just couldn't forget how much she wished she could have gone back and been able to say goodb-" Lynnie scrunched up her face, holding back tears as she quickly tapped the backspace key. She could tell it was going to be hard to finish this story, considering how personal it had been when she first conjured up the pitch.

A young roadie meets a musician she'd idolized for years, finding that the two had a connection deeper than just fan and celebrity. The idea was never hers in the first place, really. It was all his. But, he's gone now, not in Lynnie's life anymore. Lynnie lightly pushed the computer away from her, clutching a hand to her mouth. She breathed slowly through her nose, trying to calm herself. Shaking her head, she stood abruptly, walking back over to the Keurig. Grabbing the mug from below the spout, Lynnie inhaled deeply, letting the once pleasant smell tickle her nose again. Putting the cup to her lips, she took her first sip.

It was incredibly bitter, a type of bite she had never gotten from coffee. She choked on the liquid a bit before coughing it back up onto the floor. She knocked her back against counter, grabbing the edge of it to balance herself. After rattling the table, she could hear a bottle behind her wobble back and forth, about to teeter over. Quickly turning her head back around, she grabbed the bottle as it nearly fell over the edge. Holding the glass bottle in her hand, she turned it over to read the label. She flinched as she mulled over the words.

Bourbon, something she commonly liked to slip into her coffee. It was usually something she would share with him over breakfast, numbing the pain from previous endeavors. She could hear his voice chirp the familiar phrase they would share over coffee. 'A little bit of adult coffee never hurt anyone, hm?' They would chuckle together, ignorant towards how harmful they were for each other. She clutched the bottle, remembering how many times she said she'd break the habit; how many times she'd told herself to let go. One sip couldn't hurt, she thought, the bottle quaking in her hands as she shakily went to unscrew the cap.

"Mommy?" Lynnie nearly dropped the bottle as she whipped

her head to look at her daughter. She stood in the entrance of the hall, clutching a stuffed animal to her side as she rubbed the sleep from her eyes.

"Olivia, what's wrong sweetheart? Why are you up so early?" She placed the bottle behind her, obscuring it as she tried to fake a smile.

"I had another bad dream." Olivia whispered, a slight quiver to her voice. Lynnie dropped her smile, softening her eyes as she walked over to her daughter, kneeling down to her height. She took Olivia in her arms, pulling her close into a hug. She could hear her choke out a sob, burying her face into Lynnie's shoulder.

"Was it about Daddy again?" Lynnie cooed, trying to speak softly in order to sooth her. Olivia pulled away, nodding.

"He was leaving again, I tried to catch him but he was just too far away. I tried running to him but not even- not even running worked. You were there but-" Olivia was working herself up again, tears beginning to slide down her cheeks, "you were swimming, I don't know why you would be swimming. You just- you wouldn't help me." Lynnie made little shushing noises as she cupped Olivia's face, wiping away the tears.

"It's okay, Olive baby. I'm here now, it's going to be alright." Lynnie breathed, trying to force herself to make the words believable.

"Mommy," Olivia breathed out, "is Daddy coming back?" Lynnie's breath hitched, her mind racing to come up with a reassuring answer.

She tried to block out what happened, the memory fuzzy in her head. It was right after she had come home from dropping Olivia off at school. Empty bottles littered the walkway as she made her way in, greeted by the unpleasant slurring of her once lovable husband. She remembers watching him take swig after swig of the bottle of Jack Daniel's, pointing at her and shouting expletives. It's not like she wasn't used to it, she did this often herself, getting all her anger out after downing a bottle. But that day had turned out different, because instead of just passing out on the couch, he decided to storm out of the apartment. Lynnie thought maybe he was just blowing off steam, maybe he needed fresh air. She remembered her heart sinking as the landline began to rang. She remembered picking up the phone, cradling the body of it to her face. She remembered going numb from the neck down, head swimming as the color drained from her.

"I thought he was getting fresh air, just getting, just getting fresh air." Lynnie's words tripped over one another as she tried to bargain with herself. She instinctively reached to her wedding ring, wrenching it back in forth painfully. She didn't notice the burning sensation as she continued, body numb and mind in shambles. Finally dropping to her knees, she let her body release the scream that had built up, fists hitting the floor in a cocktail mix of confusion, anger, and sadness.

"Daddy is resting right now." The words felt wrong to say, guilt bubbling in her stomach as she continued. "We're going to let Daddy rest, okay?" Olivia nodded back at the reply. Lynnie gritted her teeth, wanting to explain to Olivia what happened. But not right now, not that early in the morning.

"Now, I think it's time we get you ready, hm?" Lynnie hummed, listening as Olivia groaned.

"But I don't wanna go to school, I wanna be here with you." She whined out, her face dropping further into a frown. Lynnie laughed softly, picking Olivia up.

"Olive, honey, why wouldn't you want to go to school? You get to see your friends and draw pretty pictu-" Before Lynnie could finish, Olivia started shaking her head back and forth.

"Mommy, I want to be here with you, make sure you're safe." Olivia looked up at her, giving Lynnie a nervous, almost worrisome look. A sort of guilt bubbled inside of Lynnie, watching as her own daughter felt pressured to protect her. Shaking herself a bit, Lynnie looked at her daughter with a warm smile, trying to reassure her.

"Come on, sleepy-head. Let's get you some breakfast." She suggested, trying to shift the topic. She brought Olivia over to the counter, sitting her at a chair. Lynnie went to the fridge, picking out two eggs. Walking towards the pan, she could see Olivia eyes darting around the room, the glass bottle on the table being where they decided to focus on. She saw Olivia lookup, jarring Lynnie's vision back over to the pan she was buttering. Cracking the first egg in, she heard Olivia speak up.

"Mommy, you weren't drinking again, right?" Olivia had that accusatory kid tone in her voice, like she'd been caught breaking a playground rule. Her daughter had always been a perceptive one, her curiosity becoming her best ally.

"No, sweetie. I told you I wasn't going to drink that anymore. It's not good for me." It felt more like she was speaking down to herself rather than talking to Olivia. She could feel the disappointment radiating from her daughter. Even at a young age, Olivia could understand that Lynnie's habits needed to stop before it got any worse than a few 'silly' nights. Lynnie's ears perked up as she heard Olivia whisper under her breath.

"Please," Lynnie heard, "please don't be like Daddy." She felt her heart leap up into her throat, her skin crawling as she dragged her body forward to continue.

Cracking a second egg in, she turned to look at Olivia. Lynnie couldn't help but feel motivated thinking of her daughter. She needed to live a happy, healthy life, just like any kid should. The connection the two had was equivalent to a boat and anchor; without Olivia, Lynnie would drift away without any direction. If it weren't for Olivia, Lynnie didn't even know where'd she be.

***

"Have a great day at school, sweetheart!" Lynnie shouted out the window as she watched Olivia saunter towards her group of friends. She was admittedly a little concerned to see Olivia walk out, eyes tired as she walked into the school with her little entourage. Her gaze caught the eye of Olivia's teacher who had been holding the door open. The teacher's glare unsettled Lynnie, a disappointed frown crossing her face as she ushered the last of the kids in. Lynnie just tried to shrug it off, pulling out of the drop off circle and heading on out to start her day.

"I don't have work at the diner today." She started, talking out loud in order to organize herself. Mondays, Wednesdays, Thursdays were the days Lynnie worked at the diner. Being a writer, there was only so much income she could make. The diner kept her and Olivia above water. Being a Friday, one of Lynnie's favorite days, she was able to finish up errands instead, possibly get in some writing time for herself.

"I should probably get some groceries before I begin another writing session." She clicked her tongue, rolling down the street towards the local grocery store. The best part about Fridays were getting the time to cook big dinners for Olivia. Their favorite thing to eat was always chicken cutlet; Lynnie would bring Olivia home after school, eggs, flower, and bread crumbs lined up for her to help batter up the chicken. They always had the most fun prepping, and even more fun when they had leftover cutlet for the rest of the weekend. Lynnie smiled, excited to see the excitement light up on Olivia's face after she picked her up from school that day. Maybe we'll even play a few games of Go Fish tonight, Lynnie thought, I might even get around to teaching her to play Texas Holdem. Halting at a stoplight, Lynnie put her hand in the cup holder, fiddling around for something. She pulled out a small post-it note with a small 'aha'. The paper read out a list of things she needed from the store: 'milk, eggs, apples, some things for Olivia's lunch, chicken for dinner...' Her thoughts trailed off as she pulled into the parking lot, shoving the list into her pocket.

Walking in, she tried her hardest to avoid the gaze of others. She always felt uncomfortable when people looked at her, as if she was being judged for things strangers wouldn't even know. She scurried over to the produce section, picking up what she needed before heading on towards the dairy. She passed over the eggs, stopping to pick up a carton. Opening it, she traced her fingers over a few of the eggs, checking for any cracks. She exhaled in contentment, closing the carton and looking up. She nearly dropped the eggs, catching a glimpse of a familiar man idling in the liquor aisle. She closed her eyes for half a second, opening to realize that the man wasn't anyone she recognized; just a regular man. Lynnie quickly walked past the liquor aisle, trying her hardest to ignore it. As she sped walked, she could feel the gaze of others boring into her back. She didn't know why it felt like the world was judging her for things they didn't even know. Picking up the last few things she needed, she checked out, nearly sprinting back to her car.

***

Lynnie gasped for air, one hand clutching the blanket that covered her while the other gripped the neck of a bottle. Her laptop nearly slipped off her lap onto the floor before she jutted a hand out to grab it. The story was gone, the entire document a blank slate. Her eyes widened as she clicked all over to find a previous save file, a backup copy, anything at all.

But all she found was the remaining deleted version she left for herself after a few too many sips of whatever the hell she was holding. She clenched her teeth in pain, realization of what was happening overtaking her thoughts.

"Oh my god, oh my god!" She gripped the bottle tight. Tears burned the corners of her eyes, the clock on the wall reading 4 P.M. One hand reached up to her head as she began pulling at her hair in frustration. Lynnie was late, very late to picking up Olivia. There was so much pain coursing through her body. She couldn't help but take a few swigs to help numb herself before she decided to throw a coat on. Lynnie threw open the door, running out with her keys already jingling in her hands.

Lynnie clutched the wheel tight, focusing as hard as she can in order to keep her wheels within the lines. The school had only been a couple blocks away, so it wouldn't take her long to get there. But before she could even pull up the street, she could see the flashing red and blue in the distance. Her heart jumped up into her throat as she approached closer to the building.

Several cops stood idle in front of the school's doors, one talking to a teacher while another sat by Olivia. They eyed the car as it pulled up, two of them already jogging towards Lynnie as she parked.

"Ma'am, are you Olivia's caretaker?" Lynnie stumbled out of the care, steadying herself as she started to get bombarded with questions.

"Ma'am, where have you been all this time? The school has been trying to contact y-" The officer stopped mid-sentence as he squinted his eyes. He could tell something was up as she stumbled around, cheeks red, and eyes appearing barely responsive.

"Mommy..." Olivia spoke out as she gripped the hand of the of the officers.

"Ma'am, I'm going to need you to stand still for a second." The officer's hand went to his belt as he grabbed a small flashlight. "Follow the light with your eyes, please."

Lynnie gripped the car with a hand as she tried to focus her eyes on the light. She tried to trace it with her eyes, but after one blink, she realized the flashlight had flipped sides from where she had been facing. There was no hope to fake sobriety. She felt herself stumble, laughing nervously as the officers looked down at her. Judgment was all she could see.

"Olivia-" Lynnie struggled to word out what she wanted to say. "Olivia please don't be scared. It's going to be okay, it's going to b-"

"Ma'am, I'm going to have to ask you to step into the car." The officer interrupted, gesturing for Lynnie to come with him. They blocked her view as she tried to keep contact with her daughter.

"Olivia, I'll be back, I promise!" She yelled out before the door of the cruiser slammed shut.

***

"Ms. Wright, in order to keep custody of your daughter, you are required to correct your behaviors involving the abuse of drugs such as alcohol." Lynnie bowed her head as she listened to the judge's ruling.

"You haven't had previous incidents involving abuse, nor have you had other accounts involving DUIs, so I am willing to give you a chance before sending you to a rehabilitation center." The judge wore a blank look, but Lynnie could tell he was trying to be sympathetic.

"Thank you, your honor." Lynnie said dolefully, letting out a quiet sniffle.

"The DUI stands, which will involve a $460 fine." Lynnie just felt lucky enough to be getting just a fine instead of something like a license suspension, or worse, jail time. The judge began his closing remarks, which led to Lynnie looking over to her daughter. Olivia stood next to her grandmother, holding her hand while giving Lynnie a confused look. It made Lynnie's stomach drop, the lack of control she had making her sweat.

She zoned out as she watched Olivia get escorted out of the courtroom. Crinkling up her nose, Lynnie tried to hold back tears in order to stay professional. It was hard for her to walk out of there without her own daughter. Breathing, she tried to allow her nerves to soothe, remembering she will be in the care of her own mother now. But she couldn't help but clutch her phone tight as she called up a taxi.

Her apartment was cold, as if it went from a home to an isolation chamber. Lynnie could see the bottle of bourbon still laying on the floor after countless nights of not bothering to clean it up. She could feel hot tears streaking down her face, the anger and sadness pushing her to raise her leg up and slam down on the bottle with full force. Glass shattered everywhere, the smell of liquor burning her nose. After a few seconds of stomping on the already shattered glass, she finally stopped, standing on top of the mess she had made. It took Lynnie a second to calm down before realizing the mistake she made. Turning up her foot to see the bottom, she could see shards of glass piercing straight through her shoe. After the realization came a large wave of pain.

Lynnie tried running to the bathroom, nearly falling over due to her foot feeling like it was on fire. She took the last few steps over in large hops, frantically reaching for the bathtub faucet. She sat on the toilet seat, picking glass out of her foot as she waited for the tub to fill with water. After trying to pluck one frustratingly tiny piece of glass, she eventually gave up and let out a loud sob. Curling up into a ball, she finally started to just let it all out.

Crying came in waves, coming and going as she started to dehydrate. Racking with guilt, her body trembled as if she was experiencing an internal earthquake. She eventually just decided to plunge herself into the tub instead of just her foot. The water should've felt relaxing, but all it did was remind her of the liquor. All she could think of was watching the thing pretending to be him drown her. The sheer amount of pleasure he wore on his face as she struggled to breathe disgusted her, frightened her even. The memories of the dream became too much as she began to drain the water.

Putting her hair up in a towel, Lynnie stepped out of the bathroom, limping over to the kitchen. Her eyes traced over the groceries she had previously bought that day, her sadness overwhelming even when she couldn't produce tears. After looking at the food, she turned her head to look at the bottles of alcohol that still stood in the corner. Jim Beam, Bailey's, Kahlua, and an untouched bottle of Jack Daniel's; *his* favorite. Lynnie couldn't stand looking at it, the amount of pain brought by just that single bottle of liquor. She ripped the Jack Daniel's from its place and gave it a harsh glare.

"You took everything away from me. First my husband, and now my daughter." Her voice shook as she announced this firmly to the bottle she held. Lynnie twisted the cap off, turning the bottle upside down as she hovered it above the sink. The caramel-colored liquid poured out in large glugs. She watched it go down the drain, a weird weight lifting from her shoulders as it disappeared from her sight. She glanced at the rest of the bottles.

One after another, the alcohol that used to litter her home finally began to diplete. After throwing the last bottle into the recycling, she let out a breath of air. It felt refreshing to finally have it all out of her sight, but this was just step one. Now it was just the struggle of staying clean.

***

"What a terrible waste of money." The voice sounded out again, deeper than ever before. Lynnie rose her head up, eyeing the bartender with a determined gaze. She tried not to appear intimidated as she saw the form he took on. His smile curled with his sharp teeth glinting in the dim light. His ears pointed out, fingers skin tight at the joints as he clicked his claws against the bar top.

"This little act isn't gonna work anymore." Lynnie gave the bartender a firm look, hands folded as she leaned back from the bar. "I see what you've been doing; using the appearance of my dead husband just to play with my emotions." The thing in front of her crooked its head to the side, seemingly surprised by her bluntness.

"Aw, what? Do you not miss me, Lyn? I'm standing right in front of you and you don't even want to share drinks like old times?" A shot glass manifested in his hand out of thin air. He held it with three fingers, clinking one of his nails against the side.

"I told you, this isn't going to work. I can see right through your facade." She drew back her lips as she pointed at her teeth, indicating what she saw. This only made a smile curl on his face as he revealed the rows of shark teeth that were crammed into his mouth. "So instead of continuing to pretend, how's about you just tell me who you really are."

He let out a low chuckle as he began to tear out his hair in clumps. His body went from a pale beige to a stark white, the skin clinging to his bones as it became more translucent. He blinked his eyes, revealing deep, amethyst colored eyes.

151

"Is this better?" He growled, a small pair of black horns sprouting from the skin on his head.

"What- what the hell even are you?" Lynnie said, confidence wavering as she looked over the frightening creature. "Are you the Devil?" Lynnie's remarks only made the thing laugh.

"I've been called the Devil plenty times before, but I can only really take that as a compliment. No no," he continued to click his claws against the counter top, "I've been called many names before, but I've become fond of the name Jones. I am what you would refer to as mankind's bad habits."

After reeling back a bit, Lynnie tried to compose herself. She closed her eyes tight, opening them back up to see the pale beast in front of her.

"Okay, *Jones*. I'm going to be firm about this. I'm not here to play your little drinking games anymore. I'm- I'm through with alcohol!" The last statement might have been her pushing it, but she said it with confidence regardless.

"You really think that just stating that you're through with me means I'm going away?" He made a *tch* sound with his mouth, rolling his eyes a bit before finally dropping his smile. "I am always here. Whether you want me to be here or not. I will always be here to *personally* make you screw yourself over."

"But why? What do you even get out of this!" Lynnie shouted the last part, not intending for it to even come out as a question. Regardless of that, Jones answered back.

"Because," his bony fingers carefully grasped around the neck of a low shelf bottle, "it's fun to watch you helplessly squirm." By the time the light glinting off the bottle alerted Lynnie, it was too late. The blow of glass and liquor against her head immediately knocked her out, sending her body to the floor.

✳✳✳

It felt bizarre to Lynnie to wake up in the bathtub. A wave of déjà vu overcame her as she sat in a small puddle. Confused, she hopped out of the tub and into the kitchen. She winced, a shock of pain shooting up through her leg. She carefully limped as she remembered her previous injury, leaning up against the counter to find her bar fully stocked.

"What-" Lynnie gripped the counter top, anger boiling inside of her as she snagged out from the bar like before. She tried to feel strong, exert dominance over the liquor, but all she could do in that moment was cry and drop to the floor. Her hands twitched as she constantly tried to stop herself from just opening the bottle and doing away with the pain.

Opening her eyes again, blurry from the crying, she found herself looking at Olivia's room. The door had been opened a crack, the pinks and purples dim inside. She stopped for a second, sniffling as she tried to stand back up. Catching her balance, she carefully made her way into Olivia's room.

The room could be described easily in one word; innocent. You couldn't even tell the life Olivia lived outside of that room just because it was like a world of her own. Dolls were put neatly in her playhouse, frozen in the state they were previously in. A family stood inside, a mother cooking in the kitchen, the father cleaning the living room, and the kids playing in their respective rooms. Outside the house, a dinosaur figurine stood peering inside the little girl's window. On the roof sat the dog, and outside the car lay upside down with a few barn animals dancing on top. It made Lynnie smile to see Olivia's little world. Stepping closer to the house, Lynnie felt something curl beneath her foot. She looked to see something that looked like a thin piece of cardboard. Reaching down to pick it up, Lynnie discovered a few dozen more of the same sized pieces of cardboard.

"Oh, my playing cards!" Lynnie chimed, started to pick up the set of 52. A few cards curled, a couple others bent, and one or two held a few rips. But regardless, it was still her old set of playing cards she had gifted Olivia for her 8th birthday.

"When I was your age, I played a lot of cards." Lynnie remembered saying, watching as Olivia confusedly flipped through the cards.

"What do they do?" Olivia said, not looking up as she observed the queen.

"Why, anything you'd like! They're for all sorts of games, like crazy eights, poker, and go fish!" Lynnie said with a smile.

"Fishing? How could you fish with these?" Lynnie let out a small laugh, Olivia only tilting her head with a befuddled look.

Lynnie looked at the cards with serenity, making sure she had all 52 in hand. She wondered for a second as she held them, thinking of the amount of times playing cards had helped her calm down. Something about the soothing action of playing Solitaire, or the aggressive franticicity of playing a game of Rubbish, it was almost cathartic to her. Holding the cards close to her chest, she finally had the idea she needed.

***

"Back so soon I see?" The creature wore a mocking look as it snarkily turned toward Lynnie. Its confidence was replaced with confusion as she placed the deck of cards upon the counter top.

"I think it's about time we switched it up." Lynnie began dealing out cards to the pale beast. "Let's play a card game."

"What- do you really think you can waltz back on in here and change the game? That's not how it works Lynnie." He sneered, annoyingly clicking his claws together.

"Not how it works, hm? And who really made you think you're in control? Last time I checked, we're in my head, not yours." The creature reeled back, turning to find something to help arm himself. He jumped in shock, finding that the shelves once lined with alcohol came up empty.

"What the hell type of game do you think you're playing?" He finally shouted at her, his guard faltering.

"Doesn't matter, because now it's time for me to decide what we're doing, and for you to ante up."

✳✳✳

First Flight

We were cruising above the clouds, as the plane ascended to the final cruising altitude. Taking a peek outside provided a breathtaking experience; the sea of green with the huge stretches of roads that the cars followed lay down below. The clouds were all moving slowly down below us as we cruised upward. This view was always astonishing and never ceased to amaze me. Suddenly, on one of the center screens in the cockpit, a little blue message illuminated on the display: *auto throttle disengage, throttle moved.* There was a loud beeping sound making both us aware of the situation. Looking down, he reached for the throttle quadrant and pushed it back to its proper position. The message disappeared.

Mark, the first officer, continued to with his paperwork for the flight. "Oops, sorry about that. My arm must have moved it when I was using the computer."

"No problem. It happens to the best of us." I turned my gaze back outside. "You know that little thing was how I almost crashed on my first flight." This caught Mark's attention, and he stared at me until he finally spoke, "Well are you going to tell me what happened or…" he trailed off, with an eyebrow raised.

"Oh, of course I will. Well it all started before we were airborne…"

On the way to the airport, my whole body felt numb, a light shiver running up my spine as the car approached slowly to its destination. It was the place where my father and I would sit back and stare at the aircraft from the giant windows of the airport; the place where my first flight would take place. The giant green sign above the road reminded me that the airport was only three exits away. My gut suddenly started speaking and I tried to focus my attention back on to the road. Quickly the next exit sign appeared, gazing at the green exit sign as it informed me that two more exits remained. As the exits neared and passed by, butterflies swarmed within, realizing that soon it would be my turn to pilot a plane. The sound of a small regional plane making its landing interrupted my thoughts. What is going to happen to me up there? The thought of everything going wrong appeared in my head. If any one component fails on the aircraft, it could lead to a catastrophe. My breathing became more and more rapid, the palms of my hands were wet. The wheel started to slip, and I struggled to remain in control.

The last exit sign passed by. It was time to get off the ramp and head towards the airport. It was stop and go traffic, the exit only a couple hundred feet ahead at this point. Eager to fly, the butterflies now settled down as I made my way down the exit. Another roar emanated from behind, a slightly larger plane than before. The huge menacing shadow appeared overhead, and once again the butterflies appeared. The road became winding, and I found myself drifting to the other lane. Coming to my senses, I shifted back into the proper lane and got off.

Making my way toward the big building, with a concrete tower above, I pulled up to the security booth of the airport. I told the guard there my intentions, showing him the paperwork, and he let me park in the staff parking lot, telling me how to get in from there. The doorway into the airport as unfamiliar to me. A new way into the same building I'd been in hundreds of times before. Everything was the same, the many shops and kiosk were still there, but something was off about today. A feeling so ineffable.

Slowly making my way through security, the whole thing a blur, I walked down to a man waiting at the other side, holding a sign with my name on it. He was wearing a white button up shirt, black pants and a matching tie.

"Hello, you must be Stuart, nice to meet you." he reached out and grabbed my hand as I made my way toward him,

"Nice to meet you too, Mr. Jefferson"

"Jim, you can call me Jim, no need for that formal stuff. So are you ready for your first lesson," there was a mixed feeling of excitement and nervousness that surrounded me. This has been a dream of mine since I was young. Finally getting to fly.

"I'm ready," I replied back to him nervously. My body was still shaky as we made our way to the aircraft. Glaring around the cockpit, the many buttons and switches that were in the simulator were more menacing for some odd reason. They were exactly the same, but the only difference was that this was happening in real life, not at my computer desk. The instructor made his way around, and the plane wobbled as he got in next to me. We started off with the usual checklists, the preflight, cockpit prep, before engine start. Speeding through them to get quickly off the ground, the closer and closer we got to start the engine the shakier I got. Then the time came to start the engine.

"Clear prop," the instructor yelled loudly outside to let the people walking around know to stay away from the front of the propeller. "Okay, looks clear," he told me, "turn the key to start the engine." A tear of sweat came down to the side my cheek as I slowly put pressure on the small metal thing. Click, click it went as he turned the key to the first then second position. Click it went again as the key made its way to the third position. I saw looked outside one more time to make sure nobody was anywhere near the metal blade, and he did the same and clicked it over to the start position. Slowly the engine whined loudly, and the blade slowly made its way around. It went around and around, slowly accelerating until he pushed the condition lever forward, and the engine roared to life. The roar of the engine was loud, even wearing the aviation headphones. Slowly I started to get a tingly feeling creep its way up from my feet, and the sweat across my forehead became more notable.

"Don't worry about anything, it's all going to be fine," he said trying to calm my nerves. "I know this is a new experience for you, but this will be one to remember."

"This feeling is so new to me. I have flown flight simulators before, following the checklist online. This is…"

"Trust me, you are not the only one I've seen like this. Once we are in the air, you'll feel better," he responded to me gently holding my shoulder, and nodding finally. "November Bravo Alpha Mikt X-ray, at the ramp requesting taxi to active runway," he turned his attention know to getting us in the air. Over in the headset, tower responded.

"November Bravo Alpha Mike X-ray, you are clear for taxi via Mike, November, Romeo. Winds at 287 at 8 nautical miles guesting to 14. Altimeter 30.01."

Jim responded back to the tower, all the while, I was grabbing the clipboard with the checklist and started to read each item off the list. He initiated the taxi. First he pushed the throttle in a bit, and then released the parking brake holding the plane in place. Slowly it started to roll down the yellow line, following the ATC's instructions to the letter. As we turned onto November we saw a huge line of planes waiting to takeoff, much of them bigger than us. We had to stay far behind them to avoid being pushed by the giant engines that caused them to fly. Slowly the time went by and we were up to line up and wait. First we had to wait for a plane to land. It slowly appeared into view, and it was a huge Boeing 777. It came past us at high speeds, touched down with such grace.

"November Bravo Alpha Mike X-ray, you are cleared to line up and wait caution wake turbulence from departing A318," the sudden voice of the ATC came into the headset, as Jim turned to me.

"Would you like to do the honors of taxing us onto the runway?" he asked me, seeing if the butterflies disappeared.

"I would like to try," I said, grabbing the flight controls, and waiting to hear his response.

"Alright, tell me to release the parking brake when you are ready."

I pushed the throttle in a bit, and the engine responded, speeding up the already fast blade, and turning to him, and telling him to release the brake. The plane made a small lurch, and started taxing onto the runway. I kept my hands and feet on the controls, and slowly we made our way onto the runway. Now I was staring down a long stretch of asphalt that would lead us to our first great journey.

"Okay we have some time to kill before they let us pass, can you tell me why we are waiting?" trying to pass the time, and test me on my knowledge of aviation.

"Wake turbulence," he saw me now more comfortable in my seat, no longer shaking. "Wake turbulence can cause problems in small aircraft such as this, such as causing the plane to roll suddenly, or in some cases lose altitude." As I finished talking over the headset we heard.

"November Bravo Alpha Mike X-ray, cleared for takeoff runway 30,"

"Cleared for takeoff runway 30." He slowly pushed the throttle in as he responded back to ATC, the plane again lurched us forward as the brake was released, and suddenly the butterflies in my stomach returned. We started to veer to the left, but were quickly centered back. My body started to violently jitter as we gained more and more speed, going faster and faster, toward the other end of the runway.

"This is the fun part, hold on tight," He said as he gently pulled back onto the yoke, and maneuvered the nose to point up.

Slowly outside of the window, we made our way up higher and higher. Looking out of the sea of green, and the roads as they snaked through as we made our way to our altitude where he would have me perform the various basic maneuvers for our first lesson. Slowly we performed basic banking maneuvers over the small town we were flying over, and all the while I was looking out, and admiring the view.

"Alrighty, lets make another bank to the right to heading 220, remember nice and gentle." I grabbed ahold of the yoke, and started to make the bank to the right. A loud thud was heard, and a couple of papers fell off the clipboard that he left on his lap. "Continue making the turn, and when you level off maintain level flight so I can pick these pieces of paper up."

"Wilco," I responded to sound a bit professional, and to show him that the simulator at home worked.

As he reached down to grab the paper, his shoulder pushed the throttle in to full power. This caused the engine to rev up, and cause the plane to speed up. More power meant the plane was generating more lift than necessary and in turn the pitch of the plane to raise up. In response I pushed the yoke forward, but the plane would not respond right away, and the nose continued to pitch up.

"Hey Jim, get up for a minute, and help me out here," a small tremble starting to occur through my body. He got up, and grabbed control of the yoke. He too was struggling to maintain control, and pulled the throttle out. The engine did not respond to the slight pull back, so he pulled it back farther. The engine maintained the high RPM and we had to fight to keep the plane level.

"Tower, we have a problem, our throttle appears to have stopped working," Jim spoke into his headset, updating ATC to the current situation onboard.

"Are you declaring an emergency at his time?" They asked trying to be helpful. He did not respond to them, and took a short breath and exhaled quitely. A chill ran up my spine, as my heart slowly started to beat faster, and faster. A sudden small thought that we were probably crash appeared in my head.

"Here, take this" he handed the clipboard to me. "Flip to the emergency section, and read the checklist for an engine fire."

"Are you sure? The engine appears to be running still, and not smoking." I pointed out the obvious fact.

"Well if you know planes like I do, then you should see the oil temps are rising to dangerous levels that could lead to fire." I turned and looked at the instruments in front of him, and sure enough the small little needle was pointing too close to the red. "Read the first thing on the checklist."

Flipping through the book, I found the back page, and slowly started to read off the checklist, all the while still trembling. The yoke was fighting with him hard.

"Drop the book, and help me out." He exclaimed loudly as was still struggling with it. Grabbing the yoke proved difficult as he kept moving it, but eventually I managed to hold. All of a sudden something clicked in my mind. Glancing at the instrument in front of him, I reached across his lap, and turned the turned the key. "What are you doing?" he shouted angrily at me.

"What I would do in the simulator for fun, turn off the engine and try to land at the closest airport." I looked at him, now determined to save myself from this mess. He turned to me and inhaled loudly.

"Alright, I guess it's better than an engine fire," he said as the blade was spinning very slowly now. "The closest airport is about 15 miles from our position, how well can you talk to ATC so I can control this bird?"

"Fairly well," I said and pressed the small red button on the yoke, and spoke calm, and clear to the tower. "Mayday. Mayday, November Bravo Alpha Mike X-ray, we have no thrust, requesting vectors to the nearest runway."

"November Bravo Alpha Mike X-ray turn left heading 180," tower responded quickly.

"Turn left heading 180" and before the last word exited my mouth, Jim already was turning to the heading, with a nice gentle bank, trying to maintain speed and altitude. In silence we flew, with tower giving us a couple more vectors to the runway. Before we knew it, the same runway we taken off from, was now a mile out, and flashing red and blue lights were near the runway, waiting to respond. We both looked outside, the silence deafening, only the sound of the wind, as we glided through to land. On final was the hardest to maintain the speed. Slowly we had to pitch the nose down to maintain the speed. Flaps were not even considered since it would slow us down more. Looking at the altimeter less than 500 feet till we touch the ground. The plane was still losing speed, and altitude quickly. The ground quickly approached, bracing my arms against my side, and watching Jim as he guided us in. I closed my eyes as we approached the numbers on the runway, and in a second a thud was heard, I opened my eyes to witness that we were on the ground. Seeing the airport as we passed by on the runway. Jim sighed greatly as we approached the end of the runway.

The sound of sirens approached us as we stopped, we got some of our belongings and got out quickly were police, and the National Transportation Safety Bureau was there and we were asked questions.

"They investigated this accident for a month, and the report came out. I read it, and they said that if the engine kept going it would have most likely have blown a piston, and who knows what kind of damage the plane would have occurred." I turned around to meet his gaze.

"So if you didn't make that decision to cut the engine who knows where you would be." Mark said with great enthusiasm. "Why did you continue to fly though? You must have been frightened."

"Don't get me wrong I nearly died that day, but," a small pause "these are the types of events that you learn from, and get better. You are never truly tested until put under pressure. That day I learned a lot, if not how to land, but how to act fast, and not give into the fear. That day will forever be engraved in the back of my mind as the best day of my life."

"Why the best day of your life? Clearly it should be the day you flew solo, or getting hired to fly commercial." It was no use, if it were not for that day I would never have gained the skills necessary to become the person I am today.

✱✱✱

B-Side

Nights on the street have always been the most peaceful times for me. I place myself just far enough away from the usual commotion of New Orleans' nights but just close enough to have my fair share of exposure. Closing my eyes and drifting off into freedom as chord changes fill my mind. The outside world seems to disappear and I'm left alone finding solace in my playing. No complaining here, though. People can be exhausting after a while, so some alone time is appreciated. Of course, I do get the occasional listener or two that stay for a few songs. Hell, I've even had someone bring over a saxophone to play alongside my trumpet playing. Most nights I'm out here on Miles Drive, it's my happy place. Dealing with booking gigs and crappy bars and nightclubs all day takes a toll, so I come here to clear my mind. Time always blinks by, as I look at my watch and see it's already 1 am. Packing up my trumpet into its case, I put headphones in and press play on my cassette tape of Maynard Ferguson's "M.F. Horn" to listen to on my short walk home, about a block away. I'd love to meet him one day, but doubt that'll happen with the path I'm on right now.

My apartment is less than luxurious. I barely scrape by for rent and as for necessities, let's just say that I have the bare minimum. One room, a mini fridge, a rusty bathroom, and a dusty couch is pretty much all I've got. I go through the same routine every night after playing outside, put some clean clothes on, start up a new record, and go to bed. I'm usually asleep before side A ends so side B is saved for the next night. My wakeup call is usually by phone, most of the time from my family calling to check in on me, my hope is always that it's someone looking for performers, but that has yet to happen.

I stay inside my rundown apartment for a few hours, merely scouring newspapers and websites in search of any possible place that'd hire me. If I'm lucky enough to find a new place and give them a call, it usually ends with them hanging up on me. That's the saturation of jazz nowadays, especially in New Orleans. It's an amazing place for jazz, don't get me wrong, but every bar, club, and restaurant has regular performers and don't see the need to find anyone new when they have such reliable people. I managed to get myself a few gigs at this place, Billie's Pub. Now, to the naked eye, Billie's is a fairly nice bar. Clean floors, decent staff, and the whiskey isn't too bad either. However, not many people know what's behind their facade. Walking in there the first time with hope in my eyes is probably the last time I'll walk in there happily. The manager, Billie, and I got on good terms at first, making small talk and bonding over our love for music, and in no time I had a set. First time went great, so I was invited back. Second time was even better. But the third time is where it fell apart. I was dealing with a cold, nothing major, just a runny nose and a cough. I thought I'd be fine to play and I didn't have much money so I took the opportunity. Little did I know that I'd end up playing worse than a private school's 4th grade band. It was embarrassing and horrendous, I didn't even get through the first song in my set. From that moment I knew I'd be kicked. I mean, it took Charlie Parker a year to come back from his bombed performance, and I couldn't afford to not play for a full year. I made my way backstage and tried to pack up before I saw the manager, but it was to no avail.

"Jesus Christ Lee, that has got to be the worst damn solo I have ever heard in my life! Do you take us as a joke? You really think that's acceptable here? Listen kid, you've done well here before, but after that I don't know if I can let you back in," Billie had rushed up to me before I got everything packed, he was red with anger and steam was coming out of his nose. "We have standards here, kid, and if you don't meet them, you get the boot." The smell of whiskey and cigar smoke covered by cheap cologne took me by surprise. I was too scared to say anything at that time; Billie was one of the most intimidating men I'd ever met.

Reaching 6'5, grey hair and a beard, muscle on muscle, and hands that could crush a watermelon.

"Now you got me believing that the first two times you played here were dumb luck. No excuses for playing like that kid. You're out. Come back when you don't sound like crap." After Billie left, I packed my things and headed home immediately. It took me a while to go back, but after searching for other bars and other clubs, I realized, no one else was gonna give me a shot. Despite losing the little reputation I had, they at least knew I had *some* good playing in me. If only they could hear me on the street where I played best.

✳✳✳

"Musicians Wanted: Freddie Hubbard's New Big Band. Recruiting All Instruments Now." I first caught sight of that poster walking home one day from another failed attempt at Billie's and hope gleamed in my eyes. Freddie Hubbard hosting open auditions for a band? That's unheard of! I bolted towards the poster and copied down every bit of information I needed. I had to get a head start on this, because in the blink of an eye, every audition spot can be filled. It was about 12:30 am when I found the poster. The auditions weren't for a whole week so the best thing for me would be to get rest. However, that didn't go as planned. Desperate attempts to close my eyes and relax were pointless as I just wanted to prepare. I started sifting through my stack of sheet music at the end of my couch, looking for what to play for the audition, when I came across "Giant Steps." John Coltrane's creation that caused even the best musicians to hesitate. The changes switched keys every few bars, the tempo ranged from 200-280 beats per minute, and caused Tommy Flanagan to get lost in his piano solo. Sometimes considered the most difficult jazz song ever written, it'd guarantee me a spot if I played it well. Then again, practicing it might have taken up the rest of my life. I could get it down, I told myself, there was two months until the audition, it'd be easy. My mind was my worst enemy, always discouraging me and telling me "I can't," but not that time. No way was that stopping me from getting in, or at least trying.

I used the pocket change I got from playing the street corner to pick up the Giant Steps record. It was a great album overall, but I only cared about one song which luckily was track one on side A, so it was easy to repeat over and over again. And that's exactly what I did. For two months I played that one song the second I woke up, went to bed, and every moment possible in between, engraving the chords and tempo into my head so that when I attempted to play over it, I wouldn't fall flat. I picked up a cassette, as well, to listen to on the street and practice over it. No way could I keep up with Charlie Parker yet, but something told me I would.

***

"You auditioning for Hubbard's band? I hear a bunch of people are doing Giant Steps," a short, scrawny guy about my age stood over me sitting down on Miles Drive.

"Huh?" I heard what he had said, but was thrown off by the claim and the fact that I have no idea who the guy was.

"Yeah man, practically *everyone* is doing that. They wanna impress the man himself, and what better way than playing the hardest jazz song ever written," he had a cocky tone in his voice and the way he held himself screamed egotistical.

"Oh uh- I-",

"Eh, I'm sure you'll be better than everyone else, no need to stress about it! See you at the audition!" the man strutted off as if he was a king.

Many of my mentors in life had told me time and time again that in order to be someone in the jazz scene, you need a little ego, but that guy was what I never wanted to become. The abundance of musicians with that attitude had thrown me off from getting the ego that I may have needed, leaving me a little ego that continually got trampled on.

***

There was one week until the audition when that guy came up to me, and what he said really got to me. If everyone played the same song, and my performance was anywhere near just average or decent, I'll be overlooked in a heartbeat. I needed something to set me apart from the competition. *Something... different*, those words went through my head for hours while I scoured my music, trying to find the perfect balance between difficult and unique. I had to pick something at a moment's notice. "Lightbulb," I whispered to myself, quickly running over to my records. John Coltrane's "Blue Train," track two, Moment's Notice. An iconic jazz song that wasn't insanely difficult but still challenging and there was for sure less of a chance of many people doing it. I had one week to cram in two months of practice and preparation, so immediately I went to looping the song over and over again, later practicing over the changes. I didn't have the music, so all I could do was hope that I wrote down the right chords. Back to the street I went to practice, with only two days until the audition. My heart didn't slow down for that whole week and my sleep schedule suffered greatly. The feeling of determination inside of me wouldn't let up and prevented me from sleeping, eating, and thinking about anything other than the audition. As I played on the street, my arms shook from fatigue of holding them up for hours on end, my lips showed a bright hue of red from overplaying, and my eyes stayed shut from lack of sleep, I was pretty sure I fell asleep outside the night before the audition. All I remember was closing my eyes while it was dark, opening them to light, and waddling my way to my apartment bed.

✳✳✳

I woke up in a panic as if I had just hit the ground in a dream My arms frantically looked for a watch that had fallen off, 9:30. Audition in an hour, I thought to myself, letting out a deep sigh in an attempt to calm down. Nothing seemed to work so I decided to take a hot shower; that was sure to be relaxing. Time ceased to exist in the shower, I was always late to school as a kid because of it. Apparently I never dropped that habit since the clock read 10:23 by the time I hopped out and began drying off. Piercing panic powered through my body, as anxiety took over my thoughts and the hair on my neck turned razor sharp. I'd never been that active of a guy, but I sure as hell seemed like one as clothes flew on, cologne was sprayed, and teeth were brushed within a few minutes and I made my way down a few blocks to the theater where the auditions were being held. Sprinting there, I felt as though cabs were too slow, dodging roughly 12 cars, stepping on countless pieces of gum, and nearly tripping over cans and bottles I finally made it to the theater. 10:33 my watch read as I busted through the door of the theater where I saw another trumpet player, mid-audition. Thank god, I exhaled loudly, if they had been waiting for me the chance of getting in would be even more so slim than it already was. As I listened and looked closer, I realized it guy from the street, soloing over none other than Giant Steps. I was in awe, star struck even, as this guy followed changes without missing a beat, playing some of the fastest and most stylistic rhythms I'd ever heard. My mouth dropped open even further when he decided to show off his range of a triple C, an octave above anything I could have reached. My stomach flipped when he played something familiar. Something I had heard over and over again for months. It was the lick that I practiced everyday on the street. The one I played before he came up to talk to me, and the one when he left. In fact, the majority of what he played in the second half of the solo was stuff I wrote, stuff I poured my soul into and nearly went insane over. I had to hold my breakfast in after that; it sickened me to no end. How was I gonna play my best after that, I thought as I started to shake. The thought of being there and performing anywhere near that guy made me anxious beyond belief, but I couldn't let that stop me. I had to go up there and play my heart out, no excuses.

✳✳✳

"I'm sure it wasn't *that* bad sweetie," my mother's comforting voice said over the phone. "You always are too hard on yourself with auditions, cut yourself some slack," her words went in one ear out the other. I thought I played bad back at Billie's- little did I know this would be a million times worse. The following months were all but forgotten by now. All I really knew was I slept more than I was awake. My trumpet didn't leave it's case until I got over it. The day I finally took it out to play took longer than expected-it was the longest I'd gone without playing in years and boy, did it show. Yeah, I was rusty at first but eventually, I got back on track. I missed playing, and decided to head out to my happy place. Back on Miles Drive, I lost myself in music like I had countless times before. I was oblivious to the outside world, which became clear to me when I opened my eyes after a sudden round of applause. Looking around me, I saw familiar faces from months prior, all those that stopped by for a song or two and dropped in a spare dollar if they could.

"We missed ya kid," one man said, "my walks to work were pretty boring without you here," he continued, the rest of the crowd nodded in agreement. I was in awe- had I really made an impact on these people? Before I had time to say anything to them, I caught the eye of what seemed like a ghost but was merely a man. My heart stopped as he stepped in front of the crowd, I immediately stood up.

"The names Freddie," he held out his hand for me to shake, "didn't I see you at the audition?

The Eye in the Sand

The barren landscape of endless hills seemed to stretch forever into blue nothingness as I stopped to rest. The light was beginning to fade and it was time to head home, but I was hungry, and had come too far to return without a meal. My brother had gone missing ages ago, but my search for him never ended. Food was most important, for my stomach twisted and clouded my desperate mind, but I knew he was still out there somewhere.

"I won't forget you, brother" I quietly spoke, as if he could hear me.

Judging by the unfamiliar vastness of the plains behind me, this had to be the farthest I had ever wandered from my home. There was no sign of the towering pile of rocks where my family slept, for I had been crawling across the great plains of grey silt for hours now, without a spec of food in sight. The frigid currents forced me into my thoughts. Thoughts of my home, and Father, filled my mind. This time he was too weak to accompany me. He just needs food, soon he will be strong again, I hoped, for I had never hunted without him. Alone for the first time, only my instincts guided me.

My world was slowly being cast into its nightly shadow, and now my eyes struggled to make out the shapes of creatures crawling in the distance. Every so often, my eyes would spy some passing shape above me for a brief moment, or something slither over a mound into the approaching wall of darkness. My eyes scanned the shrinking visible landscape as my stomach rumbled and my hope began to fade.

This is hopeless, I thought, but my father's hunger made me

press on. The tightening starvation pulled at my mind, and my body becoming weaker with every step. I kept thinking over and over 'won't come home without a meal.' It motivated me, but I fear that it meant I'd be searching until my last breath. Must I return? No- to return empty handed would be dishonorable. Unthinkable. My legs were tired and every shadow from the corner of my eye made me shiver, so I thought back to mother's teachings.

"The Spirit of the Ocean guides us, and with him, you shall never be lost." She would say. The memory gave me strength, He was with me, and so I pressed on.

Then my eyes came over a hill and beheld a most peculiar sight indeed. Lying on the plain in front of me was a towering monolith, the likes of which I had never before seen. It was a black and crooked box of stunning size, with a long shiny set of rings, all linked together at the top that stretched upward into the great void above.

"What in the name of-" I froze, and gazed upon the monolith of black, a structure of no origin nor meaning. Its menacing presence sparked a primal, unknown fear deep within me. "Could this be-" I remembered the stories mother would tell about the Old Gods. She would speak of their wretched contraptions, built before the Almighty Spirit had killed them at the end of the era of chaos, centuries ago.

"Great machines of metal" She would say "the cursed creations of the Old Ones," and as we laughed, she would become serious. "You doubt the wisdom of our ancestors?" She snapped, "for when the Ocean Spirit unified the heavens and cast out the Old Gods, the machines remained, to rust and decay. I have seen the solemn husks myself, they stretch into the heavens from chains of silver." When I recalled mother's solemn words, the black object's origin became clear.

"I must turn back, Mother said to never-" My empty stomach shot pain through my body and silenced the constant thought of needing food as I began to approach the towering mass. The black shape seemed to grow taller as my many tired legs pulled me towards it. My intrigue got the best of me, for my leg slipped through the fine grains of silt below and I was sent tumbling down the hill. My world was suddenly sent into a twisting blur, and as I tumbled my senses were filled with a delicious aroma. The sensation of the scent was brought to a sudden halt when my head struck a hard object, and the tumbling ceased.

"Where am- what is- ouch" Throbbing pain shot through my head as I regained my senses. Coming out of the shock of the blow, I looked upward, remembered the odd structure. Completely dazed, I noticed flakes of small red dust gently settling around me. It looked familiar, and I remembered the word mother used for the red dust that covered the metal pipes in the ground near our home. "Rust" she called it, but still my mind had trouble understanding its origin. With my vision fully regained, I looked up at the obelisk that stood before my eyes. My close proximity caused the black surface of intertwined metal bars to seemingly stretch for miles above, and I was sure that this was where that delicious smell was coming from. Despite the coating of rust that covered and filled the porous surface, many little holes lined the wall, through which I could peer. I brought my eye up to a hole and gazed within. It was then that I saw it... food! Within the structure laid a black pedestal with a thick piece of red meat that emanated the strongest, most delicious scent I had ever smelled. My stomach grumbled and my nose sniffed the aroma with excitement. I needed to find a way in!

The wind increased, and the flowing currents sent particles of rust drifting down on top of me, obscuring my view even more than the blackening sky above. Despite my fleeting vision, I scanned the menacing structure, looking for anything that would grant me entry. "Nothing." I said. "Rust and decay. I know it's on here somewhere." Again I thought of my father, old and hungry in the cave. His energy was fading; I saw it in his eyes leaving the cave.

"I won't lose you like I- just find enough for us and return safe. Do not forget what I have taught you," were the last words he spoke when we parted.

"I won't, father. With His guidance, I will find it." The holy thought motivated me, and I looked behind the structure. It was when my legs turned the corner to the back side of the thing that a massive disk was revealed, attached to the wall and hanging high from the top of the structure, much too high for me to reach. "What could you be?" I asked the hanging shape. In my hunger induced delirium, I half-expected the thing to answer. Still I approached the disk from below, and brought my eyes right up to the black wall. Closely examining the strange surface, it had no texture other than chaotic etchings and scratches in the rust. When I ran my claw down the steel bar, the rust that once covered it broke off and fell to the ground, revealing a shining metal surface that glimmered in the fading light. I stared in amazement at the shimmering color, but soon was wrenched from my trance when the tight hunger pains from my empty stomach shot through my body. Reminded of my predicament, I searched the glimmering surface, and found a peculiar groove in the steel walls. This was new, and I scratched the rust along the groove, revealing the entirety of the strange feature. It formed a square in the wall, just below the disk above me. Could this be a way in? I thought, thinking only of the prize within. Quickly my claw struck the shape, and to my delight, the square budged! The movement was quite subtle, but the ancient gateway had indeed been dislocated. Somehow I had to strike it with enough force to blow it wide open. Just like a clam, I thought, and a memory of one of mother's first lessons entered my mind.

"Swing!" She said to brother, after carefully moving him as far away from the stagnant mollusk as he could reach. He swung, much wider this time, and his claw struck the clam with a violent crack. The sharp noise echoed into the surrounding void as we pried the clam open. We ate well that night, for mother's lesson had been sufficient. After obtaining a better position, as far as I could reach, my claw swung into the loose piece of metal with all the force that my weakening body could muster. With a loud clang and a cloud of rust and silt, the door swung open. The sound of the blow rattled the cage and the surrounding darkness. Something made me hesitate before I entered, perhaps the fleeting noise as it reverberated into the metal bars, strangely resembling the distant calls of some unknown creature of this treacherous void we inhabited. When the tone finally ceased, I carefully climbed up into the conduit, entering a corroded corridor of ancient steel.

What if this ancient machine is to kill me? What if I cannot return? If only brother was here, surely he would know what to do. God, he must be out here somewhere... and if neither of us return what will happen to father? Again I thought of him, helplessly waiting for me in the cave. Then I remembered how hungry he must be. I must take this risk, for him. The flurry of thoughts was cast from my mind again when another sudden bolt of piercing pain shot through me from my empty stomach, and I was forced towards the beckoning meal ahead. The corridor soon widened, and lead me into an open chamber where the delicious meat awaited me, for at last it was mine! It rested on a podium of steel, untouched for what seemed like eons.

"What could have been the purpose of this thing?" I wondered. "A pedestal of metal bearing meat. A culinary container for the Gods perhaps?" My impatience overcame my inquiry, and my legs rushed for the prize. Without hesitation, I wrenched it from its metallic podium and pushed it into my drooling mouth, filling my senses with its delicious flavor. As I ate, my energy returned and the gnawing hunger receded. Before I could finish, I heard something... a slow, scraping noise. My eyes quickly looked up from my meal to find the pedestal that held it slowly rising above me. Its ascent seemed to pull a shiny cord that reflected the dimming green light that pierced the holes of the chamber. My eyes darted backward, following the cord, and I saw the mighty circular lid descending toward the door. The hanging shape's terrible purpose suddenly clicked in my mind, and sent me racing as fast as I could toward the shrinking conduit. The faster I ran, the farther the exit seemed to stretch away from me. The mad dash turned into an explosive leap of desperation, sending me flying towards the small spec of hope that remained of the shrinking opening. This is it, I thought, shutting my eyes tight. With my legs no longer on the ground, and the conduit quickly approaching, it was now up to fate. I felt my head crash against a hard surface, jolting my limp body backward into the corridor. The great black disk that once hung above descended upon the door completely. It began to twist, a loud scraping noise echoing through the corridor as the black rust fell from the ceiling. The floor jolted suddenly as the great twisting stopped, the object firmly sealed on the doorway. The dim light from the outside had faded into blackness, and I sat alone, in hopeless silence.

Like a floating leaf, my soul mindlessly drifted around the confines of my new prison. The scraps of meat initially saved for Father had all been eaten, to see him again now would be a miracle. Over and over I scraped and tapped the walls, hoping that maybe some undiscovered exit would somehow reveal itself. Thoughts of my family back home, hungry and worried about me, filled my hopeless mind. The thought made me sick, and all I wanted to do was sleep. "What shall happen to me now? Trapped by a machine of the old gods" I said to myself, and a terrifying thought struck me as I spoke it. "The ancient gods, might they return? No, mother couldn't lie, they were all dead! Cast out by the Ocean Spirit" It was true; mother's teaching couldn't be wrong. But despite its absurdity the thought lingered. I remembered long ago, of my family huddled together on a cold night in the rocks.

"Mother, the old Gods, what did they look like?" My brother asked. The rigid, forbidding look mother gave him frightened both of us. For a while there was silence, then finally, in a serious and apprehensive voice, she spoke.

"The dark ones were shapeless. Horrible. They had no form and were jealous of His creations, us, for He gave us solid, meaningful bodies. They corrupted and prayed on us until He cast them into the void and killed them."

"And what of-"

"Do not speak about this again. You will sleep now." And that was the last that she spoke of the Old Gods. The light had faded entirely, and I found my way towards the sealed door from where I came in complete darkness. After a few more furiously futile attempts at breaking through the metal, I could barely lift my claw to strike it again. Exhausted by my futile efforts to escape, I finally slept.

I'm back home it seems, the familiar rocks jutting out from the silt around me. Walking away from my family, their voices from within the den fade as my legs draw me further away. Where am I going? I thought, noticing the quickened pace of my steps. Something deep in my mind silenced my questions, this was where I am meant to go. And it was, for something over the hills beckoned my mind. Continuing up the hill, my little legs dig through the soft grains on silt as they ascend. Reaching the top, It comes into view. The great trench, spanning both ways into the distance, lied on the plains below. I feel it drawing me, speaking to me in ineffable calls from within its infinite depths. I must look deeper. I continue down the hill and bring myself to the edge. My eyes look down into the black, the great unknown that stretched forever into the divine abyss. It was beautiful. Voices my ears couldn't understand flow from the chasm into my mind. If only I could get closer! Even standing at the edge wasn't enough, I needed to know more. But how? I feel its rhythmic pulses of sound, its divine presence, emanating from the deep. I step even further, the very edge, and the deep pulses increase, like a predator's excited breathing as its prey draws ever closer. It isn't enough. "Take another step" said a voice from below, it's warm and loving tone made me forget entirely that there was no more ground to step on. Tempted by forbidden knowledge, I take another step. Everything I felt left my body as fast as the rocky cliff above me fell away from view. The warmness, the courage, the excitement, and all feelings of love and intrigue were gone, suddenly replaced by pure, hopeless terror as I fall into the abyss. I look above, and see nothing. It was far too late now.

Suddenly I was jolted awake, a cold, strong current coursing across my body and sliding me across my cage. The current was very brief, stopping almost as suddenly as it started, but it greatly disturbed me, and I cowered against the rusted wall. My eyes darted back and forth, frantically scanning the empty chamber. The green rays of light that pierced the porous walls lit the solemn chamber, and I deliriously came to my senses from my slumber. A peculiar cloud of silt was settling on the mound behind me, and a strange new scent was present.

"This is hopeless. This wretched machine must hide me from His light." I tried to pray, and heard no answer. Even in death the old ones confined me, and still I feared their return. Without His company, I was truly lost. Gazing out upon the barren grey plains, the feeling of hopelessness overcame any inquiry my mind had over the scent, the cloud, or the current. However, something was off, about the mound in front of me. Had it been there before? I wondered as I inspected the curious shape, somehow different from the rest. Suddenly a shiver went down my spine and I froze with fright- the mass in front of me gazed right back at me... with an eye of its own.

Upon meeting my gaze, the eye narrowed and suddenly a cloud of silt was wrenched upward, startling me and obscuring my vision. Through the falling sand, I saw the mound begin to move, and grow. What was once the light gray of the silt was now changing to red, and behind the cloud the thing continued to expand and stretch. From my helpless cage I watched a flurry of impossible shapes, struck with a deep and terrible fear, for I had no doubt in my mind that the formless entity, obscured by sand, would soon be upon me. It twisted and writhed behind the cloud and it was now a deep black. A massive shape emerged and pushed the grains of silt away as it approached me, and I was met with the piercing gaze of a massive creature, its two giant eyes staring into me through the porous walls. I heard and felt its deep breaths as it examined me, before it moved backward, revealing its towering black figure: a massive head and eight twisting tentacles below it. The giant eyes stared into me, and then I heard it. A deep, rhythmic tone emanated from the beast, as if trying to communicate. The noise only filled me with a familiar terror. I didn't understand.

"What do you want?" I yelled to it. The shapeless thing's essence suddenly unveiled in my mind. My greatest fears had been true. I screamed. "Al- Almighty Spirit of the Ocean, destroyer of evil-" The beast's noise only loudened. "Holy creator protect me from this wretched abomination, cast it back into the void-" It became unbearable. It twisted my brain and filled me with insane thoughts that could only inhabit the floating creatures mind.

"Stop this!" screamed my petrified body, and I shut my eyes tight. The maddening thoughts didn't stop. The low, haunting voice of the shape echoed in my head, the twisted vocals became images behind my closed eyes. I saw impossible landscapes of darkness, filled with tiny creatures that glowed bright colors against the deep void, and bright blue areas with a shimmering layer that rippled above everything. Eyes and faces of terrified creatures, frozen with fright looking straight up at me. Then I saw him- my brother, helplessly frozen on the plains, a look of utter terror in his eyes. "No- that's impossible" I shouted in vain as I watched a shadow descend upon his body. The horrid vision changed again; now it was only myself, hopelessly trapped in an ancient prison of rust, eyes tightly shut with fear. This was too much, I began to shout and open my eyes, but my voice caught in my throat, for the creature had silently approached, and was now mere inches from my face, against the steel walls. Without breaking its paralyzing gaze into my eyes, the monster raised one of its eight long appendages. The cage briefly shook, and from a rusted hole squeezed the long, black tentacle, passing effortlessly through the tiny opening.

I watched, paralyzed with fright, as the black shape entered my prison, and slithered across the corroded floor. Finally willing my terrified legs to move, I ran to the opposite side and clung to the rusted wall. This is it, I thought, this is the end. My eyes tightly shut with fear, could hear the thing scraped toward me with a hideous metallic screeching noise. I began to think back to my home, what would father do? God, had his hunger already taken him? I didn't even know how long I'd been trapped here, my sense of time obscured by fear and darkness. My petrified mind raced as I pondered what would happen when the slithering mass finally reached me, finding nothing, only the terrifying unknown. Filled with fear, I felt myself drifting off.

We followed our mother as she crawled over the hills, our stomachs rumbling and gnawing at our minds. We knew her hunger was worse, for she gave every tiny scrap lying on the plains to me and my brother, but that was ages ago, and we still hunted against the black sky. Mother always said to never hunt after dark, but she never told us why. The currents were getting stronger, and we struggled to climb each hill as the silt crumbled under our tired legs. In front of us, mother stopped to rest. We did the same. I turned to brother and asked

"How much longer?"

"Mother knows what she's doing. Soon we will-" He paused, looking forward with a terrified expression. I turned in the direction of his gaze, and saw mother, still resting. I didn't know why, but when I saw her a terrible shiver went down my spine. It was a moment later that I saw it... a black shape, barely visible against the black sky, looming over mother. It was a long tendril, that seemingly stretched forever into the abyss above. Before we could say anything the tendril twisted around mother's body. She frantically snapped her claws in vein as the thing tightened around her, pulling her into the darkness above. Just before we lost sight of her we heard an awful crack as mother's shell was crushed by the twisting force of the thing that pulled her away, never to be seen again. The horrid sight froze my body, I couldn't move. Brother instantly ran to where mother was, in a blind and devastated rage.

"Come back!" I desperately yelled to him, my legs still frozen to the ground with freight. "Brother!" He wouldn't listen, and ran further and further into the distance, looking for what had took our mother. I finally

willed my petrified legs to move, when suddenly a violent current kicked
up a plume of silt, sending me tumbling back and obscuring my vision.
Frantically I rushed through the wall of falling silt, searching for brother,
but he was long gone.

The scraping noise stopped. Opening my eyes, I saw the black
tendril mere feet away from my face. It twisted and moved but came no
closer. The cage began to rattle as the monster tried to squeeze further
into the cage, to no avail. The eyes narrowed and the twisted tentacle
turned red with anger as it slowly was pulled back through the hole
to its master. It let out an annoyed grunt and returned to its original
deep black hue. Then a massive cloud of silt was kicked up as the beast
quickly ascended, its eyes fixed on mine. Something fell from under it,
into the cloud of silt below. In a moment the cloud cleared, and I saw
what had fallen from the monster.

"No... it can't be-" Absolute horror overcame me, for when the
beast shot upward, a corroded piece of my brother's shell fell from the
black and twisting mass. I knew it was him, for even though the empty
husk had been sucked dry, the look of pure terror I knew all too well was
still fixed on his face.

I watched helplessly as the amorphous horror circled and inspected
my prison. I could see the hunger in its eyes as it poked and prodded the
metal walls with its tentacles. Finally, it descended upon the entrance
from which I came, the large metal lid sealed tightly on the door. I
waited as the creature carefully inspected the material with fascinating
concentration. I saw its eyes widen and its low, heavy breathing increase
as it ran its arms under a particular groove behind the lid. The mighty
arms gripped and curled around the lid as the creature pressed its body
up against my prison. The current produced by the giant's advance sent
me tumbling to the opposite side of the cage. The floor began to shake
as the sounds of metal scraping against metal echoed throughout the
chamber. The sounds grew louder and rust began to slowly fall from the
ceiling. I watched with terror as the giant lid began to twist.

Thrown into panic, I hopelessly clawed at the walls of this steel
tomb, desperate to escape my inevitable doom. I heard the scraping
metal get louder as the door spun faster. My mind was overcome by

terror and my eyes tightly shut, awaiting my end. All hope was lost. I accepted my fate. All I could do was pray.

"Spirit, holy creator in heaven, allow me to pass away from this life and return to you, for all your creations devoted to your light will live on in the great heaven above where-" Suddenly I felt the floor jerk slightly under my legs, and the sound stopped, leaving nothing but silence. My eyes slowly opened, and saw the massive circular lid drifting past the outside of the wall to my side.

***

Before taking a step, I waited. Surely this thing was playing some trick on me. My eyes darted back and forth and my heart beat furiously, the sense of imminent death still coursing through my body and mind. Moments passed, and still nothing. The gentle sound of the steady currents around my prison calmed me, and I stepped forward. Looking outward through the open doorway I saw nothing but the familiar grey hills that surrounded me. Where had the giant gone? As I began to step down into to the sand below, my body froze and a strong feeling of uneasiness filled my body. I scanned the ground and the surrounding hills but saw nothing unusual. What's wrong? Perhaps all this excitement was just getting to my nerves, the giant was gone! Slowly, I stepped out of my prison. My legs sink into the grains of the familiar ground once more. Had the creature simply freed me out of pity?

"Joy! I am free for He has answered." My voice shouted with delight. My soul yearned to run to father and tell him of this adventure! How long has it been? Father surely thinks I'm dead. I turn towards home and race up the hill that I once fell from. The steepness was difficult, but I claw and climb and finally reach the top. Realizing how exhausted everything had made me, I stop to rest on a small nearby hill. My little legs sink into the silt. They continue to sink. The same uneasiness from before creeps back into my mind, my eyes slowly peer at the ground below... and I freeze. Time itself seemed to stop as I met the piercing gaze of that same horrible eye that so hungrily glared at me from the mound. The ground turns black, and I feel things twisting around my arms. With a sudden flash of motion, I was pulled backward, and everything went black. The tendrils around my body twist and tighten, I couldn't move. There is only time for a few brief thoughts, everything happened so fast. I think of my father, never to see me return, and my mother, waiting patiently for me in the afterlife. I feel the tendrils twisting tighter, and hear my shell begin to crack. I see my brothers face again, this time he is smiling. He is with mother, awaiting my arrival. Violently the tendrils twist even more. My shell is giving in- the last thing I hear is a loud crack, my entire existence crushed into oblivion. The pain instantly ceased, and I felt myself drifting away into warm nothingness.

✳✳✳

Power

"Hey Marshall, Ms. Robin will be picking you up after school. Dad will be home at 5. Okay? Mommy will be home late, so I'll see you tonight. I love you!"

"Mhm. Bye Mom." The boy rolled his eyes and walked into the school, his shoulders slumped forward. Covering his face in order to avoid any confrontation with the other 9 year olds. He walked into the building, and out of sight from his mother.

As the mother started walking back to her car, she was interrupted by group of parents. The one in front being a well-known PTA mom. Please don't do this. Please not now. Not to Marshall, She thought

"You need to talk some sense into your son." The five moms behind her stood with their arms crossed across their chests. "He is scaring kids at school, and if he keeps this up, I will bring administration in on this."

"I'm sorry, I don't know what you are talking about. My son hasn't done anything wrong. Now please, let me get to my car." She tried pushing through the crowd, but was blocked. "Let me through, Susan"

"Your son's a terror, and I will make sure this gets to the principal. This isn't the end, Margaret." The group of aggressive moms split off and let her get to her car. Margaret fumbled to put her keys in the ignition, and drove off. Her shaky hands trembled the entire ride, her face red with anger and embarrassment.

Marshall is a good kid. They just don't understand him, she reassured herself. They are wrong. Yes, they are just wrong.

She paced around the house fists clenched, infuriated by the way she was treated. "Who does she think she is?" She put her scrubs on and headed off to the hospital for her shift.

***

"Hi, Marshall!" Robin was standing on the blacktop by the outside of the school. She was wearing her college sweatshirt and glasses. "Marshall?" He wouldn't look at her. "Okay then. Lets go home."

Once they got to the house, Robin set her laptop down on the kitchen table, and got started on her school work.

"Okay Marshall, what do you want for a snack? Your mom wants you to get your school work done before you can use the computer… Marshall? I'd like a response." Frustrated, she looked at him in the eyes, and waited for him to speak.

"Yeah." he rolled his eyes, "Can I have an apple sauce."

"Sure, I'll get it. Your dad will be here in 2 hours. Is there anything you'd like to do in the meantime?"

He looked down, avoiding all eye contact with his babysitter. Robin was confused. She'd never tried to talk to a kid about their hobbies, and not received a response. Normally, kids Marshall's age couldn't seem to stop talking, she thought to herself. Marshall looked up after 30 seconds of silence, took a spoonful of applesauce, and started staring at his feet again.

"I umm," He mumbled, almost inaudible, "I like to draw a little"

"Oh really? That's cool! What do you like to draw?"

"I just sketch cartoons and stuff." He ate another spoonful of applesauce.

Maybe he's opening up to me? She thought. "What kind of sketches?"

He looked at Robin directly in the eyes. His stare pierced through her, as he glared, annoyed. "I don't know. I just draw. Leave me alone about it."

"Oh, okay." She pushed back, not wanting to lose any progress that she made with connecting to the boy sitting in front of her. He stood up, threw out the empty applesauce container, and pulled out his green homework folder. Looking over the paper covered with fraction problems, he picked up the pencil and began working.

Woah, he's fast. How is he doing that? Robin thought to herself as she looked on at Marshall swiftly finishing each problem and moving onto the next. In no time, Marshall was halfway done with the page when she decided to chime in, "You're really fast. You must be very smart for your age."

"It's easy. Stop interrupting me, please."

✳✳✳

"Hi Marshall! How was school?" Robin was standing, once again, at the school's blacktop.

"Boring. Lets go home."

As the two walked to Robin's old car, the babysitter noticed the sheer amount of people watching them. Some kids were pointing and whispering to their moms, and others would move closer to their parents as the two passed. A few feet from their car, Robin overheard a group of moms talking in hushed voices as she and Marshall walked by.

"That must be the new babysitter. Surprise, surprise, looks like another quit. That boy is a menace."

Robyn looked over to the mothers, a startled expression plastered across her face as the group of women turned away quickly.

Robin turned to Marshall, infuriated by how they are treating him. "Okay Marshall?" She said through gritted teeth, "I want you to get in the car. I can handle this." The boy scurried into the passenger seat as fast as he could; it was almost as if he knew what was coming.

Carefully shutting the door, she turned slowly and began walking towards the group of women who had shifted their attention to the school door, presumably waiting for their children. Words spilled from her mouth before she could think of them.

"You've got quite a mouth, lady. Are your lackeys going to contribute anything to this conversation, or are they just going to copy everything you say? I heard what you said about Marshall. He's just a kid-why would you be so mean, talking about a boy?" Her eyes, moments before filled with rage grew sullen, looking at the women.

"Excuse me?" The woman was obviously offended. Crossing her arms across her chest, it became obvious she wasn't about to become defensive. As if brushing what Robin had said aside, she retorted, "Do you know who I am? I am the president of the Parent-Teachers Association. I have the principal on speed dial. It would be in your best interest to stop talking."

"Try me."

The two got closer and closer. Their faces almost touching. The angry mother's breath overtaking Robin's senses.

"Is everything alright here?" The school's crossing guard interrupted.

"Sure is, Mr. Jim. I was just leaving." The mom was still holding her gaze on Robin. She whispered so faintly, so only Robin was able to hear, "I will not stand to keep a creep like him in this school. I will make your life a living hell, along with that stupid kid and his parents. I am friends with everyone here. You are alone."

The group casually walked to their cars, as the kids ran to their respective parents and drove off, leaving Robin at the crosswalk next to her car. Slumping into the seat, she looked over at Marshall.

"Hey kid. Those people are crazy. Don't listen to what they said. I think you are pretty great." He was hiding his face.

"Thanks, Robin. Lets go home" The boy looked down, pulled his hood over his head, and leaned against the window.

"Yes. Lets. Hey, how would you like some of my homemade hot chocolate? I know it's not that cold outside, but hot chocolate can help anyone on a rough day."

"I'd love that, thanks."

✳✳✳

Walking into the house, they put their stuff down on the kitchen table, almost as if it was a tradition at this point. Robin got to work on the hot chocolate, as Marshall got to work on his math homework.

"So who were those kids anyway? Do you know them?"

"Yeah, that was Jake Stevens. His mom is the head of the PTA. She's crazy. Mom talks about her all the time and Jake is able to get away with anything because she runs basically every school event."

"Well that's not fair at all." She was surprised by how much Marshall was sharing especially after their interactions the day before.

"Yeah, two months ago, Jake threw Sean's phone in a puddle and then nothing happened to him. Instead, Sean started going to another school across town. It's not fair."

"That sounds very suspicious."

As Marshall finished his homework, Robin began pouring two cups of hot chocolate. The two sat at the table sipping their drinks, occasionally looking up with remnants still on their upper lip.

"Hey, yesterday you said you liked to draw. Do you mind showing me some of them? I'm very curious." Marshall hesitated, chocolate still on his lip. He wiped it off with a napkin, and contemplated showing her.

"I'll show you them, but you can't tell anyone about it. Even my parents. Pinky promise."

"I promise." Their fingers interlocked and the boy grabbed a notebook from his bag.

Opening it up revealed pages of elaborately detailed cartoon drawings of people. Most of the pages filled with different classmates or teachers, each one having a short bio of what they were like, alongside an exaggerated caricature of how Marshall perceived them. Next to the caricatures were misshapen and deformed cartoon drawings. "How do you do this? These are so good!"

The boy hid behind his sweatshirt hoodie. "I don't know, I just draw them in class."

"What are those things on the side?" She started flipping through each page, revealing a new creature every time

He flipped to the front page and pointed to the caricature. "This is Jake, or what he portrays himself as, at least." His finger slid over to a sketch of a snake with a backpack on, and a school in its coiled tail. In the background, there was at least a dozen graves with flowers at their base. "This is him on the inside."

Robin was speechless. This was just the first page, yet it depicted Jake in so much detail. She was filled with overpowering curiosity as she longed to see the other pictures.

The two spent the rest of their time looking at each and every drawing in the book, laughing occasionally at the somehow accurate doodles of their personalities on the side.

Suddenly, the door opened, and Marshall's dad walked in. He was wearing a buttoned shirt and tie that was loosened after the long day of work.

"Hey, Marshall. Hey, Robin. How were your days today?"

"It was great. I made hot chocolate and uh," Robin caught herself, remembering the promise she made, "We had a great time."

"Well, I'm glad to hear that. Oh yeah, Robin. Here's your pay. I almost forgot." He handed her the cash, but as he was doing that, managed to catch sight of his son heading off to his room with his hood covering his face and his notebook in hand. The father leaned in to make sure Marshall didn't over hear him.

"Was he really alright today? He never talks to me or his mom about anything anymore."

"We both had a great time together. He's opened up to me a lot over the past few days." She whispered back, "There was this incident at school today-"

"Did he do anything bad? Please tell me he didn't."

"No, actually. It was with a parent."

"Ooooh. Let me guess, was it Jake's mom? Margaret rants about her all the time."

"Yeah, but I think I handled it well. She will definitely be coming back, though. The only reason I wasn't jumped by her gang of PTA thugs was because a crossing guard saw us and broke it up."

"I'm terribly sorry you had to go through that. She has too much power, and her kid's not any better." He smiled, but it quickly faded when he thought about the kid's mom again. "Anyway, there's literally nothing we can do. The other parents are afraid of her, yet she somehow keeps getting elected as president. Avoid her at all costs, and try to not get on her bad side."

"You got it. I need to leave; my mom is making dinner tonight, and I don't want to be late. I'll be here tomorrow."

The next day, Robin was getting ready to leave to pick up Marshall, when her phone started to ring. Her smartphone read "Margaret: Marshall's mom".

"Uh, oh," She muttered. "She's at work. This can't be good." She answered the call.

"He what?" Robin couldn't believe what she was hearing. Maybe her phone service cut out for a second and she misheard.

"Marshall was sent to the principals. I need you to pick him up there instead of the normal exit. You are able to represent me for him. They didn't tell me much, but from what I heard, it's bad" Margaret's voice sounded worried.

"Ok I'll be there. Don't worry, Margaret, I got this."

***

At the principal's office, there were six chairs in front of the menacingly large desk. Three boys sat in the chairs, and there were empty ones on either side of them. Marshall was in the middle. He was scraped up pretty bad, but much better off than the other kids. On his left, was a small, skinny boy with a ripped shirt and bruised all over. On his left, Jake. He was covered in mud from head to toe.

"Now that our parents and," he looked right over at Robin, "guardian are here, we can start talking about this incident together. We can start by going down the line and seeing everyone's perspectives. Now, Jake, what happened?"

"Umm Dr. Shan. I was just talking with Sam, and then Marshall ran up, pushed me, and shoved my head in the mud. I told him to stop, but he didn't listen. I would have died if it weren't for Sam telling him to stop."

"That's not true!"

"Quiet, Marshall. Let Jake speak."

"He pinned Sam against the wall and was going to hurt him!"

"Quiet, Marshall." The principal was getting impatient.

Susan took her opportunity to speak. "My son would never do anything like that. I am astounded you would even think up such things!" She glared at Robin, who was still trying to absorb what was going on around her.

"Jake, is there anything else you remember?"

"No sir."

"Now, Marshall, what did you see happen?"

Marshall was extremely uncomfortable having to talk to strangers like this. He sat in silence for a moment, not knowing how to phrase his testimony. Robin leaned in, "You need to talk to them. If you tell the truth, it will be over sooner, but if you stay quiet, you could get in trouble from his lies. I know you were protecting Sam. Look at his shirt. Just tell them what you did."

Marshall took a breath. "Sam is in my math class. He didn't come in from recess, so Mr. Santos sent me to find him. I saw him and Jake out by the side of the school. No one was around to see, but Jake was grabbing Sam's shirt and screaming at him. Sam was crying and afraid. I just ran and slammed Jake off of him. He fell right into the mud."

"That's not true! My son will never do such a thing!"

"Mrs. Stevens, please."

"Don't *Mrs. Stevens* me. My son's not a monster! That kid is!" She pointed at Marshall. "He's always hiding his face and staring at people."

Dr. Shann ignored her. "Sam, what happened from your perspective."

Both Jake and his mom were glaring at Sam with fiery eyes. As he looked down, it was obvious by his behavior he was nervous from the pressure. Marshall looked over at Sam and reassured him. "It'll all be okay. You don't need to be worried."

"I just wanted to play with the ball, but Jake wanted it." Sam started, "I said he could have it after me, but then he shouted louder. He didn't want his friends to see him give up the ball so fast, so he kept on persisting. Eventually, the bell rang, and everyone left."

"I-"

"Hush, Jake. I'm sorry Sam, please continue."

"Well, Jake kept getting closer to me, and then he slammed my body against the wall. I was scared. He just kept yelling and pushing me into the wall. Then Marshall came. He pushed Jake off and he flew into a puddle of mud."

"I-"

"Please, Jake. Stop interrupting. Lets look at the big picture here. There were no other witnesses other than the three of you. We have gone over security tapes, and there are no cameras in that area. Sam's shirt is ripped and he's bruised and has scratches up his back. The only way that could happen is if he's being pushed up against a wall."

"But it could have been Marshall!"

"It was you, Jake! Stop lying!" Sam's outburst caught everyone by surprise.

"My son would never do that!"

"You weren't there!"

Robin and Sam's dad stayed quiet through the whole argument. They, along with the principal, knew Jake and his mom were wrong, so they didn't add to the volume of the room. Since they weren't there to witness the scene, they thought to only chime in when necessary.

"Silence everyone!" Dr. Shann was getting impatient with Jake and his mom. "I will not tolerate bullying in our school. Jake, you will have a one-week suspension. Hopefully you will learn your lesson from that."

"You can't do that to him!" Susan screamed. "I am the president of the PTA. I demand you drop this!"

"You don't have that kind of power, Mrs. Stevens."

"You'll see," She pointed at the man in the suit. "You'll see." She grabbed her son by his collar and pulled him out the door.

"I am so sorry for what happened today, boys. I just hope you know we try our best to make this school as safe as possible."

"Thank you Dr. Shann." The two boys said in unison.

✳✳✳

Sam, his dad, Marshall, and Robin walked to their cars in the parking lot. Ahead of them, they all witnessed Susan yelling at her son. The little boy had tears streaming down his face, and she was yelling a mere inches away from him.

"Mommy, I like this school-"

"No, I will not stand for this, I am transferring you out."

"But mommmmm-"

"No!" Jake went silent, and obediently got into the car.

Sam nudged Marshall's arm. "Looks like we won't be seeing him anytime soon. Good bye!" the two boys laughed as they were walking,

Robin and Sam's dad watching them. "I haven't had the chance to tell you this, but thank you. I was in trouble there, and you saved me."

"Oh, it's no problem man, I was just doing what I thought was right." He nudged Sam's arm. "Looks like we won't need to deal with him ever again."

The boys went into their respective cars, as they began driving home, leaving the parking lot, where Susan's car was still parked.

The entire ride home, Marshall was silent. The only sounds audible were the sounds of the car, the road, and his pencil frantically scraping across the page. Robin knew to not interrupt him when he was drawing, so she just carried on driving him home.

As she pulled into the driveway, Marshall took the page and ripped it out of his notebook.

"Why would you do that?" She asked, confused as to why he would tear a page out of his precious notebook. He looked right into her eyes, took his hood off, and handed her the piece of paper.

"Here you go. Thank you." Marshall opened the door and headed into the house.

Robin sat with the folded piece of paper in her hand. She slowly unfolded it, not knowing what it could possibly be. On the left side of the page was a funny looking caricature of herself. She had her usual navy blue hoodie and her laptop in her hand. It looked funny, but she understood they were more comedic jabs than anything mean. On the right, where the usual gruesome sketch went, was instead a pleasant garden with a gardener in a navy hoodie. She smiled to herself while placing the drawing into her pocket and following Marshall inside.

✳✳✳

Condor

The forest swayed gently with the whistle of leaves. Sunlight pierced through the blanket of green that spanned the canopy. Dried moss stuck to the large rocks resting upon the thick trunks of the trees. As the wind blew, the leaves on the ground were carried away into the clear skies. Stepping out of my nest, built into the hollowed trunk of a tree, my feet kicked away the twigs and grass strewn outside. As the light broke the horizon, the songs of birds began to bounce back and forth from one tiny avian to another. My head turned, trying to follow the melodies that ricocheted from their mouths. The noise disturbed the calm ambiance of the morning, and as more birds joined in the cadence, I grew increasingly irritated.

"Shut up," I demanded, peering into the multitude of birds perched on their branches. My voice pierced the melodies, and soon the volume swiftly dwindled. Being the biggest bird of the forest had its perks. With my size, the status of being the toughest and most intimidating bird was unequivocally given to me. The forest was under my control. Although my nest was below and the birds looked down upon me from their branches, my gaze shadowed over them all from the skies. I turned around and headed back to the hollow, hoping to catch a few more hours of undisturbed sleep. One brave soul, however, stopped me in my tracks with their shout of defiance.

"No!" the voice said, turning heads to the source. The voice came from a plump robin, its ruffled feathers covering most of its round body. That's not a bird, I thought, that's a cotton ball.

Another voice from the side called out, "Jerry, hush!"

The robin hesitated before speaking up once more, "We're tired of living under your wing! A condor like you shouldn't even *be* in this forest!"

I glared straight into Jerry's beady eyes. Jerry's head shrunk into his body, visibly shaking in fear. "I-I'm not scared of you," he managed to spew with all his swiftly diminishing courage.

Though my eyes threatened the robin, my mind could only focus on his ridiculous shape. His fluffy exterior was incredibly prominent, and it vastly contrasted from the tense air swallowing the forest. An actual cotton ball is talking to me, I thought.

Suppressing my thoughts, I began my greatest intimidation tactic. Clearing my throat and deepening my voice, I boomed, "You dare look down on me from that measly perch?" Steadily, my posture straightened and my breast puffed out. The shape of my wings revealed themselves from the veil of its thick feathers, slowly stretching them out to their full length. Fully asserting my dominance with a striking pose, I extended a foot forward as though I was preparing to launch. The bird was paralyzed, its beak shut tightly.

"You will regret—" I said, but my sentence was left incomplete as the robin spread his wings, fleeting his branch hastily. In his rush, however, Jerry failed to turn away from an incoming tree. My beak was left hanging as a gentle thud filled the ears of every surrounding bird, watching helplessly as Jerry plummeted to the ground.

A moment of silence passed before a neighboring bird exclaimed, "Oh my, thunderbird!" High-pitched cries echoed throughout the forest. "Jerry, no!" Their discordant chirping was distinctly worse than this morning's song.

I returned my wings and condensed my breast. Still dazed from the recent occurrence, I turned around and headed for the river hurriedly to avoid the commotion and escape any responsibility for an accidental death from here on after. Besides, I need to search for sustenance! Nutrition is important, too.

In my time living in the forest, the first attempts in hunting for food were difficult. A bird's greatest asset is their wings, and a bird hobbling around on the forest floor was an uncommon sight. With a wingspan that could guard the wide entrance of my hollowed tree, the ordinary forest bird would think that my wings were the greatest blessing the world could give. My wings were feared and honored among the masses, granting me the position I held to this day. One flap from these wings, the birds said, could send a gust of wind strong enough to make the forest dance.

With all that said, I refused to use these feathered arms for their purpose. My wings do not scare me—heights do. If my options were to choke on fish or take flight above the canopy, my throat would be filled. Life has been one great challenge, yet life has found a way for me to keep moving forward, even now. Not to mention, I had already been too far in the act to actively seek help. At this point, the best option was to go with the flow and pretend that flying was a lowly bird's burden.

I chased rodents and rabbits with my wings tucked in, but their speed outmatched mine. Often, my talons would get caught on the raised roots of the trees and the ground would gladly feed my mouth. Through multiple trials, I learned to let the air envelop my wings as my speed would increase. One small leap and I began to glide for short intervals, but enough to gain a much greater distance than running. The critters of the land, however, climbed the trees upon realizing they could no longer outrun me.

One time, in the midst of pursuing a rabbit, the sound of smooth, rushing water caught my ears. Intrigued, I stopped in my tracks and headed towards the source. The dirt became softer as the sound grew louder. The dense population of trees became lighter till it reached a slight decline. The trees that bordered the decline bended towards a river, now within my sights. Inching closer, carefully making my way down the low hill, there was a broad patch of gravel that easily supported my weight. The river was vast, growing deeper in color further beyond. Fish, I thought, would be a good alternative to my diet.

Although my eyes could spot clusters of fish skimming the surface, most of them were swimming where the river was deepest. Walking would be no easy task. Gliding was another option, but it risked being carried by the current and expended too much energy if the fish were feisty. Off in the distance, however, I spotted what seemed like a weathered, drifting log. When it began to move and grow arms, its shape was more identifiable. It was an otter.

This was my chance, I thought. Seeking the opportunity, I called out to the otter, "Hey, you there!" Without control, my right wing began waving in the air almost too enthusiastically. I tucked the wing in immediately before the otter turned around.

"Me?" the otter pointed to himself.

I needed to exert my presence. Clearing my throat and deepening my voice, I said, "I demand your assistance." With my chest puffed out and my back straightened, the river was no match for the rush of confidence that was flowing out.

The river otter kept staring straight into my eyes as he drifted closer to me. Not once breaking contact or blinking, my lungs began to have trouble breathing normally. Still stuck in the pose, my mind tried to concentrate on other parts of the otter as he moved closer. His paws were gently laying over his body. Past the plump exterior, something seemed off about the otter. His relaxed state was an unusual response from my domineering stature.

As the otter stopped in front of me, he finally responded, "Yeah, no." With that, he began waddling his tail and swam back towards the center of the river.

My head jerked back, and I was too stunned to react immediately. This otter denied me without hesitating. Shaking my head from the shock, I broke the act and called out, "Wait, wait, come back!"

The otter made his way back as if time was of no concern. "Hello," he said, waving a paw.

"How did you, uh—"

"Know it was an act?" the otter said. "You look like you need to fart." His eyes widened as he gasped, covering his nose immediately upon a sudden realization. "You're not gonna fart—"

"No, I'm not gonna fart on you," I retaliated. "Birds can't even do that." The otter kept staring at me with his nose still hidden behind his paws. For a few seconds, neither one of us failed to break eye contact. I thought that informing him of my intestinal functions would break his stance, but fear and caution still glossed over his face.

The air around us finally became easier to breathe in, provided that no gases were expelled. "My name's Stewart," he said finally breaking the tension.

"Condor."

"No way." His head jerked forward at the reveal of my name.

"Not lying."

"Your parents named you after your own kind?"

My feet were kicking a few rocks around, shying my eyes away from Stewart's gaze. When it came to my parents, our times together as a family were suboptimal at best. "They were more direct with me than my brothers," I said.

Stewart was eyeing me up and down. It seemed my body language was too upfront to hide anything. "Daddy issues?"

"Hey."

"Right, my bad. I'm pushing it." The sound of the river's flowing water took the space that our words used to fill. "Well, listen, if you need someone to talk to, I'll always be swimmin' 'round in this river." My chest felt lighter and my shoulders began to relax. It came upon my memories that this warmth in my heart had not been felt for years since departing my family's nest. "You know, I've been wondering since you arrived. What are you doing here?"

"Needed food. I thought fish would be easy targets." My heart raced, unsure of what to say next. The otter had an easygoing aura that made him seem like someone easy to hold a conversation with.

"Should be easy then, right? You've got those mighty wings to help you out." Stewart flapped his arms, imitating a bird flapping their wings. He laughed at himself, imagining how ridiculous he may have looked.

As his laughter erased my doubts, I said, "Yeah, I guess. I just can't use these wings."

"Oh." Stewart's concerned tone filled my heart with shame. "Childhood injury, or something?"

"I'm…" Taking a deep breath, I let out a defeated sigh and continued, "I'm afraid of heights."

"Oh." His tone switched closer to amusement. "Well, that's some cosmic irony for you, eh?" He let out a laugh from deep in the bottom of his stomach. I laughed along nervously, uncertain of what to do next. "Don't worry, Conrad."

"Conrad?"

"I'm an expert at hunting fish. I wouldn't mind helping you out, especially in the situation you're in." He dived below the surface and rose immediately with a fish in his mouth under two seconds. Stewart placed the freshly caught prey by my foot, flopping around on the dry gravel. Our eyes followed the fish as it bounced back and forth from its spot, trapped in a river of air. "So, how did the locals take it in?"

"I, uh, haven't told anyone yet."

"Really?" the otter said. "You are one surprise after another."

"They think I'm some veteran bird of the wild with how menacing I look, so I act like it to avoid trouble."

"You could play the part better." Once again, I was shocked at his response. There was no incentive for an otter to help a troubled condor. Stewart, however, still had the heart to give advice to threaten the birds of the area. "If you can't use your wings to fly, then use them to scare others."

I thought about the idea for a while, trying to imagine a clear image of a more threatening posture. Once I decided to execute the idea, my chest puffed out and my back straightened out. Then, my wings stretched out far, covering an area large enough to cast a shadow that swallowed all of Stewart's body. "Like this?" I asked.

Stewart was astonished. His mouth was agape and his eyes sparkled in wonder. "There you go!" he said. Hearing the otter's praise showered me with pride.

"Thanks, Stewart."

He nodded. "Anytime, Cody. Now, take the fish and skedaddle."

Before taking the fish, I said, "You know, it's Condor—"

Stewart raised his finger before I could finish my sentence. "Let this be our trade. Fish and a lifelong secret for a bit of your dignity." With that said, he waddled away from the shallow bank, the sound of his chuckle slowly being drowned out by the river. Shaking my head, I turned back and accepted the agreement with the fish in my mouth.

Now, nearing the edge of the river once more for my daily intake of fish, I scanned the surface for my reliable friend. "Stewart?" My eyes detected a sleek figure swimming elegantly underwater. Its head bobbed up, breaking through the surface. "Ah, there you are." The river otter placed the fish in his mouth by my foot.

"Connie!" he said. I rolled my eyes. The sign of our friendship was still ever-present in the otter's antics. "How's it goin' man?" Stewart began to drift slowly off the edge, letting the water lead him.

"I blew it." My feet kicked the gravel around, and my head hung limply. The otter's eyes drilled into my guilty conscience.

He gasped. "Oh, no. Did they find out?"

"No, not that. I may have pushed the act too far and injured a robin."

"You must be getting real good at being intimidating, eh?" Stewart's words trailed off into the air, now drowned by the river. He swam back to the edge, swishing his tail side to side to propel himself. The otter placed his paw on my foot and began stroking one of my toes. Mildly in discomfort, I brushed his paw away with my wing. "Listen," he said. "Maybe it's time to be more honest with ourselves. This whole dilemma's weighing down on you, and it shows on your face each time you come to visit.

"That's easier said than done."

"The more you fake it, the more it'll get worse. It's not in your *nature*."

"My *nature* is supposed to be strong and confident. You know, bold and manly, like
my father would always say."

"No, no," Stewart shook his head. His paw reached out for my foot once more, but
this time I let his soft paw caress a toe. "*Your* nature. Who cares if you're not what people expect you to be?"

Time seemed to extend before my response. "My parents would."

"But they're not here, now, are they?" Stewart's words made me reconsider my recent behavior. For a moment, I stood in silence, unsure of what to say. "Your food's over there, by the way." He pointed to a mound of leaves.

"Thanks," I said. Stewart began drifting off into the river once again. Taking several half-bitten fish in my beak, I headed towards my nest to relax. Stepping over the shallow bank, the smell of freshwater no longer filled my nostrils. It was back to the earth and its damp leaves with a hint of fish carcass. With each step, my beak kept losing its grip from the glossy flesh of the fish. I pointed my head up to reposition the fish, but instead, missed and hit the ground as my eyes spotted a group of birds flying towards the river. It was no flock, either. A mass group of birds of varying kinds were flying hastily towards one direction.

Their behavior was suspicious, but not outlandish. I paid no significant attention to the group, picked up the dirt-riddled fish, and ambled opposite of their destination. The next key point in my path were two, dry bushes growing beside the roots of a tree. Before crossing the line, however, the shadows of even more flying birds caught my eye. The shapes headed for the same direction the earlier group of birds were traveling towards. This group was distinctly more vocal, shrieking in the air. My foot froze midway its step when my ears picked up a name.

"Jerry?" the birds repeated. Jerry? That flying wad of cotton? "Jerry, where are you?" Their concerned calls wrapped chains around my chest. As the robin's name swarmed my thoughts, many possibilities played out in my head. Did they form a search party? Too many birds were flying away from their homes. Why were they all headed in one direction, then? In the midst of my thoughts, the birds above were only met with silence. After hearing no response, they moved further towards the river. Something was going on, and it blared danger.

Just as the birds fled, my eyes caught the position of the sun. It was nearing high noon, yet the sky itself was not its full, crisp blue that would contrast the light of day. Looking to the river, then to the way back home, the blue above merged into a bright orange beyond the trees that creeped further and further towards the sky. The pieces were coming together inside my head. The fleeing birds, the missing robin, and the abnormal color of the sky at noon. Before reaching a conclusion, however, I let the fish slide out of my beak and made a beeline towards the growing orange within the forest.

A mild wave of heat struck me, crawling between the barbs of my feathers. The intensity grew at an alarming rate the further I went into the forest. Light tendrils of smoke were emanating from within, invading my nostrils. Breathing became a greater task to maintain as the smoke contaminated my lungs. It spiked my already tired breaths, ragged from panic and physical exhaustion. The scent of the earth was drained by the remains of scorched leaves, most of which still floated in the air as glowing embers. The burning lights seemed to dance around as I ran deeper into the forest. Few, tiny sparks would pelt my body, but a cloak of air would snuff them out as soon as they made contact. The low-hanging branches of the trees began to snap off as the moisture within them evaporated. The wave had become immense, and I had to squint to shield out the heat that were drying out my eyes.

Upon arriving, the atmosphere had become dense and brimming with danger. There were no birds or screams of bloody murder filling the air. I set the fish down in my nest and looked around, scanning every branch. Not a single bird was perched, nor a single nest attended to. For some, there were eggs left to be abandoned. The screeches of birds echoed in my mind, and I looked up to find larger groups heading away from the source. Looking opposite of the direction, massive plumes of smoke contaminated the sky.

"Fire," I whispered under my breath. The heat crawled closer, and my body shivered with fear. My head pivoted frantically, searching for a safe exit. I panicked as bright flames and billowing smoke blocked every possible escape route.

The talons on my feet dug through the ground as I desperately waddled towards the hollow. Heavy smoke blocked my vision and subsequently hindered my breathing. The nest was still several meters away, but I could determine its shape past the smoke. Still racing, I stretched my wings out and felt the flow of the air. I leapt and began to glide, covering a much greater distance in such short time. Finally clearing the thick wall of smoke, the nest was directly in sight. The fire was dangerously creeping in on the nest, however. Almost there, I told myself.

Just then, I heard the roaring crack of a thick branch. I could only watch in terror as it plunged straight down, crashing onto the entrance. Distracted by the dirt and ember that sprayed out, I lost control of my flight and began to wobble in the air before striking the ground.

I shivered in fear of the sudden realization that befell my quivering body. The sky, I thought. It pounded inside my head, screaming through my jumbled thoughts. There were no other possible options to flee from the growing fire. If not by land, then by sky. I needed to fly.

***

My father's words rang inside my head. "Jump."

"Frederick!" my mother exclaimed. "Just give him some time!" She took me under her wing, stroking my head gently to ease the stress.

"His brothers have already learned to land *safely* on the ground, and he has not left the nest *once!*" My mother looked out and below to check her babies.

She laid still for several moments before finally saying to my father, "Frederick."

"What, Helen?"

"One of them's not moving."

"Helen, wh—huh?" I join my father and look out the edge to spot one of my brothers, Braelynn, pecking the still body. The belly jiggled with each peck.

My mother called out to my conscious brother, "Braelynn? Sweetie?"

Braelynn yelled back, "I think Tanner's—" He looked back down. "Oh, no, wait." Tanner stood up and quickly shook to rid his feathers of debris. "He's fine!"

"I'm okay!" Tanner followed. My mother sighed in relief.

"See, they're fine," my father said. Helen scoffed and turned the other direction. "Listen, son," he continued. "You have to learn now, or else you'll be left behind! Just look at your brothers." I leaned out once again to spot Tanner sunken halfway into a mound of dirt while Braelynn kept pounding him into the ground with his weight. Braelynn laughed with glee as Tanner coughed violently, desperate to get the dirt out of his mouth. My father turned my cheek away and had our eyes meet. "They are on their way to manhood," he said, running his feathers over my cheek. "Now, you have to become a man, too!" My head drooped down, and I began to think over my words. From my perspective, the nest was supposedly perched high enough to avoid the dangers lurking on the land.

I mustered up the courage to respond. "What if I don't want to be a man?"

"What? That's ridiculous," my father said, dismissing my concerns. "You're a condor. The manliest of birds!"

I was confused, but more so worried. In regards to my father's logic, my next question arrived with genuine curiosity. "Then, does that mean mom is a man?"

"Excuse me?" My mother joined in, suddenly aware of the conversation.

"Wha—no, son," my father replied. He fought to keep his composure, though it was visibly fading away fast with my mother's glaring eyes. "Your mother is a strong, independent *woman*, and you will be just as strong and independent as your mother and I."

Great excitement filled my innocent soul and I uttered, "I'm gonna be a man *and* a woman?"

"Oh, great Horus, he's hopeless."

"Frederick!" Helen exclaimed.

"Come on, Helen, you have to help me out here," Frederick said. His face showed defeat, and his plea for help convinced my mother to finally make her move.

I faced my mother and was greeted with a warm, gentle smile. Her voice became hushed, and in an instant, I was locked in a bubble with just the both of us. She began, "Sweetheart." At the sound of her voice, my heart and mind came to full attention. "Your father has good intentions. I want the best for you, too."

✳✳✳

Great pillars of yellow filled my peripheral vision. With every turn, the towering plumes of flame snapped back wildly, the loud cracks of roasting branches whipping my train of thought into panic. The sweltering heat was crushing me from every angle, the light of the flames stabbing the pupils of my eyes and through my head. The fire greedily drained the air out of my lungs, and it took longer and longer to take one full breath.

Soon, I found myself trapped within a ring of fire. The heat had gotten intense to the point where each step I made caused the once, soft ground to sizzle. The skies above were the only way out of this heated mess. Every conversation and every thought of doubt had come to this point; a test given by the world to determine my fate. My wings stretched out to their full glory, flapping rhythmically in great arcs to ready the muscles. Debris was blown away with each beat, visible circles pulsing away from where I stood. Against the roaring flames, my voice breaks out as adrenaline filled me to the brim, "This is for you, mama!" My knees bended back and my body lowered. With one final flap, my feet thrust me upwards into the air.

For one moment, the charred embers seemed to fall slowly and the flames gently puffed as my wings continued their rhythm. The sound of my wings swimming through the flow of air muffled the thunderous crackles of burning wood. Each flap brought me to a higher altitude and the tips of the trees grew nearer and nearer. The air below my wings felt as if it had already paved the way towards a safer place, guiding me to the same path the birds were going. In that one moment, I felt just as wild and daring as the inferno that consumed the forest. I was flying just as my parents had envisioned through their dreams and words.

At last the tops of the trees were in my view. My beak hung open as my eyes carried the world that it had long wondered to see. "Oh, great Horus," I muttered beneath my breath. Not long after, however, gravity weighed my head down and was introduced to the view below. Immediately, I caught my breath and my stomach felt hollowed out. The familiar sense of slimy fish was curiously filling my throat. The fear smashed into me just as hard as that robin hit the tree. Struggling to stop myself from extinguishing the fire with vomit, my focus slipped and my wings began to flap out of sync. The once merciful air that lifted me from the ground suddenly vanished from beneath, and there was no longer a force to support me in the air. This is the end, I thought. I closed my eyes, bracing myself for death as my wings slowly came to rest.

A voice from behind yelled out, "Flap steadily!" Death's grasp loosened on my mind. Upon instinctively pulling my wings out once more, my body became upright. "Steady, and keep your eyes looking ahead!" Following the voice, my neck stiffened up and I kept my head locked forward. They began to approach closer, the faint, rapid fluttering of their wings coming closer till they were in my field of vision. The pudgy figure racked my mind.

"Jerry?" I said, in shock. "Everyone's been looking for you!"

"I come out of being unconscious and as soon as I wake up, the world's on fire." His cheeks puffed out as he continued his angry ranting. "I was convinced I'd gone straight to he—"

"Look, can you help me out?" I said, desperate for options. "I've never been this high up."

"Yeah, I can tell." Jerry gazed at me, bewildered. "You're wobbling. I can't believe this is the same bird that's been terrorizing the forest." My face turned away from the robin's stare. "You'll fry in here long before you can make it out. Copy me and follow my lead."

Nodding, my wings retain a steady rhythm before finally being able to move forward. I kept my eyes directly focused on the robin. The situation felt farfetched in my head, having a bird like Jerry teach a condor to stay in the air. My face became relaxed and my chest felt lighter, weirdly enough, as I imagined how things would play out now that my cover's been blown.

Jerry led me farther from the fire, the intense heat losing its hold on our bodies as the river came into view. "We'll land on the other side of the river," he said. He masterfully pulled his body back and let his wings stretch out perpendicular to the flow of air, effectively slowing down quickly. His feet stretched out below, softening the impact as he landed smoothly on the ground. I decided to follow suit in a pristine manner.

The robin looked back and called out in sudden realization, "Wait, you do know how to land, right?" I did not know how to land. The determination I once carried quickly morphed into panic as my body dipped too far back, feet kicking the air helplessly. Jerry watched as my face hit the earth flat. It left a trail on the rugged rubble of the river bank as friction led me to a stop. His small foot nudged my sore body. "Well, there's a first for everything."

A Long Walk Home

The sound of high pitched beeps caused a shock through my body. Without thinking, my arm reached out, smacking the nightstand until it landed on the familiar round button, causing the noise to stop. The only light in the room was coming from the alarm clock that read 6:30 in bright red. I rubbed my face in circular motions in order to force myself from falling back asleep. With groggy movements, I found my way out of bed and over to the large desk on the other side of the room. There was an all too familiar binder sitting on top of a pile of random papers.

"Sofia's Tuesday." I let out in a quiet mumble as my fingers traced the rainbow stickers

and glitter covering the smooth purple plastic. My feet guided me to the light switch as I flipped to the first page in the binder. I looked up once more to make sure everything was in its proper place. The bright pink walls were covered with posters of different animals and cartoon characters. At the end of the bed, there was a large bin with an assortment of different stuffed animals, the majority being either a shade of pink or covered in sparkles. By my door, there were seven pairs of shoes lined up perfectly in rainbow order.

"Perfect." I let out in a yawn before heading towards the kitchen and placing the binder open on the table. My eyes glanced down at the open page, the idea of breakfast suddenly filling my mind. I walked to the left of my kitchen and made my way around, grabbing a spoon, a bowl, a box of cereal, and then grabbing the milk from the fridge. I carefully set everything down on the table. The bowl was first, then the spoon just to the right of it, the milk had to go directly above the spoon, and the cereal to the left of the milk. Finally, I picked up my binder and placed it to the left of the bowl. A smile formed across my face at the sight of the perfect set up. As I took my seat, I turned back around and looked at a clock on the wall.

"6:39, not yet." I told myself, watching the second hand tick by. *Tick...Tick...Tick....* I knew better than to go against the schedule, something usually went wrong if the schedule wasn't followed perfectly. The moment the second hand finished its rotation, my arm was already reaching out for the cereal box. There was just enough in the box to fill the bowl before it ran out. I grabbed the shopping list from the inside cover of the binder along with my sparkly pink gel pen and made a note to buy cereal while at work. Once I had started eating, my eyes scanned the contents of the binder, first going to a heavily starred and highlighted section.

Without thinking I began reading it out loud,

"Hi! This is the schedule of Sofia King. If you find this unattended, look for a girl with short ginger hair who is around 5'5. Please return immediately! Thank you - Sofia." Everything seems in order, I thought to myself while scooping up more cereal. My eyes drifted back to the clock that now read 6:50 which meant five more minutes before moving on to the next part of the day. My instincts kicked in as I drifted around my kitchen, putting everything back into its proper spot. If something was in the wrong spot, it was like alarms going off in my head that just got louder and louder until it was corrected. My schedule allowed me to do things on my own without the constant alarms. Once the clock struck 6:55, I made my way back to my room, schedule in hand, and already reading the next step.

✳✳✳

My red rain boots seemed almost too big for my feet as I stepped off the bus and began walking down the sidewalk. Each step caused my foot to slip forward, making the walk rather uncomfortable. I grabbed one of my heart shaped sticky notes and began writing,

"When rainy...wear two...pairs of socks." I peeled it from the pack and stuck it into my binder. The sky was a sad shade of gray, but everything else seemed to pop against the gloom. Puddles were scattered throughout the road and sidewalk, which made it even harder to walk. As I approached each puddle, my reflection looked back at me. Everything looked strangely wavy, slight alarms beginning to go off since it was Tuesday which meant it was a striped shirt day, not waves.

"8:56." I whispered out, after glancing at my watch, which meant four minutes until my shift started. My legs began moving faster; there was no way I could allow myself to be late. The little market was just in the distance, only a bit more to go. Every puddle turned my clothes into the wrong pattern, every step was shaky and uncomfortable, every second inched closer to 9:00. I hadn't even noticed the harsh mutters that began escaping my lips.

"Waves. Tuesday. Alarm. Slide. Shoe. Alarm." My knuckles grew more white around my binder with each comment. My eyes darted to each puddle, hoping one would show the correct outfit for the day.

"Waves. Tuesday. Ala-" Without realizing it, my boot got caught in a pot hole in the sidewalk, sending me flying. I hit the ground with a hard thud that knocked the wind from my chest. Breathe, just breathe, that one-line kept repeating in my head until I was able to roll onto my back. I glanced down at my shirt, soaked in certain spots but still stripped. My hands ached from trying to stop the fall, they were covered in red scratches and glitter. Glitter? Why is there glitter? Then I gazed down at my lap and noticed the empty spot.

"Where is my schedule!" It came out as a demand rather than a question, despite no one being around me. The alarms in my head began, but only quietly at first. Standing up, I brushed myself off and scanned the ground around me until my eyes landed on it. The once glittery and sticker covered binder sat in a puddle in front of me. I ran to it, no longer noticing the incorrect waves and the awkwardness of the boots. My knees hit the ground in front of the schedule as I placed it in my lap. The array of once colorful designed now bled down the sides of the binder, onto my pants. As I stared down, unsure of what to do, the only thing I could think about was what a problem this was and all I could hear were the alarms going off in my head.

"No, no, no, no." The binder cover squished out water from my grip. I slowly opened to the first page. Everything stopped. There was nothing. Nothing in my head and nothing on the once colorful schedule. It looked as if the paper had cried for hours on end. What do I do? The schedule doesn't say what to do right now! My breaths began to quicken with each comment, and with each breath, the alarms got worse. The binder closed as I brought my hands to my ears and my eyes slammed shut, I had to stop the alarms. I just kept imagining my waved shirt in the puddles, how my feet felt too small in my boots, and how lost I was. Nothing was making sense, I tried clenching my ears and eyes tighter but to no avail. My lungs filled with as much air as they could and before I knew what was happening, I screamed. Louder and louder, the air left my body because in that moment, it was the only thing that I could do.

"Sofia! Sofia! Stop screaming!" The kind voice caused me to let go of my ears and look up. I was met with kind blue eyes, jet black hair, a nose ring which seemed painful, and a gold necklace that read Meg. The alarms got quieter at the sight of her. Meg would be able to help, she helps me at work all the time.

"Sorry, Meg," I began to wipe away the tears that finally stopped running down my face, "I didn't mean to." Meg looked down at me, her brows furrowing together.

"Okay Sofia, explain to me what happened." I clenched the binder as I tried to explain everything to her, trying not to show my annoyance that she didn't understand what just happened to me.

"It's a stripe day, and the puddles were wrong, and I need more socks, and I'm lost." Meg's eyebrows raised slightly at my explanation which caused my hands to tighten even more on the binder. This makes perfect sense; how could she not get it. To try to help, I began slowly flipping through the schedule, avoiding a tear on one of the moist pages.

"Oh...you're lost." She said in almost a whisper as I closed the soaking mess. A long sigh escaped my lips as I looked down at my hands. They were covered in a different colored stains and tons of glitter. Meg wiped her hands off on her jacket before gesturing back towards the market.

"Why don't we get you cleaned up first?" I nodded back at her and soon we made our way over to the market. As I walked over to the door, my eyes connected with my reflection one last time. Before the alarms could sound off I mumbled, "It's Tuesday, no waves."

*** *

Meg and I sat in the employee's lounge looking down at the binder that sat open on the table between us. The binder was flipped open to the last page which was the least damaged from the water, my phone next to it. We stared at the two remaining phone numbers on the list. I wouldn't meet Meg's gaze; she wouldn't understand why we couldn't make the call.

"Sofia, hear me out," Meg was standing now, which made me I look down at my arms that were crossed against my chest. "This is the only thing left in your binder that is fully legible and it's a phone number! And it's your par-"

"I can't," I huffed out, "There is another number on the page!" I pointed to the second number on the page, the phone number was visible but the name before it was long gone. Meg let out a long sigh as she also pointed towards the numbers on the page.

"Yes, but we don't know if they can help! Your parents can help!"

"They can't know what I did!" The room went quiet as I finally locked eyes with Meg. I could feel the tears begin to well up as my mind raced with all the different possibilities of what could happen if mom and dad found out what I did. Their kind faces flashed across my mind, causing a jolt through my body.

"They trust me...If I call, then they come back." I looked back down at a sticker that was now resting on the table. It was a small blue and purple butterfly with a glitter border. My mind wandered back as I picked up the little sticker.

"There, that should do it!" Mom had placed the last sticker onto the cover of the binder. She turned and smiled at me, I couldn't help but reach over and hug her, sending a breeze of lavender from her hair towards me. The sound of rummaging could be heard coming from my kitchen as dad stepped out with a fresh cup of tea. He lowered his glasses over his light brown eyes as he examined the cover. A smile formed as he let out a chuckle.

"You certainly have outdone yourselves, it looks amazing." I found my way over towards him to give him a hug as well.

"Thanks dad." The words came out muffled as I spoke into the navy sweatshirt. His hand was warm on my back from his peppermint tea. Sparkle from the binder's cover caught my eye as dad let go of me. 'Sofia's Tuesday' was spelled out right in the center of the purple cover with silver foam letters, and an assortment of bright colored stickers surrounded it. I picked up the binder and stroked the smooth back cover as I walked over to a pile of two other binders. A bright blue binder with a different collection of decorations sat on the top that read 'Sofia's Monday'. With extreme care, I placed the Tuesday schedule gently on the top, making sure not to knock off any sparkles or stickers. Mom chirped up as I made my way back towards her.

"Next is the red binder, right?" I nodded in response as she reached under the table and pulled out a bright red binder from a plastic bag. Dad took a seat beside mom, his knuckles seemed to tighten around his mug as he spoke.

"Soon you will be able to do all this on your own." A grin exploded across my face,

"Yes! No more help!" I reached into the same bag under the table and pulled out a different array of stickers and foam letters, "I can do it alone." Mom and dad looked at each other as I carefully placed the first 's' down in the cover.

"Sweetie," mom's voice was suddenly very quiet, "you know we trust you, right?"

"Yes, mom." I didn't even look up as I added the next few letters to the cover. There was silence throughout my whole apartment as I placed the last letter to 'Sofia's' down. I smiled at my precise work as dad piped up.

"Just know if you ever need anything, you can call us." My head shot upwards as he finished his sentence.

"No," alarms started going off in my head, "you trust me, I trust me, so no calling." They sighed in unison before mom reached over and started opening the first pack of stickers.

"Whatever you say, honey." Mom nearly whispered as she started carefully placing the stickers around my work.

The sound of buzzes brought me back to the employee's lounge. My phone had gotten a random notification from one of the many games. I picked up the phone and found the keypad, the white screen glaring into my eyes as my mind raced. Meg still stood across the table from me, watching as my thumbs twitched above the screen. I could call mom and dad, I thought, but that would mean no trust, and that would mean they would come back, but they would know what to do, they always do.

"I don't know, I don't know." I began mumbling to myself as the alarms began to rise, Meg must have noticed my struggle as she finally spoke up,

"Well, if the second number is in your binder, it must be important right?" I looked away from the phone screen and towards Meg. Our eyes met and it was as if her presence helped the alarms seem a little quieter. Without answering her, I began punching in each number to the keypad. I stared at the call button for a moment, alarms still going off in my mind. What if this wasn't what the right thing to do? What would my schedule tell me to do? What if I make things worse? Why is the number dialing? My thumb had landed on the call button on accident and by instinct, my hand brought it up towards my ear. My body began to rock back and forth as I waited for an answer, Meg quietly made her way closer to me, also waiting to see who we called. The sound of the ringing from the phone began to mix with the alarms. It just seemed to get louder with each passing moment, I began to bite my lower lip to distract myself. My weight kept shifting from toe to heel, toe to heel, until the ringing stopped.

"Hello this is Julie from the Speech Language Pathology Center, how may I help you?" The alarms shut off, the only sound was a laugh that was coming from my mouth. There was a chuckle from the other end of the call as well,

"Well hello, Sofia," Julie's voice was smooth and gentle as she spoke, "what can I do to help you?" I was jumping up and down now, Meg took a step back to avoid me hitting her. Julie sat at the front desk whenever I had my speech lessons. Every day she put out a new little bowl of candy that she let me have after my lessons. Before speaking, the soaking wet binder caught my eye and all my laughter quickly stopped.

"Julie, I'm lost, I was walking to the market, and I didn't have enough socks on, and the alarms wouldn't stop, and now my schedule is ruined." The whole time I was talking, there was a sound of keys clicking coming from Julie's end. Once she had stopped typing, she replied.

"Well, lucky for you, Ms. Russell is free from 11am to 2pm if you want to come by. She can help make a new schedule for you, does that sound good?" Another laugh erupted at the thought of Ms. Russell. She was the best speech teacher, she helps me every week during our lessons and we get to have fun. I looked over at a large clock that was hanging on the wall.

"10:46...Yes, yes, yes!" The jumping had started again, but Meg had started waving her arms which caused me to look towards her as she whispered.

"You have to ask for the address and directions."

"Oh right! Julie, Meg told me I need directions." Julie began typing again, I glanced at Meg who gave me two thumbs up. While smiling back at her, Julie asked,

"So how is Meg? Is she helping?"

"Oh yes, Meg has been very helpful, the alarms are quieter with her."

"That's good," she finally stopped typing before continuing, "now, do you have any paper with you Sofia?" The binder was completely soaked, so none of it was good to write on. There was a fridge over on the back wall that was covered in multiple papers being held up by magnets. I reached into my pocket and pulled out a sparkly silver gel pen and then rushed to the fridge. The papers were a mix of different colors, but one was purple. I pulled it off, the back was empty but the front read 'Tuesday's shifts". A smile grew on my face, it was the same purple as my binder. I brought it back over to the table and sat down.

"I have a paper now, Julie." She began going step by step on how to get to her building. Each word was written slowly and carefully, there was no way I could ruin the only purple paper. Julie made sure to read through the list two times just to make sure I had everything down perfectly. Once everything was done, I thanked Julie again.

"Of course Sofia, Ms. Russell and I will be waiting for you for when you arrive, alright goodbye."

"Goodbye, Julie!" With that, the call ended and I was already running out of the lounge with Meg close behind. With the new list in one hand and the binder in the other, Meg and I zoomed past all of the aisles and various customers. As I ran, each foot landed perfectly in the square tiles to avoid landing on any cracks. Customers seemed to be watching me with occasional groans whenever I would nearly avoid running into them. Nothing ran through my head except for the idea that soon everything would be fixed; Ms. Russell was going to help get rid of the alarms. The glass sliding doors were just ahead, but my eyes were looking down at my new schedule, once through the doors, I had to take a right back to the bus stop. Then there was a shout followed by a loud crash.

"Look what you've done!" A tall woman stood in front of a puddle of pickles and broken glass, her son was crying in the shopping cart seat. The cries were like nails on a chalkboard, and it didn't help that the woman was yelling at me. I covered my ears to try to calm myself, but the alarms began.

"You need to watch where you are going, what if the glass hit my son!" Stop, please stop, my head began to ache. As the woman stepped closer to me, her son began to cry louder. My voice could barely be heard as I whimpered out,

"I'm sorry, I'm so sorry, I didn't mean to." There was too much, I glanced around me, Meg was gone. The directions were shoved deep into my coat pocket and my free hand was now trying to block out any sound, but the lady just got closer and louder.

"Get your hands away from your ears! Listen to me when I talk to you! Why would this place even let someone like you-"

"Excuse me ma'am," an older man with gray and white scruff towered between the woman and I, "what is the problem?" He glanced down at the broken pickle jar, then my ruined binder before looking back at me with a soft smile.

"Well," she looked at his nametag before going on in a very exaggerated tone, "Chris, I want to speak to your manager about *her*." She didn't even look at me as she said it. I was still clenching my ears as I did another scan of the area. There was now a crowd of people watching the scene that had unfolded and other people just trying to push by, but no Meg. Where could she have gone? Why would she leave me at a time like this? I began to slowly step away from the growing puddle of pickle juice, seeing my reflection would only make the alarms worse. Chris seemed to notice what I was doing, but he managed to stay as calm as possible as he gestured the woman towards her cart.

"You are talking with him right now, I am willing to answer any questions and to clean up this mess, but could you come with me to a less crowded area?" The group grew even more from the commotion, I couldn't help but notice everyone staring at me. Chris kept trying to walk the lady to her cart, where her son was still wailing. Both of her hands suddenly shot down to her hips in tight fists.

"No," she pointed at me while still glaring at Chris, "you need to do something about this retarded girl right now!" As the lady brought her hand back to her side, her face became an entirely new shade of red. My hands grew shaky as the other shoppers around me began to murmur. There were so many eyes, so many voices, the lady just kept staring at me as my legs also began to shake.

"Look at her! She can't even compose herself!" Tears streamed down my face but I couldn't get my hands to move from my ears to wipe them away. Vibrations could be felt through my boots as Chris stormed towards the woman and basically pushed her towards her cart. He began to speak to her, but it came out in almost a growl,

"I'm going to have to ask you to leave right now." The crowd finally began to diminish as the lady kept muttering angrily to Chris. My hands finally unclenched from my ears and began wiping the tears away.

"Thanks Chris, I didn't mean to do it." I said as I finally caught my breath, Chris looked back at me and said,

"It's okay, you can go, I'll handle this." I smiled at him before turning back towards the exit of market.

***

The bus stop was just at the other end of the street from the market. More cars drove by in search of places to find lunch before heading on their way back to where ever they came from. Various colored apartment building lined the sidewalks, and there was an occasional tree near the edge of the road. Every once and awhile someone would walk towards me as stranger danger rang through my mind until they had passed me. But I still checked to see if any of them were Meg, how could I have lost my Meg? It wasn't to bad, I still had the schedule from Julie in my pocket. The watch on my wrist gave off a quiet beeping noise, which meant it was noon. I took the pen out of my pocket and wrote on my hand to get lunch after seeing Ms. Russell. Once at the bus stop, I removed the crumpled purple paper and read the next step quietly to myself.

"Get on the bus and wait for three stops to get off at Jefferson street." The sound of the approaching bus forced me to look down the street, but instead of seeing the bus there were piercing blue eyes and a nose ring.

"Meg! There you are! I thought I lost you!" Meg giggled at my statement.

"You can be so silly, Sofia, all you have to do is call when you need me."

The bus came to a slow stop in front of us, as the door opened, I pulled out exactly $1.50 and then stepped inside. I made my way over to my usual seat in the front, right behind the bus driver. Meg took a seat next me right before the bus jerked forward. Neither of us spoke as I leaned my head against the cool window and watched the town roll by. The engine gave of a soft humming sound that also vibrated the windows just slightly. My thumb ran back and forth across the damp cover of the binder that sat in my lap as I thought about Ms. Russell. Her warm and happy face when I showed her my schedules for the first time popped into my mind. She carefully flipped through each page, reading every aspect of it.

"Sofia, this is wonderful," she placed the last binder down on the table between us, "I just have one question for you." I pulled the binder closer to me and placed it on top of the pile by my feet before responding.

"Of course Ms. Russell, what is it?"

"What would you do if forgot your schedule or forgot how to do something without the schedule?" My head shot up while the rest of my body went stiff. I nearly shouted at Ms. Russell.

"No! Nothing bad can happen, mom and dad have to trust me!" Ms. Russell held her hand up.

"Sofia, remember your indoor voice. Don't worry, nothing is wrong with the schedules right now, but I have an idea to help you prepare for an emergency." She began searching through her bag that sat beside her chair until she found a large folder. The cover had big black letters that read memory emergency guide. A giggle began to escape from my lips as I read the cover, from my angle it looked like it spelled out Meg. Ms. Russell didn't seem to mind and started talking,

"I think this will help you just in case something was to happen to one of the binders and you needed to remember what to do next," she placed a number of worksheets and flashcards on the table that looked like blank schedules, "what do you think?" The thought of mom and dad coming back to help me sent a shiver through my body. I looked at Ms. Russell, she was wearing a cozy brown sweater that matched her eyes, and her bright red glasses sat right on the edge of her nose as she gazed back at me.

"I'd like it, can we call it Meg?" She gave me a big smile while handing me a worksheet to fill out.

"Whatever helps you the most, Sofia."

The bus came to a less graceful stop as the bus driver called out to everyone.

"This is Jefferson street!" I quickly gathered my belongings and rushed off the bus. My eyes skimmed the next part of the directions before scanning my surrounds. Meg was no longer by my side, but no alarms went off. Instead I started smiling and said to myself,

"I trust me." With my binder in one hand and the paper in the other, I made my way down the sidewalk, no longer noticing the remaining puddles or the sliding of my feet in my boots.